Jayne Ann Krentz is the critically-acclaimed creator of the Arcane Society world, Dark Legacy, Ladies of Lantern Street and Rainshadow Island series. She also writes as **Amanda Quick** and **Jayne Castle**. Jayne has written more than fifty *New York Times* bestsellers under various pseudonyms and more than thirty-five million copies of her books are currently in print. She lives in the Pacific Northwest.

Visit Jayne Ann Krentz online:

www.jayneannkrentz.com
www.facebook.com/JayneAnnKrentz
www.twitter.com/JayneAnnKrentz

D1056134

Jayne Ann KRENTZ

Trust No One

piatkus

PIATKUS

First published in the United States in 2015 by G. P. Putnam's Sons,
A member of Penguin Group (USA) Inc., New York
First published in Great Britain in 2015 by Piatkus
This paperback edition published in 2016 by Piatkus

1 3 5 7 9 10 8 6 4 2

A CIP catalogue record for this book
is available from the British Library.

ISBN 978-0-349-40155-3

Printed and bound by CPI Group (UK) Ltd, Croydon, CR0 4YY

Papers used by Piatkus are from well-managed forests
and other responsible sources.

MIX
Paper from
responsible sources
FSC® C104740

Piatkus
An imprint of
Little, Brown Book Group
Carmelite House
50 Victoria Embankment
London EC4Y 0DZ

An Hachette UK Company
www.hachette.co.uk

www.piatkus.co.uk

For Frank. I positively love you.

One

The note pinned to the front of the dead man's silk pajamas was a one-sentence email printed out from a computer: *Make Today a Great Day the Witherspoon Way.*

Grace Elland leaned over the blood-soaked sheets and forced herself to touch the cold skin of Sprague Witherspoon's throat. His blue eyes, once so brilliant and compelling, were open. He stared sightlessly at the bedroom ceiling. A robust, square-jawed man with a mane of silver hair, he had always seemed larger-than-life. But death had shrunk him. All of the charm and electrifying charisma that had captivated the Witherspoon Way seminar audiences across the country had been drained away.

She was certain that he had been gone for several hours but she thought she detected a faint, accusing question in his unseeing eyes. Shattering memories splintered through her. At the age of sixteen she had seen the same question in the eyes of a dead woman. *Why didn't you get here in time to save me?*

She looked away from the dead eyes—and saw the unopened bottle of vodka on the nightstand.

For a terrible moment past and present merged there in the bedroom. She heard the echo of heavy footsteps on old floorboards. Panic threatened to choke her. This could not be happening, not again. It's the old dream, she thought. You're in the middle of a nightmare but you're awake. Breathe. Focus, damn it, and breathe.

Breathe.

The mantra broke the panic-induced trance. The echoing footsteps faded into the past. Ice-cold adrenaline splashed through her veins, bringing with it an intense clarity. This was not a dream. She was in a room with a dead man and, although she was almost certain that the footsteps had been summoned up from her nightmare, there was still the very real possibility that the killer was still around.

She grabbed the nearest available weapon—the vodka bottle—and moved to the doorway. There she paused to listen intently. The big house felt empty. Perhaps the footsteps had been an auditory illusion generated by the panicky memories. Or not. Either way, the smart thing to do was get out of the mansion and call 911.

She moved into the hallway, trying to make as little noise as possible. A fog of shadows darkened the big house. There were elegant potted plants everywhere—vibrant green bamboo, palms and ferns. Sprague had firmly believed that the abundant foliage not only improved indoor air quality, but enhanced the positive energy in the atmosphere.

The curtains that covered the windows had been closed for the night. No one had been alive to draw them back that morning. Not that it would have done much good. The Seattle winter dawn had arrived with a low, overcast sky and now rain was tapping at the windows. On days like this, most people turned on a few lights.

No one rushed out of a doorway to confront her. Gripping the neck of the vodka bottle very tightly, she went down the broad staircase. When she reached the bottom, she flew across the grand living room.

She knew her way around the first floor of the house because Sprague Witherspoon had entertained lavishly and often. He always invited Grace and the other members of the Witherspoon Way staff to his catered affairs.

The vast great room had been furnished and decorated with those events in mind. The chairs, cushioned benches and tables were arranged in what designers called conversational groupings. There was a lot of expensive art on the walls.

Sprague Witherspoon had lived the lifestyle he had tried to teach in his seminars, and the motivational business had been good to him. With Sprague it had been all about positive thinking and an optimistic attitude.

But now someone had murdered him.

She whipped through the front door and out into the beautifully manicured gardens. She did not stop to pull up the hood of her jacket. By the time she reached her little compact waiting in the sweeping circular driveway her hair and face were soaked.

She got behind the wheel, locked all of the doors, put the vodka bottle on the floor and gunned the engine. She drove through the high steel gates that guarded the Queen Anne mansion and out onto the quiet residential street.

Once outside the grounds she brought the car to a halt and reached into her cross-body bag for her phone. It proved amazingly difficult to enter 911 because her hands were shaking so hard. When she finally got through to the operator she had to close her eyes in order to concentrate on getting the facts straight.

Breathe.

"Sprague Witherspoon is dead." She watched the big gates while she rattled off the address. "At least, I think he's dead. I couldn't find a pulse. It looks like he's been shot. There is . . . a lot of blood."

More memories flashed through her head. A man with a face rendered into a bloody mask. Blood raining down on her. Blood everywhere.

"Is there anyone else in the house, ma'am?" The male operator's voice was sharp and urgent. "Are you in danger?"

"I don't think so. I'm outside now. A few minutes ago I went in to check on Mr. Witherspoon because he didn't show up at the office this morning. The gates were open and the front door was unlocked. The alarm was off. I didn't think anything about it because I assumed he was out in the gardens. When I couldn't find him outside, I went into the house. I called out to him. When he didn't respond I worried that he had fallen or become ill. He lives alone, you see, and—"

Shut up, Grace. You're rambling. You must stay focused. You can have a panic attack later.

"Stay outside," the operator said. "I've got responders on the way."

"Yes, all right."

Grace ended the connection and listened to the sirens in the distance.

It wasn't until the first vehicle bearing the logo of the Seattle Police Department came to a stop in front of her car that she remembered a fact that everyone who watched television crime dramas knew well. When it came to suspects, cops always looked hard at the person who found the body.

She had a feeling that the investigators would look even more closely at a suspect who had a history of stumbling over dead bodies.

Breathe.

She looked down at the bottle sitting on the floor of her car. Dread iced her blood.

Don't panic. A lot of people drink vodka.

But the only things she had ever seen Sprague drink were green tea and expensive white wine.

She found a tissue in her bag and used it to pick up the bottle. Not that it mattered much now. Her fingerprints were all over it.

Two

"I suppose the three of us can only be thankful that we've all got reasonably good alibis," Millicent Chartwell said. She sank languidly against the back of the booth and regarded her martini with a forlorn expression. "I didn't like the way that cute detective was watching me today when I gave my statement."

"He wasn't exactly smiling at me," Grace said. She took a sip of her white wine. "In fact, if I weren't the optimistic type, I'd say he was looking for an excuse to arrest me for Sprague's murder."

Kristy Forsyth put down her wineglass. Tears glittered in her eyes. "I can't believe Mr. Witherspoon is gone. I keep thinking there must have been a horrible case of mistaken identity and that he'll come striding through the door of the office tomorrow morning the way he always does, with some fresh-baked scones or doughnuts for us."

"There was no mistake," Grace said. "I saw him. And Nyla Witherspoon identified her father's body. I was still at the house talking to the police when she arrived on the scene. She was seriously distraught. In tears. Shaky. Honestly, I thought she was going to faint."

It was just after five o'clock. The three of them were exhausted and, Grace knew, still dazed. A close encounter with murder had an unnerving effect on most people. She and her office colleagues had not only lost a great boss, they had just lost their jobs. They were all of the opinion that working for the Witherspoon Way had been the best thing that had ever happened to them, career-wise. Their lives had been turned upside down by Sprague's murder.

After giving their statements, Millicent had suggested going for a drink. There was unanimous agreement. They were now seated in a booth in their favorite after-work spot, a cozy tavern and café near the Pike Place Market.

The day was ending the way it had begun, with rain and gloom. The winter solstice had passed a few weeks earlier. The days were becoming perceptibly longer—Seattleites were keen observers of the nuances in the ever-changing patterns of sunlight—but the early evening twilight made it seem as if it was still December on the calendar.

Millicent sipped her martini and narrowed her eyes. "If I were the police, the first suspect on my list would be Nyla Witherspoon."

As Sprague's bookkeeper and financial manager, Millicent had a tendency to go straight to the bottom line, regardless of the subject. She was a vivacious, curvy redhead with a taste for martinis and the occasional bar hookup.

Millicent had been working for Sprague for nearly a year before Grace had joined the Witherspoon Way team. On the surface, she seemed to have it all—film star–level glamour and a computer for a brain. She had used both to make her way in the world. What Millicent did not have was a family. Her past was murky. She did not like to discuss it. But she had once said that she left home at the age of sixteen and had no intention of ever returning. She was a survivor. In spite of the odds against her, she had landed adroitly on her stiletto heels.

Kristy blinked away a few more tears. "Nyla does have the most to gain from Sprague's death, doesn't she? But she's his daughter, for heaven's sake. We all know that she had issues with him. It was a troubled relationship. Still, murdering her father?"

Kristy was the most recent member of the Witherspoon team. Born and raised in a small town in Idaho, she had moved to Seattle in search of adventure and—as she had explained to Grace and Millicent—more options in husbands. With her light brown hair, warm eyes and pretty features, she was attractive in a sweet, wholesome way that went down well with the Witherspoon clients.

Unlike Millicent, Kristy was close to her family. Although she had confided to her coworkers that she did not want to marry a farmer, it was clear that she had a deep and abiding affection for the bucolic world she had left behind. She was forever regaling the office staff with humorous stories about growing up on a farm.

Grace and Millicent had privately speculated that Sprague had felt sorry for Kristy, who had found herself struggling in the big city. Perhaps giving her a job had been, in part, an act of kindness back at the beginning. But somewhat to everyone's amazement, Kristy had quickly displayed an invaluable flair for travel logistics and an ability to charm clients. As the demand for Witherspoon Way seminars had grown, so had the work involved in coordinating Sprague's busy schedule. Business had been so brisk lately that Sprague had been on the verge of hiring an assistant for Kristy.

"It wouldn't be the first time an heir has hurried things along," Millicent pointed out. "Besides, we know that Nyla was furious with Sprague. They argued constantly. Things between them only got worse when Mr. Perfect came along. Sprague didn't approve of him and that just made Nyla angrier. I think she was ready to do just about anything to get her hands on her inheritance. She hated Sprague for putting her on an allowance."

"Well, she is an adult, not a child," Grace pointed out.

"If you ask me, she decided she didn't want to wait any longer for the money," Millicent said. She swallowed some more of her martini, lowered the glass and fixed Grace and Kristy with a grim expression. "I think there's something else we should keep in mind."

Kristy frowned. "What?"

Millicent plucked the little plastic spear out of the martini and munched the olive. "It's true that Nyla had issues with her father but she wasn't very fond of the three of us, either. We had better watch our backs."

Kristy's eyes widened. "Jeez, you're serious, aren't you?"

"Oh, yeah," Millicent said.

Grace picked up her glass and took a sip. The wine was starting to soften the edgy sensation that had been riding her hard all day but she knew from experience that the effects would not last. She told herself to think positive but she had a bad feeling that the old dream would return that night.

She studied Millicent. "Do you really think Nyla is a threat?"

Millicent shrugged. "I'm just saying it would be a good idea to be careful for a while. I'm telling you, Nyla Witherspoon is unstable. She and Sprague had what can only be called a fraught relationship but the capper was the new fiancé."

"Burke Marrick," Kristy said. She made a face. "AKA Mr. Perfect."

"You know what?" Millicent said. "Burke Marrick was Sprague's worst nightmare. Sprague was always worried that some good-looking, fast-talking con man would come along and sweep Nyla off her feet. Why do you think Sprague insisted on paying her bills and keeping her on an allowance? He was trying to protect her."

Kristy sniffed. "Small countries could live on Nyla's allowance."

"The actual amount is beside the point." Millicent aimed the olive spear at Kristy. "If there's one thing I know, it's money, and I know how people react to it. Trust me, no one ever thinks they have enough. Nyla couldn't stand the thought that the bulk of her inheritance was tied up in a special trust that she could not access until her father's death. And I've got a hunch Mr. Perfect was pushing her hard to get ahold of the money."

A grim silence settled on the table. Grace reflected on the fact that they had all had their run-ins with Sprague's temperamental daughter. Nyla had seemed jealous of the three of them. Now she would have her inheritance to go with her charming fiancé. From a certain perspective, life was suddenly looking quite rosy for Nyla. And for Mr. Perfect.

Grace cleared her throat. "You do realize what you're saying, Millicent. If you're right, that means that Burke Marrick is also a suspect."

Kristy put her glass down very quickly. "What if Nyla and Burke planned Sprague's murder together?"

Millicent shrugged. "Wouldn't surprise me."

"I think we had better hold off on the conspiracy theories," Grace said. "If you're going to make a list of suspects, you'll need a really big sheet of paper."

Kristy and Millicent looked at her.

"What do you mean?" Kristy asked. "Sprague was so nice. So generous."

Understanding gleamed in Millicent's eyes. "You're right, Grace. After Nyla and Marrick, the next name on the list just has to be Larson Rayner."

"We all know there was not a lot of positive energy lost between Larson and Sprague," Grace said. "Nothing like a falling-out between business partners to create motive."

"That's true," Kristy said. "Remember how Larson stormed into the office last month and accused Sprague of stealing his clients?"

"Professional envy and a strong dose of jealousy, not to mention a decline in revenues." Millicent smiled. Her green eyes gleamed. "Great motives for murder." She looked at Grace. "I wonder if Larson realizes that you're the reason why Sprague's business took off a year and a half ago."

Grace felt herself turning pink. "That is a gross exaggeration. I had a few ideas and Sprague let me run with them, that's all."

"Bullshit," Millicent said cheerfully. "Before you came along, Sprague Witherspoon was just another motivational speaker in a very crowded field. You're the one who launched the business into the big time."

"Millicent is right," Kristy said. "If poor Sprague hadn't been murdered last night, he would have become the number one self-help guru in the country within a few months, thanks to you."

"The Witherspoon Way was doing well before you came along," Millicent said. "But the really big money didn't start rolling in until after the cookbook was published. The affirmation-of-the-day blog caught fire after that. During the past few months, Kristy couldn't confirm speaking engagements and seminars fast enough. Isn't that right, Kristy?"

"Yes." Kristy smiled reminiscently. "Sprague was on the road every week. I don't know how he did it. But he never complained when I booked back-to-back seminars."

"He loved it," Grace said. "He thrived on the travel and the crowds. He had so much charisma and such an incredible ability to communicate with an audience."

Kristy nodded sagely. "But it was the cookbook and the affirmation blog that put the Witherspoon Way over the top. You're the one who came up with both projects."

"The cookbook and blog would never have worked if they hadn't been done under the Witherspoon name," Grace said. "All I did was dream up some marketing ideas that suited Sprague's approach to positive thinking."

"It's called branding," Millicent said. "I wouldn't be surprised if you get a call from Larson Rayner soon making you an offer you can't refuse."

Kristy brightened. "Maybe he'll offer all three of us positions in his firm. We are, or rather, we *were* Sprague's team. Larson must realize that we've got exactly the qualifications he needs to take him to the top."

"True," Grace said. "But you might want to rethink that career path if it turns out that Larson Rayner is a suspect in Sprague's murder. Could be tough to book future seminars for him."

Kristy winced. "There is that little problem."

"As for that list of suspects we were talking about," Grace said, "it doesn't end with Nyla, Burke and Larson Rayner. You'll have to add those odd and disgruntled seminar attendees—the folks who emailed Sprague to complain because their lives did not undergo a dramatic change after they started practicing the Witherspoon Way."

"Well, shit," Millicent said. "You're right, Grace. That would make for a very long list."

Kristy sighed. "It may be sort of tacky under the circumstances but I can't help noticing that if Larson Rayner is on the suspect list, our pool of potential employers is going to be extremely small. I don't imagine there are a lot of folks out there looking for people who possess the skills required to manage the office of a motivational speaker."

"On the other hand," Millicent said, going very thoughtful, "if Rayner is cleared as a suspect, he's going to need us. I wonder if he knows that?"

Grace picked up her wine. "Time for some serious positive thinking, as Sprague would say."

"We need a Witherspoon affirmation for successful job hunting," Kristy announced. She gave Grace a misty smile. "You're the affirmation writer in the crowd. Got one for us?"

Millicent laughed. "Well, Grace? What would be a good Witherspoon Way saying for those of us who find ourselves suddenly unemployed?"

Grace ran one fingertip around the rim of her wineglass and gave the problem some thought.

"If Sprague were here he would remind us that no one finds an interesting future by staying indoors and waiting for a sunny day," she said *"To discover your future you must go outdoors and take a walk in the rain."*

"That sounds about right," Kristy said. Her warm eyes turned somber and serious. "Don't know about the rest of you, but working for the Witherspoon Way really did change my life." She raised her wineglass. "Here's to Sprague Witherspoon."

"To Sprague," Millicent said.

"To Sprague," Grace said.

Millicent downed the last of her martini and signaled the waiter for another round.

"I probably shouldn't say this," she said, "given how much money I made working for the Witherspoon Way and absolutely no offense intended toward you, Grace, but I have to tell you that I really detest those dumbass Witherspoon Way affirmations."

Three

The dream was lying in wait for her . . .

. . . The wind shrieking through the old, abandoned asylum caught the door at the top of the stairs and slammed it shut.

The darkness of the basement closed in around her. It was suddenly hard to breathe. She knew she could not allow her own fear to show. She had to stay strong for the boy. He was unnaturally calm, the way people are in dreams. He clung to her hand and looked up at her.

She knew that he was waiting to see if she would save him. That was what adults were supposed to do—save little kids. She wanted to tell him that she wasn't a real grown-up. She was only sixteen years old.

"He's coming back," the boy said. "He hurt that lady and he's going to hurt us, too."

She aimed the cell phone flashlight at the long bundle on the floor. Her first thought was that someone had left an unrolled sleeping bag in the basement. But it wasn't a sleeping bag. The eyes of the dead woman stared up at her through the thick layers of plastic.

Heavy footsteps thudded on the wooden floor overhead. Hurriedly she switched off the flashlight.

"Hide," she said to the boy in the language of dreams.

The door at the top of the steps opened. The entrance to the basement was once again illuminated with an empty gray light. Soon the monster would appear.

"It's too late," the boy said. "He's here now."

There was a small prescription medication container on the floor near the dead woman. Next to it was a liquor bottle. She could not see the brand on the bottle but she could make out the word vodka.

The only way out was through the door at the top of the stairs . . .

The ping of the email alert brought her out of the nightmare on a rush of adrenaline that tightened her throat and iced her blood. For a few seconds her heart pounded to the dark rhythm of the killer's footsteps. She hovered in the murky terrain between the dream state and the waking state.

Breathe.

It had been a while since the dream had haunted her nights but she had long ago made the breathing exercises a daily routine. It was one of three rituals that she practiced regularly. All were related to the nightmare of the past.

She sat up quickly on the edge of the bed and focused on her breath. But the edgy, fight-or-flight sensation threatened to overwhelm her. She could not sit quietly so she got up, went out into the living room and started to pace. Sometimes it took a few minutes to calm her nerves.

The gentle glow of night-lights illuminated every room in the small apartment. In addition, the drapes were open to allow the city lights to pour in through her fifteenth-floor window. She did not turn on any of the regular lamps and ceiling fixtures because she did not want to further stimulate her already overstimulated senses.

Breathe.

The images of the dream flashed and flared, clawing at her awareness in an attempt to drag her down into the dark, seething pit of raw panic. Her skin prickled. Her pulse pounded.

As she paced, she made the promise that she always made to herself during a bad attack. If she did not get things under control she would take a dose of the anti-anxiety medication the doctor had prescribed. In the past few years that vow, combined with the breathing exercises, was usually sufficient to get through even the worst episodes.

Just give the breathing exercises a chance to work. The meds are in the drawer. Don't worry, you can have one if you really need it. You knew tonight would probably be a bad night.

Breathe.

She needed to go through the door. She had to get outside.

She unlocked the slider. Cold damp air swirled into the room. She stepped out onto the balcony. The rain had stopped. The jeweled cityscape of Seattle sparkled around her. The Space Needle glowed reassuringly, a giant torch against the darkness.

She focused on the exercises.

The thud-thud-thud of the killer's footsteps faded back into memory.

Gradually her pulse steadied and her breathing returned to normal.

When she was sure she was back in control she returned to the living room. She closed and locked the slider.

"Crap," she said aloud to the silent room.

And everyone wondered why she had never married, why she never let any man spend the night. Panic attacks were like earthquakes. It wasn't a matter of *if* there would be another one. It was only a question of when it would strike. She had discovered the hard way that it might be weeks, months or even years between attacks. Or it could be tomorrow night. How did a woman explain that to a potential lover?

Maybe, if her social life ever progressed beyond the short-term-relationship pattern she had developed, she might find a man she could entrust with her secrets. But somehow that had not yet happened.

She had overcome the shivery jitters but she knew she would not be able to go back to sleep, at least not for some time. On the other hand, there was no job waiting for her in the morning, she reminded herself. She was free to sleep late. Now that was a truly depressing thought because she always got up early, even after a bad night. She was doomed to be a morning person.

She went to stand at the window. Although there were a number of condo towers, apartments and office buildings scattered around her, she could see a wide slice of the Queen Anne neighborhood. The hillside was dotted with the lights of the exclusive residences that had been built there to take advantage of the views. Tonight one of the big houses was dark and empty. Sprague Witherspoon's body was probably in cold storage in the medical examiner's office, waiting to be autopsied. The hunt for his killer had begun.

She thought about the vodka bottle that she had found at the scene. Another wave of anxiety whispered through her nerves. It had to be a coincidence. There was no other explanation.

She suddenly remembered the ping that had shattered the nightmare. She went back into the bedroom and picked up the phone. When she saw the sender's name she almost plunged straight into another full-blown panic attack. For a few beats she simply stared at the screen in stunned disbelief. This could not be happening.

Sprague Witherspoon had sent her an email from beyond the grave. The message was a macabre twist on one of the Witherspoon Way affirmations:

Each day brings us another opportunity to change the future.
Congratulations, your future will soon be very different.

Four

Well, that was the most awkward evening I've spent in some time," Grace said. "And I include the night of my high school prom, during which I discovered that my date was deeply depressed because the girl he had wanted to be with had turned him down."

"You want awkward?" Julius Arkwright asked. "Try the annual business dinner and charity auction I'm scheduled to attend later this week."

Grace gave that some consideration. "I don't think that qualifies as awkward. A business dinner and charity auction sound boring, not awkward."

"Yeah, boring, too," Julius agreed. "I will have to make casual conversation with a bunch of people who are as dull as I am. But the really awkward part comes later, when I deliver the most boring after-dinner speech ever written. The charity auction isn't so bad. I'll be stuck buying a piece of art that I don't want but that isn't exactly awkward. That's just costly."

He didn't seem to care about the financial cost of the event, she noticed. Interesting.

She had been introduced to Julius for the first time that evening. She barely knew him but she was already certain that he ranked as the least boring man she had ever met. That was, however, beside the point, she told herself. They were talking awkward, not boring, and she doubted that any business dinner could have been as unnerving as the blind date that she and Julius had just endured.

And the date was not over—not until she got back to the lake house. To get there she had to clamber into the front seat of Julius's gleaming black SUV. She hated SUVs. They were not designed for women who were frequently obliged to shop in the petite department.

She tucked her trench coat around herself and tried to discreetly raise the hem of her pencil-slim skirt so that she could position her left high-heeled sandal on the floorboard of the vehicle. Reaching up, she grasped the handhold inside the cab and prepared to haul her body-weight up into the passenger seat.

There was no hope of negotiating the business gracefully. Even if she had been wearing jeans and athletic shoes she would have had a problem. Dressed in a snug-fitting little black dress and heels the best she could hope for was to make it up and into the seat on the first try with as little bounce as possible.

She tightened her grip on the handhold and pushed off with her right foot.

"Watch your head," Julius said.

Before she realized what he intended she felt his hands close around her waist. He lifted her as easily as if she were a sack of groceries and plopped her on the passenger seat.

She tried to control her trajectory and landing but she bounced, anyway. Her coat fell open, exposing a lot of inner thigh. By the time she got things under control Julius was closing the door.

Crap.

The awkward night was not showing any signs of improving. There was probably an affirmation for a blind date gone bad but what she really wanted was a therapeutic glass of wine.

She watched Julius round the front of the SUV. For a moment his hard profile and broad shoulders were silhouetted against the porch lights of the Nakamura house. In spite of all the warnings she had been giving herself that evening, an unfamiliar and decidedly danger- ous sense of anticipation sparkled through her. For the duration of the short drive home she was going to be alone with Julius. That was probably not a good idea.

He opened the door and climbed behind the wheel. She watched him angle himself into the seat with the easy grace of a large hunting cat settling into high grass to wait for prey.

Well, of course he had made the process look easy. It wasn't as if someone had literally tossed him up into the seat.

He closed the door. An ominous but rather exciting sense of intimacy seethed in the dark interior of the SUV. At least it seemed ominous and exciting to her. Julius appeared blissfully unaware of the edgy vibe. He was no doubt eager to dump her on her doorstep.

She focused her attention on their hosts for the evening. Irene and Devlin Nakamura waved cheerfully from the front porch of their home.

Irene was a tall, attractive blonde who could trace her heritage back to some of the many Norwegians who had settled in the Pacific Northwest at the end of the nineteenth century. She was the kind of woman who could handle being the wife of a man who worked in law enforcement. She was also a very sharp businesswoman with a fast- rising local company that specialized in high-end cookware.

Devlin Nakamura bore the unmistakable stamp of a man others looked to in a crisis. Which was a good thing in a police officer, Grace told herself—unless he was looking at you. He radiated determination and a stern will and he had cop eyes. It was easy to imagine him kicking down a door, or reading you your rights. If you were a criminal, he was not the investigator you wanted on your trail. Grace shivered. She had not been surprised to discover that Devlin and Julius Arkwright had once served together in the Marines.

"I'm sure Irene and Devlin meant well," she said.

Julius fired up the SUV's big engine. "Do you always say things like that after someone has ambushed you with a blind date?"

"Don't be so melodramatic. It wasn't that bad. Just . . . awkward."

Grace was certain that Irene's motives had been well-intentioned. She and Irene had grown up together. They had been close friends since kindergarten.

Devlin's motives, however, were questionable. He was relatively new in Irene's life. The pair had met shortly after Devlin moved to Cloud Lake a year ago to become the town's new chief of police. Grace had been Irene's maid of honor at the wedding.

Grace liked Devlin and she sensed that he was a committed husband. But tonight she'd had the uneasy impression that he was watching her with the same cold speculation that she had seen in the eyes of the Seattle homicide detective who had questioned her after Sprague's murder ten days earlier.

"Okay," Julius said. "We'll go with awkward as a description of the date. For now."

The amusement that etched his dark, deep, deceptively easygoing voice sent another chill across her nerve endings. She glanced at him. In the otherworldly glow of the car's interior lights his face was unreadable but his eyes were a little tight at the outer corners, as if he was preparing to pull the trigger of a rifle.

Not that she knew much about guns or the type of person who used them, she thought. The only man of her acquaintance who actually carried one was Devlin. But given his job, she supposed that he had some business doing so.

She had to admit that she was probably at least partially responsible for the atmosphere of impending doom that had hung over the small dinner party that evening. The problem was that she was not doing a really great job of thinking positive these days.

Stumbling onto a murder scene was bound to have some unpleasant repercussions. Still, it had been ten days since she discovered Witherspoon's body and the darkness was not lifting. It hovered at the edge of her consciousness during the day. At night it swept in like the tide. In spite of a lot of meditation and positive self-talk and the three rituals, the bad energy seemed to be getting worse, affecting her thoughts and her dreams. Both were growing darker and more unsettling.

And the disturbing emails from a dead man were still arriving every evening.

Julius eased the SUV out of the driveway and onto Lake Circle Road with the cool, competent control that seemed to be at the very core of his character. The man would make a really good friend or a very bad enemy, she thought. She doubted that he was the positive-thinking type—more likely a tactical strategist.

She refused to contemplate what kind of lover he would be.

Whatever you do, don't go there, she thought.

She had been too tense—too aware—of Julius all evening to consider the reasons why he disturbed her senses. The best she could come up with was the old warning about icebergs—the most dangerous part was hidden under the surface. Her feminine intuition told her that Julius Arkwright had a lot going on under the surface. So what? The same could be said of everyone. There was no reason to dwell on Julius's concealed issues. She had her own issues these days.

The only hard facts that she knew about Julius were the bits and pieces that had come out in the course of conversation that evening.

He was a venture capitalist—a very successful venture capitalist, according to Irene. Other investors routinely entrusted gazillions of dollars to Julius to invest on their behalf.

Not that she had anything against making money, Grace thought. As it happened, figuring out how to generate some future income was right at the top of her To-Do list at the moment. Nothing like losing a job to make a person appreciate the value of steady employment. She should know—she'd lost count of the number of jobs she'd had since leaving college to find herself.

The position at the Witherspoon Way headquarters had lasted longer than any of her previous careers—a full eighteen months. She knew her mother and sister had begun to hope that her ever-precarious job situation had finally stabilized. She'd had a few expectations that might be the case, as well.

Julius drove at a surprisingly low rate of speed along the narrow, two-lane road that circled the jagged edge of Cloud Lake. The surface of the deep water was a dark mirror that reflected the cold silver light of the moon.

The silence in the front seat became oppressive. Grace searched for a way to end it.

"Thank you for driving me back to my place," she said. She struggled to assume a polite tone but she knew she sounded a little gruff.

"No problem," Julius said. "It's on my way."

That much was true. The lakefront cottage that Julius had recently purchased was less than half a mile beyond the house in which Grace had been raised. Nevertheless, she hadn't anticipated the ride home with him. She had fully intended to drive herself to the Nakamuras' that evening but Devlin had offered to pick her up. She had assumed that he would be the one to take her home. But when Julius had pointed out that he would be going right past the Elland house and said it would be no trouble to give Grace a lift, there had been no gracious way to refuse—not with Irene and Devlin both nodding encouragingly.

Dinner would not have been nearly so uncomfortable, Grace thought, if it hadn't been so obvious that Irene had been trying her hand at matchmaking.

Oddly enough, now that she found herself alone with Julius, she could almost see the humor of the situation. Almost. She settled deeper into the seat.

"Did you know ahead of time that Irene and Devlin were setting us up?" she asked.

"I was told there would be another guest." Julius's mouth edged upward at the corner. "Like you said, they meant well."

"Now that it's over, I suppose it's sort of funny."

"Think so?"

"I'm used to people trying to set me up with blind dates," Grace said. "My mother and my sister have made something of a hobby out of doing that in the past couple of years. Now Irene appears to be giving it a whirl. Between you and me, they're all getting desperate."

"But you're not interested?"

"Oh, I'm usually interested," Grace said.

"Just not tonight, is that it? Got a problem with the fact that I'm divorced?"

His tone was a little too neutral. So much for making light conversation. This was getting more awkward by the moment.

She tried to sidestep.

"Nothing personal, really," she said. "It's just that I've got a few other priorities at the moment. I'm trying to come up with a new career path and that requires my full attention."

Julius did not appear interested in her job issues.

"Any idea why things haven't worked out with any of your other dates?" he asked.

She was starting to get the deer-in-the-headlights feeling.

"It's just that nothing has ever clicked," she said, very cautious now. "My fault, according to Irene and my family."

"Why is it your fault?"

"They tell me that I have a bad habit of trying to fix people. If I'm successful, I send them on their way and I move on, too."

"And if you can't fix them?"

She tapped one finger on the console that separated the seats. "Same outcome. I send them on their way and I move on."

"So, you're a serial heartbreaker?"

She did laugh then. "Good grief, no. I'm pretty sure I've never broken any man's heart. Men tend to think of me as a friend. They tell me their troubles. We talk about their problems. I offer suggestions. And then they go off and date the next cute blonde they meet in a bar or the good-looking coworker at the office."

Julius gave her a short, sharp look. "Has your heart ever been broken?"

"Not since college. And in hindsight, it's a good thing he did break my heart because the relationship was a disaster for both of us. Lots of storm and drama but no substance."

Julius was quiet for a moment. "Looking back, I don't think there was any storm and drama in my marriage."

"Not even at the very end?"

"We were both relieved that it was all over, as I recall."

That was hard to believe, Grace thought, but the last thing she wanted to do was dig into the subject of his failed marriage. She was not going to try to fix Julius Arkwright.

"Mmm," she said instead.

"Don't worry, I won't spend the rest of the drive to your place unloading on you. You don't want to hear about my divorce and I don't want to talk about it."

"Whew." Grace pretended to wipe her brow. "Good to know."

Julius laughed.

Some of the tension went out of the atmosphere. She relaxed a little more and searched for a neutral topic.

"How long will you be staying here in Cloud Lake?" she asked.

"I plan to use the house year-round. I have a condo in Seattle but most of my work is done online. With some exceptions, I can work here as well as I can at my office. Cloud Lake is only an hour from the city. I'll commute a couple of times a week to make sure things stay on track."

She reminded herself that Julius was a very *successful* venture capitalist. He probably bought lakeside cottages and city condos the way she bought new shoes and dresses. Not that you would know that to look at him, she thought. In recent years the Pacific Northwest had proven fertile ground for start-ups and the savvy investors, like Julius, who funded the businesses that hit big. There was a lot of new money walking around the region these days and very little of it gave off a flashy, rich vibe. Most of it blended in very well with the crowd that shopped for deals at Costco and bought mountain bikes and all-weather gear at REI.

Grace was quite certain that Julius's money was not the old kind. He had the edge of a self-made man—the kind of man who was accustomed to fighting for what he wanted.

"The house you bought used to be owned by your neighbor, Harley Montoya," she said. "I was surprised to hear that he had sold it. He's owned that property and the house he lives in for nearly a decade."

"Harley says it's time to downsize. What about you? Planning to stick around Cloud Lake?"

"For a while. Now that I'm unemployed I need to watch every penny. Mom kept the lake house after she and Kirk retired but they only use it during the summer. They suggested that I save rent money by living here until I figure out my new career path."

"Where do they live now?" Julius asked.

"They moved to Scottsdale a couple of years ago. Mom sold her gift shop here in Cloud Lake and Kirk turned over his insurance business to his sons. At the moment Mom and Kirk are on a world cruise."

"Irene said you have a sister?"

"Alison, yes. She's a lawyer in Portland."

"So you intend to stay here in Cloud Lake only until you get your act together?"

"That's the plan," Grace said.

"What's your strategy?"

She blinked. "I thought I just explained my plan."

Julius shot her an amused glance. "I'm talking about your strategy for finding a new career path."

"Oh, that." She flushed. "I'm still working on it."

She didn't owe him any explanations, she reminded herself.

"You must have some thoughts on the subject," he said.

"Actually, no, I don't," she said, going for a frosty, back-off tone. "My life has been somewhat complicated lately."

"I know. Must have been tough finding the body of your boss the way you did."

She hesitated, not sure she wanted to go down that particular conversational path.

"I try not to think about it," she said coolly.

"The Witherspoon Way will collapse without Witherspoon at the helm."

She crossed her arms and gazed fixedly at the pavement through the windshield.

"Trust me, all of us who worked for Sprague Witherspoon are aware of that," she said.

"You need a job. Sounds like your problem is pretty straight-forward."

"Is that right? And just when, exactly, was the last time you found yourself out of work?"

To her surprise he pondered that briefly.

"It's been a while," he admitted.

She gave him a steely smile. "In other words, you really have no idea whatsoever about the current job market, let alone how complicated my particular situation might be."

"How did you find the job with Witherspoon?"

The question caught her off guard. "I sort of stumbled into it. That's usually how I find a new job."

"You stumbled into working for a motivational speaker?"

"Well, yes. A year and a half ago I was looking for a new direction. I decided to attend a Witherspoon Way seminar hoping to get some ideas. After Sprague Witherspoon talked to the audience I waited around to speak to him."

"About what?" Julius sounded genuinely curious.

"While Sprague was giving his seminar on positive thinking, I came up with some ideas about how he could take his concepts in different directions." She unfolded her arms and spread her hands. "To my surprise, he listened to me. The next thing I knew, he was offering me a job. Once I was on board he let me have free rein. Working for the Witherspoon Way was the best job I've ever had."

"Just how many jobs have you had?"

"A lot." She sighed. "It's embarrassing, to tell you the truth. And it makes for a sketchy résumé. Some job-hopping is okay but beyond a certain point it makes you look—"

"Flighty. Unreliable. Undependable."

She winced. "All of the above. My sister knew that she wanted to be a lawyer by the time she was a senior in high school. But here I am, still searching for a career path that will last longer than eighteen months."

"You've got a problem," Julius said. "You need a business plan."

She stared at him. "A business plan for landing a job?"

"As far as I can tell, everything in life works better if you have a good, well-thought-out plan."

It was all she could do not to laugh. He sounded so serious.

"Are you talking about a five-year plan?" she asked lightly. "Because I don't think Mom will give me free rent for five years."

"Not a five-year plan—not for finding a career. More like a three-months-at-the-outside strategy. If you're serious about this you need to set goals and meet them."

"I've never been much of a long-term planner," she said.

"No kidding. I would not have guessed that."

She gave him a cold smile. "Sprague Witherspoon said that one of my assets was that I think outside the box."

"There's thinking outside the box and then there's failing to be able to find the box in the first place. You can't appreciate the new model until you understand the old one and why it isn't working anymore."

Irritation sparkled through her. "Gosh, maybe you should go into the self-help business. That sounds a lot like one of the Witherspoon Way affirmations."

"What's an affirmation?"

"It's a shortcut to positive thinking. A good affirmation helps focus the mind in a productive, optimistic way."

"Give me an example," Julius said.

"Well, say you had a bad day at work—"

"Let's go with something more concrete. Say you found yourself at a dinner party with friends who set you up with a boring blind date.

What kind of affirmation would you use to help you think positive about the situation?"

She went very still. "Probably better not to get too concrete."

"I'm a businessman. I deal in concrete facts."

"Fine," she shot back. "You want an affirmation for this date? How about, *Things are always darkest before the dawn*? Will that work for you?"

"I don't think that's a Witherspoon Way affirmation. Pretty sure it's been around for a while."

"Got a better one?"

"I don't do affirmations. I've got a couple of rules that I never break but neither of them fits our current situation."

"Here's my place," she said quickly.

But he was already slowing for the turn into the tree-lined driveway that led to the small, neat house at the edge of the lake. He brought the SUV to a halt in front of the wraparound porch and shut down the engine.

The lights were still on in Agnes Gilroy's house next door. The drapes were pulled but Grace was certain that Agnes was peering through the curtains. Agnes possessed a deep and abiding interest in the doings of her neighbors. She was bound to have heard the unfamiliar rumble of the car in the driveway.

"Thanks for the ride home," Grace said. She unbuckled her safety belt and reached for the door handle. "Nice meeting you. I'm sure we'll run into each other in town. Don't bother getting out of the car. I can manage just fine on my own."

She could tell that he was not paying attention to her less-than-sparkling chatter. He sat, unmoving, his strong, competent hands resting on the wheel, and contemplated the house as if he had never seen one.

"I had a career plan by the time I was eleven years old," he said.

"Yep, I'm not surprised." She got the car door open, grabbed the edges of the trench coat and prepared to jump down to the ground. "I had you pegged as one of those."

"One of those what?"

"One of those folks who always knows where he's going." She gripped the handhold and plunged off the seat. For an instant she hovered precariously in midair. Relief shot through her when she landed on both feet. She turned and looked back at him. "Must be nice."

He popped open his own door, uncoiled from behind the wheel and circled the front of the vehicle. He got to her before she reached the porch steps.

"It helps to know what you want," he said. "It clarifies choices and streamlines the decision matrix."

The cool, calculating way he watched her sent a little chill down her spine. Or was it a thrill? The possibility made her catch her breath. *Wrong time and probably the wrong man. Send him on his way.*

"What was your career plan at eleven?" she said, instead.

"I wanted to get rich."

She paused to search his face in the porch light. "Why?"

"Because I figured out that money gives a man power."

"Over others?"

He considered that and then shrugged. "Maybe. Depending on the situation. But that wasn't why I wanted to get rich."

She watched him closely. "You wanted control over your own life."

"Yeah, that about sums it up."

"That's a perfectly reasonable objective. It seems to have worked out well for you. Congratulations. Good night, Julius."

She hitched the strap of her purse over her shoulder and walked quickly toward the front porch steps. The relentless crunch of gravel behind her made her stop in mid-stride. When she turned to confront him, he stopped, too.

"It's okay," she said briskly. "You don't need to see me to my door."

"I said I'd take you home. You're not home until you're inside the house."

For some reason, anger crackled through her. "I'm not your responsibility."

"You are until you're home." He waited.

She gripped her keys very tightly. "I can't believe I just snapped at you because you're trying to do the gentlemanly thing. I apologize. Jeez. Where are my manners? Sorry. I'm a little tense these days. Thank you."

"You're welcome." He stood there in the moonlight as if he was willing to wait until dawn for her to make the next move.

"Right," she said. "The door."

She turned again and hurried up the steps. Julius followed her across the front porch, keeping a little distance between them, careful not to crowd her.

She dug the keys out of her purse, got the door open, stepped across the threshold and flipped the wall switch. Two lamps came up, revealing the warm, casually comfortable space. Her mother had been in what Grace and Alison referred to as her Rustic Retreat phase when she last redecorated.

The wooden floors were burnished with age. Two overstuffed chairs and a deep sofa upholstered in dark brown leather were positioned on a honey-colored area rug. A large brass basket on the stone hearth held kindling for the cold, dark fireplace.

Several landscapes featuring quaint cottages, wooden docks and old boathouses around the shores of Cloud Lake hung on the walls. Visitors rarely noticed that there was no painting of the most picturesque structure on the lake, the long-abandoned Cloud Lake Inn.

Grace turned around a second time to confront Julius. In the glare of the front porch light his gold-brown eyes were heavily shadowed.

She could see that he was drinking in every detail of the living room behind her. She searched for a word to describe what she thought she detected in his expression and came up with *hungry*.

Don't go there, she told herself. If you feed him he might hang around. This was not a good time for her to be taking in strays. She was not here to fix Julius Arkwright. If she did, he would probably walk away like all the others.

And this man just might be the one she would regret setting free.

She opened her mouth to thank him politely and bid him good night.

"Would you like to come in for some herbal tea?" she heard herself say instead.

Five

T hanks," he said. He moved across the threshold and closed the door. "I don't think I've ever had herbal tea. Sounds . . . interesting."

For a few seconds she could only stand there, shocked at what she had just done. When she realized that he was watching her, waiting for her to make the next move, she pulled herself together. She hadn't offered to feed him, she thought. It was just tea.

"Tea," she said. She turned on her heel. "Kitchen."

She dropped her clutch on one of the overstuffed chairs and went into the big, old-fashioned kitchen. Through the airy curtains she could see the moonstruck surface of the water. Here and there the lights of some of the lakefront houses glittered in the trees. A long necklace of low lamps marked the footpath that circled the lake.

She discovered she had to concentrate just to remember how to boil the water in the kettle.

She switched on the gas burner and reminded herself again that it was just tea. The fact that for some reason she was feeling a little rush of edgy exhilaration was probably going to be a problem later. But at that moment she did not care.

Julius lounged against the tiled countertop and folded his arms. He somehow managed to make it look as if he was entirely at home in her kitchen—as if he was in the habit of spending a lot of time there. He watched her pluck two tea bags out of a glass canister.

"What's in that tea you're fixing?" he asked.

"Chamomile," she said. "It's supposed to promote restful sleep."

"I usually use a medicinal dose of whiskey."

She smiled. "I've been known to resort to that particular medication on occasion, myself."

"Had some bad nights recently?"

Very deliberately she positioned the tea bags in two mugs.

"A few," she conceded. "You were right. Finding my employer's body was a shock."

"I followed some of the reports in the media," he said. "The story caught my attention because the Witherspoon Way was a rising star in the Pacific Northwest business world."

She shook her head. "And now it's all gone. Everything that Sprague built will soon disappear."

"That's the problem with any business that is founded on a personality rather than a product. Celebrities, athletes, actors—same story. They might rake in millions while they're working but if something happens to them, the whole company implodes."

The teakettle whistled. Grace switched off the burner and poured the hot water into the mugs.

"When it comes to the motivational seminar business, it's definitely all about the charisma of the person at the top," she said.

"So you're unemployed."

"Again." She put one of the mugs down on the counter next to Julius. "I'm an underachiever. No other word for it. It's time I got my act together. I just wish I knew what I really wanted to do in life. Every time I get a glimmer of a career path, something happens to make me swerve in another direction."

"Like the closing down of the Witherspoon Way?"

"Well, yes."

"I planned out a future once."

"You said you knew where you were going from the age of eleven." She blew on her tea. "You wanted to be rich. What set you on that career path?"

"My parents split up. Dad remarried and moved across the country. Never saw much of him after that, except once, years later, when he came around asking for a loan. My mother worked hard to keep a roof over our heads. She sacrificed everything for me during those years."

Grace nodded. "That's when you realized that money could make a huge difference. It could buy you the kind of power you needed to change your mother's life."

Julius smiled faintly. "Are you trying to analyze me? Because if so, I'd like to change the subject."

"Irene said that you are a very successful venture capitalist. She told me that in Pacific Northwest business circles they call you Arkwright the Alchemist because when it comes to investments, you can turn lead into gold."

"I'm good," Julius said. "But I'm not that good."

"Good enough to get very rich, though, right?"

"Rich enough."

"I assume your mother is doing okay?"

"Mom's fine. After money was no longer an issue she did what she always wanted to do—she went back to school to finish getting her B.A. Wound up marrying one of her professors. They live in Northern California. Doug teaches at a community college. Mom works in the counseling office. They're going to retire soon. I manage their investments."

She smiled. "I assume they will both enjoy comfortable retirements?"

He shrugged that off as if it were no big deal. "Sure."

She raised her eyebrows. "Are you satisfied with your current financial status?"

"I've got all the money I'll ever need and then some. How many shirts can one man wear? How many cars can he drive? How many houses does he really want to maintain? Yes, Grace, I'm rich enough."

She studied him for a moment.

"Do you know, I don't think I've ever heard anyone say that he had enough money," she said. "Granted, I've never met many truly wealthy people. But I was under the impression that after a certain point people use money as a way to keep score."

"That works." Julius cautiously swallowed some of the chamomile tea and lowered the mug. "For a while."

She raised her brows. "Would you rather go back to being non-rich?"

He smiled slowly. "No."

"But it would be no big deal if you lost it all tomorrow. In fact, I'll bet you would find the situation interesting."

"Interesting?"

"As in, not boring. Starting over would be a challenge for you."

"Maybe," he said. "For me. But I'm no longer the only one involved. If I lost everything tomorrow, several small, promising start-ups would crash and burn. A lot of people who work for those little companies would be unemployed and so would the folks who work directly or indirectly for me. And that's not counting the people who trust me to invest their money, like my mother."

She leaned back against the counter beside him and took another sip of the tea. "You're right, of course. You're riding the tiger. You don't have the option of choosing to get off. If you do, you'll be okay but a lot of other people will get eaten."

"You didn't expect me to consider that aspect of the situation?"

"Now, on that front, you're wrong. I would absolutely expect you to consider your responsibilities as an employer. Irene has been my best friend since kindergarten. I know her well enough to know that she wouldn't have tried to set me up with you if she didn't think you were a good man."

Julius's mouth twitched at the corner. "I could give you a list of people who would disagree with that opinion."

"Oh, I don't doubt but that you've made a few enemies along the way."

"Making enemies doesn't make me a bad person?"

"Depends on the enemies," she said.

A muffled ping sounded from the front room. She froze. Julius looked at her and then glanced toward the doorway.

She took a steadying breath. And then she took another. The jittery sensation receded.

"My phone," she said quickly. "Just email. I'll deal with it later."

He nodded once and swallowed more of the tea.

"Now I've got a question for you," he said.

"About my nonexistent career plans?"

"It's a little more specific. Did you kill Sprague Witherspoon?"

She stared at him, utterly blindsided. Her brain went blank. Words failed her. First the email ping and now this.

She heard the crash when the mug she had been holding hit the floor but she could not make sense of the sound for a few heartbeats.

Julius watched her the way an entomologist might watch a butterfly in a glass jar.

"Get out," she whispered, her voice hoarse with anger. "Now."

"All right," he said.

He set his unfinished tea down as calmly as though he had just re-marked upon the weather. He walked across the kitchen and went into the living room. She pushed herself away from the counter and pursued him, literally chasing him out of the house.

At the door he paused to look back at her over his shoulder.

"Good night," he said. "It's been an interesting evening. I don't get a lot of those."

"No shit," she said. "I think I can tell you why."

"I already know the answer." He opened the door and moved out onto the porch. "I'm pretty boring when you get to know me. Hell, sometimes I even bore myself. Don't forget to lock your door."

He went down the porch steps.

Infuriated, she crossed the porch and gripped the railing with both hands. "I didn't kill Witherspoon."

"I believe you." He opened the SUV door. "Got any idea who did?"

"No. For heaven's sake, if I did, I would have told the police."

"According to Dev's information, the Seattle police have an over-supply of suspects, including an angry adult daughter, the daughter's fiancé and a few pissed-off seminar folks who don't think they got their money's worth from the Witherspoon Way. Then there are Witherspoon's employees."

"Why would any of us murder our employer? We were all making a lot of money working for the Witherspoon Way."

"Dev says that there is reason to believe that someone involved in the Witherspoon Way was siphoning off a hefty amount of the prof-its and using phony investment statements to cover up the missing money."

"*What?* Are you serious?"

"Ask Dev. He says he got the news from the Seattle cops this morning. There's a lot of money missing. In my world, that counts as a motive."

She stared at him, outraged. "Are you implying that I embezzled money from the Witherspoon Way?"

"No. I had a few questions earlier in the evening but I doubt very much that you're an embezzler."

"Why not? Because I'm not a financial wizard like you?"

He smiled. "This may come as a shock but it doesn't take a lot of financial wizardry to figure out how to skim a great deal of money off the top of a successful business like the Witherspoon Way. In fact, it's dead easy—especially if no one is paying close attention."

"That is insulting on several levels."

"I didn't mean it that way," he said. "Just stating facts."

"Here's a fact you can take to the bank—this blind date is officially over." Out of the corner of her eye Grace saw the curtains twitch in Agnes Gilroy's living room window. "Crap."

She turned on her heel, stalked back inside the house and slammed the door. She whirled around and shot the new dead bolt. Then she secured the chain lock.

For a moment or two she stood listening to the sound of the SUV rumbling back down the drive toward Lake Circle Road.

When she knew that Julius was gone she exhaled slowly. Then she went into the kitchen and grabbed a wad of paper towels off the roll that sat on the counter next to the stove.

She wiped up the spilled chamomile tea and contemplated the possibility that someone had been draining off the profits of the Witherspoon Way. Even if that turned out to be true—and given that Devlin was a cop there was no reason to think his information wasn't accurate—how did that relate to Sprague's murder?

Unless Sprague had uncovered the embezzlement and confronted the embezzler.

She finished mopping up the tea and collected the pieces of the broken mug. She got to her feet and dumped the wet paper towels and the bits of pottery into the trash.

Earlier that day she had done her breathing meditation. It was time for one of the other three rituals that helped her deal with the nightmares over the years.

She walked methodically through the house, checking the shiny new locks she had installed on the doors and windows. Next she looked inside the closets and every cupboard that was large enough to conceal a person. She was annoyed with herself, as usual, when she got down on her knees and looked under the beds in the three small bedrooms. She had no idea what she would do if she actually did find someone hiding in a closet or underneath a bed but she knew she couldn't sleep until she had verified that she was the only one in the house.

When she had completed the walk-through, she poured herself a glass of wine, sat down in one of the big chairs and took her phone out of her purse. She opened her email with the same degree of reluctance she would have felt reaching into a terrarium to pick up a snake.

The email was waiting for her. Another night, another note from a dead man. The first line was familiar.

A positive attitude is like a flashlight in a dark room.

But whoever had sent the email had altered the second line.

You can use it to see who's waiting for you in the shadows.

Six

Congratulations, Arkwright. You really know how to screw up a date.

Julius brought the SUV to a halt in the driveway in front of his house. He shut down the engine and sat for a moment, contemplating the darkened cottage and the mystery of Grace Elland.

The cottage was modest but it was infused with the comfortable patina that only several generations of occupation could impart. It held a few very nice surprises, such as the brilliant view of the lake and the extraordinarily lush gardens. A man could be content with a house like this for the rest of his life.

Grace Elland held a few surprises, too. It was difficult to believe that any intelligent individual could take seriously all that nonsense about positive thinking and the power of affirmations. It was one thing to do a good job. He didn't blame her for working for a self-help guru. A job was a job. You did what you had to do. He admired competence and hard work regardless of the nature of that work. But tonight he'd gotten the impression that Grace had really bought into the

Witherspoon Way fantasy. She actually did seem to believe that positive energy was a force for good in the world.

Either she was for real or she was one of the most clever con artists he had ever met—and in his line, he'd encountered some very good ones.

Mentally he cataloged his impressions of her. She was on the small side. Even in the ridiculously high, incredibly sexy high-heeled shoes she'd worn tonight she barely topped out at a point just a little above his shoulder. But she moved like a dancer. There was something light and graceful about her—and a subtle strength, as well. He'd felt the feminine power in her when he lifted her up into the passenger seat of the SUV. The memory of holding her for that brief moment stirred his senses.

Her hair was the color of aged whiskey. Tonight she'd twisted it into a knot high on her head, probably in an effort to give the illusion of height. The style enhanced her eyes, which were an interesting shade of amber and green. When she looked at him he got the unsettling sensation that she could see a lot more than he wanted her or anyone else to see, things that he kept hidden from the world.

Theoretically she was the kind of woman you didn't look twice at on the street. But tonight he had definitely looked twice—more than twice—and he wanted to look at her—be near her—again. There were questions hanging in the air between them. He would not be satisfied until he got answers.

Some alchemist. He had turned a golden blind date into lead. Now he was stuck with the problem of figuring out how to reverse the process.

He opened the door and climbed out of the vehicle. Harley Montoya emerged from the neighboring house and came out onto the porch.

"How'd the big date go?" Harley bellowed.

There was no need to raise his voice. The two houses sat side by side, separated only by the narrow drive that Harley used to haul his beloved boat out of the water for maintenance. Sound carried well in the stillness of the winter night. But Harley was going deaf in one ear and he tended to assume that everyone else was hard of hearing as well.

As far as anyone knew his first name was a Montoya family name that had been bestowed on him by his parents. But back in the day when he had made his fortune in the construction and development business the rumors circulated that the name was derived from a certain brand of motorcycle. There was no getting around the fact that he was constructed along the lines of a Harley-Davidson. He was in his eighties now and had softened somewhat over the years but he still possessed the solid, muscular build that brought to mind images of the famous bike.

"It was a blind date," Julius said. He closed the door of the SUV. "It didn't go well. They rarely do. And is everyone in Cloud Lake aware that Grace and I were set up tonight?"

"Pretty much," Harley said. "You're home early. Figured you'd screwed up. What went wrong?"

"I made the mistake of asking her if she murdered Witherspoon. She got pissed."

"No kidding." Harley snorted. "Why in the name of hell did you have to go and ask her a thing like that?"

"I was curious to see what her reaction would be."

"I guess you got that question answered. I told you Grace Elland was no killer. You're an idiot when it comes to women."

"I'm aware of that."

"Well, don't worry too much about screwing up," Harley said. "Looks like you and Grace will both be in town for a while. Play your cards right and you'll get another chance."

"In other words, I should try to think positive, is that it?"

"Hell, no." Harley snorted. "I'm talking about smart strategy, not that positive-thinking bullshit. Strategy and planning are your strengths, son. Use your natural-born talents."

"Thanks for the advice. I'll keep it in mind."

"You do that."

Julius walked across the lawn and went through the small gate. He moved out into the narrow rutted lane that separated the two houses.

"You weren't living here in Cloud Lake at the time of the Trager murder, were you?" he asked.

"No," Harley said. "Still too busy making money in those days. Most of what I know about it and about Grace Elland comes from Agnes."

"A bad scene like that would sure as hell leave a few scars, especially on a girl who was only in her teens at the time."

"What are you gettin' at?" Harley asked.

"Just wondering why Grace never married, that's all."

"They say a lot of young women are waiting longer to get married these days, if they marry at all."

"Wow. You're an expert on modern social trends?"

"Nope, but Agnes keeps me up to date," Harley said. "She says Grace has just been waitin' for the right man to come along. We were both sort of hopin' you might be him."

"What the hell made anyone think I might be the right man?" Julius asked, genuinely surprised.

"No idea, come to think of it."

"Were you and Agnes Gilroy coconspirators with Irene and Dev when it came to planning the blind date?"

"Course not." Harley sounded affronted. "Do I look like a matchmaker to you? It was Irene Nakamura's idea. She and Grace have been friends since they were little kids. I hear your old buddy Dev went along with the notion. Go blame him if you want to blame someone."

"Thanks. I'll do that." Julius started walking down the lane toward the dock and the boathouse. "Good night, Harley."

"Don't give up, son. I think Grace is the kind of woman who would give a man a second chance."

Julius paused and looked back at Harley. "Are you sure you haven't fallen into the clutches of some motivational guru?"

"Are you laughing?" Harley demanded.

"Trust me, I'm not laughing."

Julius walked to the end of the lane and stepped out onto the floating dock. Water lapped gently at the planks. Cloud Lake didn't reflect clouds at night, just moonlight—at least it did on a night when the moon was out, like it was tonight. The water was a sheet of black glass streaked with silver under the cold, starry sky.

The weathered boathouse loomed on his left. He moved past it and came to a halt at the end of the dock. Although the trees crowded close to the water's edge, the lights of some of the houses and cottages could be seen from where he stood.

The Elland house was only about a quarter of a mile away if you drew a straight line from point to point across the lake. He could see the lights of the kitchen and back porch. As he watched, one window went dark but another suddenly illuminated. The bedroom, probably. Grace was going to bed. It was, he discovered, an unsettling thought; the kind of thought that could keep a man awake at night.

He took out his phone. Devlin answered on the fourth or fifth ring. He sounded irritated.

"This had better be important," he said. "We keep early hours here in Cloud Lake. This isn't the big city."

"You said you wanted my impressions of Grace Elland."

"Hang on."

There was some rustling. Julius heard Devlin mutter something about business—probably speaking to Irene—and then a door closed.

"Okay," Devlin said. He kept his voice low. "I'm in the kitchen getting a glass of water. Talk fast."

"For what it's worth, I don't think Grace killed Witherspoon."

"Good to know that you and Irene agree on that. Grace does have a fairly good alibi."

"Not iron-clad?"

"In my experience there are very, very few iron-clad alibis. My contact at the Seattle PD confirmed that the video from Grace's apartment garage camera shows that she arrived home at seven o'clock that evening and did not leave until seven-thirty the following morning. The ME said Witherspoon was murdered shortly after midnight."

"Curiosity compels me to ask, what would you accept as an iron-clad alibi?"

"If the suspect could prove that he or she was dead when the victim was killed I might go for it. But even then I'd look at the alibi real hard. It's not that difficult to come up with a scenario that has someone setting up a murder-suicide in which the suicide takes place before the murder."

Julius thought about it for a moment, intrigued by the problem. "I can imagine a couple of other ways a dead man could commit murder. A delayed-action weapon like slow poison, for example."

"I've told you before, you think like a cop."

"Pay is better in my line."

"Can't argue with that," Devlin said. "All right, let's say for the sake of argument that you and Irene are right when you tell me that Grace couldn't have killed Sprague Witherspoon—"

"I never said she couldn't have done it. I said I don't think she did it."

There was a short pause on the other end of the connection.

"You really think she's capable of murder?" Devlin asked finally. He sounded curious.

"You're the cop. As I recall you have told me on more than one occasion that everyone is capable of committing murder under the right circumstances."

"There is that," Devlin conceded.

"Don't underestimate Grace Elland. Underneath that optimistic, glass-half-full exterior, there's a tough streak."

"No doubt about it. I'm the one who told you the story of what happened here in Cloud Lake all those years ago, remember?"

Julius watched the lights of the Elland house. "I remember."

"Grace is something of a local legend in this town. It's one of the reasons I asked for your take on her. You're an outsider. I knew you wouldn't be swayed by the story from her past."

"She says she's here to think about her future and make some decisions regarding a career path."

"Yeah, Irene explained that Grace has spent the past few years hopping from one job to another," Devlin said.

"I'll tell you one thing," Julius said. "When Grace finally does decide what she wants in life, I would not want to be the one standing in her way."

Unless I'm what she decides she wants.

The thought came out of nowhere, startling him so badly that he almost dropped the phone.

"Damn," he said.

He said it very softly but Devlin heard him.

"You okay?" Devlin asked.

"Yeah, fine. Just a little phone issue."

"So, how did the date go tonight?"

"It went swell up to a point. Got asked in for tea."

"Tea?" Devlin's tone suggested that he had never heard of the substance.

"Some kind of herbal stuff."

"I guess that sounds promising. What went wrong?"

"What makes you think something went wrong?"

"You obviously got home early," Devlin said patiently. "You're talking to me on your phone so, ace detective that I am, I deduced that you were no longer with Grace."

"You're good. You're also right in your deductions. The date ended somewhat abruptly when I asked Grace if she killed Witherspoon."

"You asked her?" Devlin repeated in a neutral tone.

"Yep."

"Point-blank?"

"Uh-huh."

"You're an idiot."

"Harley said something along the same lines."

"I assume she denied it?" Devlin said.

"Sure. That's when she kicked me out of the house. But here's the thing, Dev, there's something really wrong with this picture. She's scared."

"Of what?"

"Damned if I know. But I saw what I'm sure are brand-new locks on the front and back doors of the house. While we were in the kitchen the email alert pinged on her phone. She jumped. Make that flinched."

"She's a woman living alone," Devlin said. "Good locks make sense. As for the email alert, I've been known to flinch when I hear mine ping, too."

"There's something else going on, Dev. I can feel it."

"As Irene keeps reminding me, finding a dead body is bound to be a traumatic experience for someone who isn't in the business of finding them."

"You're in that line."

Devlin exhaled heavily. "You know as well as I do that for those of us who do stumble across dead bodies every so often in the course of our jobs, it's never routine."

"That attitude is what makes you a good cop."

"Why do you think I took this nice, cushy job here in Cloud Lake? I got tired of finding dead bodies in the big city."

"I know," Julius said.

There was silence at both ends of the connection for a few seconds.

"All right, back to Grace Elland," Devlin said finally. "Here's what the Seattle people have: She walked into her boss's house and found him dead in bed, shot twice with a handgun that was reported stolen."

"Someone bought it on the street to use on Witherspoon. Grace doesn't strike me as the kind of woman who would know how to buy a gun in a back alley."

"Got news for you, it's not that hard to buy a stolen gun," Devlin said. "Nothing was stolen from the house. It was not a burglary gone bad. As I was saying, the SPD people figure the most likely scenario is that the killer is probably someone connected to Witherspoon. Grace knows that. So if she's innocent—"

"She is."

"Then she's probably coping with the fact that at some point her path crossed with that of the killer," Devlin concluded. "It's not surprising that she might decide to take a few extra precautions with her own personal safety now."

"But flinching just because she got an email?"

"Could be a million reasons why it startled her," Devlin said. "She might have been anticipating a note from a boyfriend—maybe an old one she doesn't want to hear from or a new one she's hoping will call. And there you were standing in her kitchen when she got the ping. Maybe it was your presence that made her tense."

"She's tense, all right, the question is why. Okay, that's my report.

I'm going to do some work on the computer and then I'm going to bed. Thanks for dinner, and tell Irene she doesn't need to set me up with any more blind dates. One is more than enough."

Devlin cleared his throat. "There is the little matter of the money that somehow disappeared from the Witherspoon accounts. Setting aside the question of murder, do you think it's possible that Grace is the embezzler?"

"I considered it but if she was sitting on a big pile of money, why would she be holed up here in Cloud Lake trying to figure out how to get another job?"

"Always assuming that's why she's here."

There was another short silence.

"So," Devlin continued, "you got as far as the kitchen, right? I can tell Irene that much?"

"I'm going to hang up now, Dev."

"Hard to see you drinking herbal tea. Was there any chanting or incense involved?"

Julius cut the connection.

Seven

He stood at the end of the dock, watching the moonlight on the water and thinking about how Grace had flinched when the email alert sounded. Then he thought some more about the new locks on the doors.

He checked the Elland house. The lights were still on.

What the hell. Nothing to lose. He'd already screwed up the evening.

He opened the phone again and hit the newest name on his short list of personal contacts.

Grace answered on the first ring. "Who is this?"

The tension in her voice made him go very cold. He realized she probably hadn't recognized his number.

"It's Julius. Sorry. Didn't mean to scare you. Just wanted to make sure everything was okay."

There was a brief pause. "I'm fine. What made you think I might not be okay?"

"Four new locks on your doors."

Another pause. Longer this time.

"Very observant of you," she said.

"You sound surprised."

"I decided to upgrade the locks because I'll probably be here for a while and I'm living alone. Cloud Lake is no longer the small, sleepy little town it once was."

"According to what I heard, it wasn't the safest place on the planet back when you were a kid."

The moment of silence hummed with tension.

"Someone told you about what happened at the old Cloud Lake asylum," Grace said eventually.

It wasn't a question. She sounded resigned.

"Harley Montoya and Dev both mentioned it," Julius said. "I was curious so I pulled up a few of the newspaper stories from that time. But according to Harley, Dev and the reports, it happened at the old Cloud Lake Inn up at the north end of the lake, not an asylum."

"The inn was originally built as a private hospital for the mentally ill. That was back in the late nineteen hundreds. After the asylum was closed, it went through several different owners who all tried to turn it into a hotel or resort. The last owner named it the Cloud Lake Inn. The place has been boarded up for years."

"The story I heard is that you stumbled onto a murder in the basement of the place when you were sixteen. You confronted the killer."

There was another long silence on the other end of the connection.

"Just how much research did you do?" she asked, clearly wary.

"You rescued a little kid. Damn near got yourself killed in the process. But it was the killer who died."

"It was a long time ago," Grace said. "I try not to think about it."

"Is that what you positive-thinker types do? Try to forget the bad stuff?"

"Yes," she said very firmly. "Where are you going with this?"

"Ten days ago you came across another murder scene."

"So?"

"Finding Witherspoon's body must have dredged up a lot of unpleasant memories. And in Witherspoon's case, the killer is still at large, so I'm guessing you're having a hard time trying not to think about the past."

"What's going on here?" Grace asked. "Are you the one playing analyst now?"

"Just looking at facts," Julius said. "Connecting dots."

"You don't need to remind me of any of it, believe me."

"You're scared."

Another silence stretched across the distance between them. For a moment Julius wondered if Grace would deny her fear.

"I'm . . . uneasy," Grace said eventually. "I didn't think I would be so nervous, not here in Cloud Lake."

"Because you're not in Seattle, where the murder occurred? I get the logic. But it's deeply flawed and, therefore, not working. Want to tell me why you jumped as if you'd touched a live electric wire when your phone pinged you about a new email?"

"I did not jump."

"You flinched and not in a good way."

"There's a good way to flinch?" Grace asked coldly.

"Let's use your word. Uneasy. The ping made you uneasy." He decided to try out one of the theories that Devlin had mentioned. "Old boyfriend giving you trouble?"

"Oh, no, nothing like that," Grace said.

She said it so matter-of-factly and with such assurance that he was inclined to believe her. But it also brought questions. There must be a few old boyfriends scattered about in her past.

"Someone else who is bothering you?" he pressed.

There was another short pause.

"I've been getting weird emails at night," Grace said finally. "The messages are short, just snide little variations of the affirmations taken from the Witherspoon cookbook and the blog. I would say it was just some disgruntled client but the creepy part is that they're all coming from Sprague's personal account."

A chill went through him, heightening all of his senses in the old, unpleasant way. He was acutely aware of the crisp night air, the featureless surface of the lake and the soft rustle of tree branches. You had to assume that the enemy could be anywhere.

"You're right," he said. "That is very creepy."

"There's something else," Grace said. "The day I found Sprague's body, there was an affirmation pinned to his pajamas. Someone, presumably the killer, had printed it out from a computer."

He got the feeling that now that she had blurted out the truth she wanted to keep going.

"You told the cops about the affirmation at the scene?" he asked.

"They saw it for themselves," Grace said. "I didn't touch it."

"Did you report the emails that you've been receiving?"

"Of course," Grace said. "I was told that someone would look into the matter. Every time I get one I forward it to the detective in charge of the investigation but I think he believes I might be sending them to myself."

"Motive?"

"To enhance my appearance of innocence." Grace exhaled deeply. "The bottom line is that the cops haven't come up with anything so far."

"Do you have any idea who is sending the emails?"

"Maybe," Grace said. She was speaking more slowly now, choosing her words. "Sprague did not have a good relationship with his adult daughter, Nyla Witherspoon. In her own weird way I think she was jealous of those of us who worked in the Witherspoon offices—especially me."

"Why you in particular?"

"It's . . . complicated."

Julius felt as if he had just fallen off the dock into the cold, dark waters of the lake.

"You were having an affair with Witherspoon?" he asked without inflection.

"Good grief, no." Grace sounded astonished, not offended. "What in the world would make you think that?"

"Gosh, I dunno. Not like there's any history of bosses sleeping with the women on their office staff."

"Are you speaking from personal experience?" she asked. This time there was an edge on the words.

The lady had claws. Julius smiled, oddly satisfied. Good to know she hadn't been sleeping with Witherspoon. Good to know she could draw blood if you pushed her too far.

"No," he said. "A long time ago I was warned not to get personally involved with the people who work for me. *That way madness lies.*"

Grace startled him with a burble of laughter. "Oh, wow, you get your affirmations from Shakespeare. Not sure the Witherspoon Way affirmations can compete."

"It's a strict policy, not an affirmation, and I didn't get it from Shakespeare. I got it from my next-door neighbor."

"Harley Montoya? What does he know about the dangers of office relationships? I thought he was devoted to his fishing and his garden. He and my neighbor, Agnes, have been rivals in the annual Cloud Lake Garden Club competition ever since he moved to town."

"Harley wasn't always retired."

"Of course not," Grace said. "Sometimes I forget that he was a successful businessman before he moved here."

"The quote about the dangers of getting involved with employees isn't an affirmation, just a realistic assessment of the potential risks. I don't do affirmations. I have a couple of rules instead."

"Really?" She sounded intrigued. "What are they?"

"Rule Number Two is *Everyone has a hidden agenda*."

"I'll bet that's a hard rule to live by."

"Actually, it's pretty damn useful. You can't be successful in my world unless you know what is really motivating your clients, your competition and the people who work for you. When it comes to closing the deal, you need to know everyone's real agenda."

"I thought money was at the top of the list for people in your world."

"Everyone involved will certainly tell you that," he said. "People like to think they base their high-stakes business decisions on rational financial logic. But that's not true. They make decisions based on emotion, every damn time. Afterward they can always find the logic and reason they need to back up the decisions."

"And you take advantage of that insight to make lots of money, is that what you're telling me?"

"I don't always win but I usually know when to cut my losses." Time to change the subject. "You said you think Nyla Witherspoon might have been jealous of you and the other members of Witherspoon's staff. Are your colleagues receiving those emails?"

"I asked Millicent and Kristy that question. Neither of them has received the emails but they agreed that Nyla is the most likely culprit."

"Did you get anything from Witherspoon's estate?"

"Heavens no," Grace said. "No one on the staff was in Sprague's will. He paid us all very well but he left his entire estate to Nyla."

"And now a large chunk of it has gone missing."

"It's news to me but if you and Devlin know that, then it's safe to say that Nyla is also aware of the embezzlement by now. But I started getting the emails immediately after Sprague was murdered—before anyone realized that someone had been stealing from the Witherspoon Way accounts."

"If she started emailing you because she wanted to take out some of her anger and jealousy on you, then the missing money would have served to enrage her all the more."

"A cheerful thought. You really are not a glass-half-full kind of man, are you?"

He watched the moonlight ripple on the jewel-black lake for a moment.

"Have you talked to Dev about the case?" he asked.

"Some," Grace said. "But I haven't gone into great detail. The thing is, I don't know Devlin very well. Between you and me, I think he has some doubts about my innocence."

Julius decided that it was not a good time to confirm her theory.

"Does Dev know you've got a stalker?" he said instead.

"I haven't told him about the emails, if that's what you mean."

"Yes, it's exactly what I mean."

"This isn't his case," Grace said. She sounded defensive.

"Did you mention them to Irene?"

"No. I don't want to make her any more concerned than she is already."

"Dev is the chief of police in this town. He needs to know what's going on. Talk to him tomorrow morning."

Grace hesitated. "Okay. But there really isn't anything Devlin can do about this."

"Dev's a good cop. He might have some ideas. Meanwhile try to get some sleep."

"Oh, sure, easy for you to say."

He couldn't think of a response to that. He had a feeling he wouldn't get a lot of sleep, either.

"Good night," he said again.

"Hang on, I've got a question. You said that your father came around asking for money after you got rich."

Should have kept my mouth shut, he thought.

"That's right," he said. "So?"

"Did you give him the loan?"

"He and I both knew it wouldn't have been a loan because he would never have repaid it."

"Did you give him the money?" Grace asked quietly.

Julius looked out over the water. "What do you think?"

"I think you did a deal based on emotion. You gave him the money and I have a hunch it was never repaid."

Julius's mouth twitched at the corner. "Right on both counts. It was the worst investment I ever made. Still don't know why I did it."

"The why is easy," Grace said. "He was your dad. You broke Rule Number Two for him."

"No surprise that it turned out badly."

"You did what you had to do."

"Good night," he said.

"Wait, what's Rule Number One?" she asked.

"Trust no one."

He ended the connection and clipped the phone to his belt. He stood at the end of the dock for a while longer, meditating on the conversation.

It hadn't really been phone sex, he decided. But talking to Grace had seemed a lot more intimate than any of the sexual encounters he'd had since his divorce.

• • •

He was right about one thing—sleep was hard to come by. At two-fifteen he got up, pulled on his jeans and a jacket and went outside into the cold night. He walked to the end of the dock and looked across the expanse of dark water toward the Elland house.

The back porch light was still on and a weak glow illuminated the curtains in all the windows. He knew the night-lights would still be on at dawn when he went past the house on his morning run. They had been lit up all night, every night since Grace had arrived in Cloud Lake.

Eight

The phone rang just as Grace dropped a slice of multi-grain bread into the toaster. She glanced at the screen, saw her sister's name, and took the call.

"Are you calling to tell me that you're pregnant again?" she asked. "If so, congratulations."

"I'm calling," Alison said, "because I just saw the news about the embezzlement at the Witherspoon Way Corporation. Are you all right?"

Alison was using her crisp, no-nonsense lawyer voice. That was never a good sign.

"Word travels fast," Grace said. "And, yes, I'm fine."

Phone in hand, she walked to the window. It was her favorite time of day. The late winter sun was not yet up, but there was enough early light in the sky to transform the surface of the lake into a steel mirror. As she watched, a man dressed in gray sweats came into view. He was running at an easy, steady pace, as if he could run forever. He followed the public path that traced the shoreline. The lights were on in her kitchen. She knew that if he looked at the house he would see her. She waved.

Julius raised one hand, acknowledging the greeting. For a few seconds she could have sworn he actually broke stride, perhaps even considered pausing to say good morning. But he kept going.

She had been living in the lake house for nearly a week. Although she had met Julius for the first time last night, she already knew his running schedule. He went past her place every other morning just before dawn. This was the first morning that she had waved at him. Until last night he had been an interesting stranger. Today he was a man with whom she had shared some secrets.

"I'm worried about this new development," Alison said. "Embezzlement is dangerous territory. There's a strong possibility that it was the reason for Witherspoon's murder."

Grace watched Julius until he was out of sight. When he was gone she switched the phone to speaker mode and put the device down on the counter. She reached for the jar of peanut butter and a knife.

"In a horrible way it would be almost reassuring to know that there was a logical motive like money involved," she said. "Otherwise Sprague's death makes no sense."

She glanced at the clock. The early morning call was unlike Alison, who lived a well-scheduled, well-organized life that revolved around home and work. Even the birth of her first child a year earlier had done little to disturb the efficient household. She balanced career and family with an aplomb that made other women marvel.

Grace knew that at that moment Alison was putting the finishing touches on breakfast, after which she would dress in one of her tailored business suits before heading to her office. Alison looked great in a sharp suit. Actually, she looked terrific in just about anything, Grace thought. Her older sister was tall and willowy. But as a successful lawyer who specialized in estate planning, Alison elected to project a conservative air. She wore her dark hair pulled back in a strict twist that emphasized her classic profile. Sleek, serious glasses framed her eyes.

"The problem with the embezzlement motive is that it points to someone who was working directly for Witherspoon," Alison said grimly.

"That had occurred to me." Grace took the lid off the jar of peanut butter. "You're worried that the cops will think I was the one doing the embezzling, aren't you?"

"You're the one who made Witherspoon so successful."

"That's not true," Grace said. "Why do I have to keep explaining that Sprague Witherspoon was the genuine article—a man who truly wanted to do good. And, yes, he had been doing very well financially in the past eighteen months. But that's just it. Why on earth would I want to kill him? Why would any of us in the office want to murder him? He was making himself and everyone around him quite wealthy. Besides, we both know I wouldn't have a clue how to go about constructing an embezzlement scheme."

"Embezzlement is a lot easier than most people think," Alison said. "There are so many ways to siphon off money from a successful business like the Witherspoon Way."

"Oddly enough you are not the first person to mention that to me lately."

"I can't believe you walked in on another murder," Alison said. "Statistically speaking, the odds of a person who isn't in law enforcement or connected to the criminal world stumbling into two different homicide scenes must be vanishingly small."

"Statistics was never my best subject. I keep reminding myself that coincidences do happen. That's why they invented the word."

"How are things going there in Cloud Lake?" Alison asked.

"Okay. I'm not making much progress on finding a new career path, though."

"Give yourself some time. It's not like you haven't had a couple of major shocks lately, what with the murder and then finding yourself unemployed."

"Tell me about it," Grace said. The toast popped up in the toaster. She removed it, set it on a plate and spread some peanut butter on it. "But as much as I'd like to blame my lack of momentum on those things, I don't think that's the real problem."

"What is the real problem?"

Grace hesitated, unsure of how much to confide to Alison. There was nothing her sister could do except worry. But they were family, after all. They had never kept secrets from each other, at least not for long.

"The dream is back, Alison. And so are the anxiety attacks."

"Damn. I was afraid the trauma of Witherspoon's death might drag everything to the surface again. Maybe you should make an appointment with Dr. Peterson."

"I already know what she would say. She would remind me to practice rewriting the dream script before I go to bed and to remember to use the breathing exercises and meditation techniques on a regular basis and, if necessary, take the meds. I'm doing all of that. It's just that—"

A small amount of peanut butter dropped off the knife and landed on the counter.

"Hang on," Grace said. She reached for a paper towel.

"It's just what?" Alison pressed.

Grace used the towel to wipe up the peanut butter. "It's just that I can't shake this weird feeling that there's some connection between Witherspoon's death and the Trager murder."

There was silence from Alison's end.

"It's the bottle of vodka, isn't it?" she said finally.

"Yes."

"Perfectly understandable, given what happened in the past. But you said that the police found a charge for it on one of Witherspoon's credit card statements. Sprague Witherspoon bought that bottle of vodka a few days before he was murdered."

"He didn't drink vodka, Alison."

"Maybe not, but he entertained frequently, right?"

"That's true," Grace said. "The police did say that there was a large selection of liquor bottles in his kitchen. But I told you, this particular bottle of vodka was sitting on the nightstand beside the bed where I found the body."

There was a long silence on the other end of the line. Grace took a bite out of the slice of toast that she had just slathered in peanut butter.

"Grace, do you want to come and stay with Ethan and Harry and me for a while?" Alison said after a moment. "You can work on your résumé here in Portland."

"Thanks, but I really need to stay focused on my job hunting in the Seattle area. I can't do that from Portland."

"Have you got any idea what you might want to do next?"

"Zip." Grace ate some more toast. "I've been told I should come up with a business plan for finding my next career."

"A business plan for job hunting? I suppose there's some logic to that. Who gave you that advice?"

"A man I met on a blind date that Irene arranged for me last night."

"The two of you wound up discussing business plans?" Alison chuckled. "Sounds like a typical blind-date disaster."

"His name is Julius and he was a lot more interesting than anyone else I've dated recently."

"That isn't saying much, is it? Your social life hasn't exactly been the stuff of legend lately."

"Let's face it, my social life has never been legendary."

"Your own fault," Alison said. "You're going to have to stop sending out vibes that attract men who are looking for a sister or a best friend."

"I'll work on that as soon as I get a new job."

"Mom's worrying about you again," Alison said. "She thinks you're too old to be ricocheting from one job to another trying to find yourself. She's right."

"I found myself a long time ago. It's finding a career that is giving me problems. I've got to tell you, the job at the Witherspoon Way was the best position I've ever had. I would have been happy to stay there."

"Well, that's not an option now, is it?"

"Careful, you're starting to sound like Mom."

"I'm just doing my job as your older sister," Alison said. "You know that as far as Mom and I are concerned, Sprague Witherspoon took advantage of you."

"That's not true. He gave me opportunities."

"You wrote that cookbook and blog that took him to the top of the self-help-guru world but it was his name on both."

"I've explained to you that it is not unusual for successful people to pay others to write their books and blogs," Grace said.

This was not the first time Alison had raised this particular argument. Grace decided that she did not have the patience for it this morning. She was working on a plan that had popped into her head a few minutes earlier when Julius had run past the house. Time was of the essence.

"Sorry," she said, "I've got to go."

"Where are you going at this hour of the morning?"

"I'm going to focus on the first stage of my new career plan. Inspiration just struck."

"You sound serious," Alison said. "I'm impressed. And, may I say, it's about time you settled on a realistic career path. I was starting to worry that you would end up working as a mime out in front of Nordstrom's."

"Thanks, Big Sister. You do know how to motivate a person. Now I really do have to hang up and get busy."

"Doing what, exactly?"

"I told you, my date last night suggested that I build a business plan designed to help me find a career path. He just went past the house on his morning run."

"So?'

"He'll turn around at the southern end of the lake where the path ends at the marina."

"I'm not following you."

"That means he'll be coming back this way in a few minutes. I'm going to intercept him."

"Why?" Alison asked.

"I'm going to ask him if he will consult for me."

"On what?"

Alison sounded dumbfounded now.

"On a business plan," Grace said. "Evidently he's an expert on business strategy and stuff like that. Talk to you later."

"Wait, don't hang up. What do you know about this man you're going to intercept?"

"Not nearly enough," Grace said.

Nine

Grace ended the call and glanced at the clock. Given Julius's pace and his adherence to his running routine she thought she had about ten minutes left to prepare. She opened the refrigerator and took out two hard-boiled eggs and a bottle of spring water. Next she went into the pantry and found the old wicker picnic basket.

Eight minutes later she was ready. She bundled up in her down jacket, picked up the picnic basket and went out onto the sheltered back porch. A light rain was falling. She pulled up the hood of the coat.

She crossed the porch, went down the steps and hurried through the simple winter garden. Now that her mother and Kirk were spending a good portion of the year in sunny locales, the landscaping around the house had been reduced to the basics. The hardy shrubs and the trees that remained made a stark contrast to the glorious greenery that surrounded Agnes Gilroy's pretty little house. But then, Agnes was a serious Pacific Northwest gardener.

As if she had been alerted by a psychic intercept, Agnes came out onto her back porch and waved.

"Good morning, dear," she sang out. "Lovely day, isn't it?"

Agnes had always been one of Grace's favorite people. Agnes was a relentless optimist but Grace's mother had observed on more than one occasion that beneath her cheery exterior the older woman was not only smart, she was also a shrewd judge of character.

She wore her long gray hair in a bun at the nape of her neck and dressed mostly in baggy denim jeans, flannel shirts and gardening clogs. She had been born a free spirit and had evidently lived the life-style. A botanist by training, she had traveled widely in her younger days collecting plant specimens for academic and pharmaceutical research. If her stories were to be believed, she had also gathered numerous lovers along the way. Grace found Agnes's reminiscences entirely credible.

After retiring Agnes had devoted herself to competitive gardening in Cloud Lake. She had never married and had made it clear that she preferred to live alone. But shortly after Harley Montoya had moved to town, that situation had been somewhat modified.

The competition between Agnes and Harley had led, perhaps inevitably, to a discreet, long-term affair. Without fail, Harley's truck was seen parked in Agnes's driveway every Wednesday and Saturday night. It was always gone before dawn.

"It's risky to let men spend the entire night, dear," Agnes had once explained to Grace. "It gives them the notion that you're going to start cooking and cleaning for them."

Grace paused halfway across the garden. "Hi, Agnes. Yes, it's a great day."

The rain was getting heavier but Grace knew that neither of them was going to mention that little fact. There was some natural, built-in competition between positive thinkers, just as there was between gardeners.

"Going to waylay Mr. Arkwright, dear?" Agnes asked. "I saw him go past a while ago."

"I thought I'd give it a whirl," Grace said.

"I take it the blind date went well, then." Agnes sounded gratified. "I was pretty sure it had when I heard you chase him out of the house last night. That sort of activity early on is always a sign of a promising start in a relationship."

"Does everyone in town know about my blind date with Julius?" Grace asked.

"I expect there are a few folks who haven't been paying attention," Agnes said, "but for the most part I think it's safe to say it's common knowledge. You're rather famous around here, dear, at least among those of us who have lived in Cloud Lake for a while. Have a wonderful day, dear."

Agnes went back inside. The door banged shut behind her.

The little wrought iron garden gate was designed to be decorative. It was not a security device. Grace unlatched it and stepped out onto the path. Her timing was perfect. She could see Julius coming toward her.

When he saw her he slowed his pace. By the time he was a few yards away he was walking.

He came to a halt in front of her and smiled a slow, wicked smile that was reflected in his eyes. He suddenly looked younger and almost carefree.

"Well, if it isn't Little Red Riding Hood." His smile widened into a wolfish grin. "And to think I never believed in fairy tales."

Grace glanced down at her red jacket. She felt the heat rise in her cheeks.

"Okay, the red coat and hood thing is sheer coincidence," she said.

"If you say so."

Julius was drenched with sweat and rain. The front of his gray pull-over was soaked. His hair was plastered to his head. Rivulets of water mixed with perspiration streamed down his face.

Normally she was not keen on sweaty men. She knew some women were attracted to males who looked as if they had just emerged from a cage fight but she was not one of them. But Julius Arkwright drenched in sweat was an altogether different beast. Standing this close to him aroused something primal deep inside.

Focus, woman.

"You probably wonder why I'm out here in the rain, barring your path," she said.

"I'm going to take a flying leap and say the picnic basket has some significance."

"Yes, it does," she said. "Here's another clue, I am not on my way to Grandma's house."

"That leaves us with a high probability that you have deliberately intercepted me."

"A very strong possibility," she agreed.

He glanced at the closed lid of the wicker basket with an expression of deep interest. "What have you got in there?"

"A bribe."

"Who do you plan to bribe?"

"A consultant, I hope."

He raised his brows. "You are in need of a consultant?"

"Apparently so."

"What do you want the consultant to do for you?" Julius asked.

"Help me work up a business plan that will enable me to find a new career, one that I will find challenging, exciting and fulfilling—preferably a career that will last longer than eighteen months. I want to find my true calling."

"I thought you were just trying to find a job."

"My aspirations are actually somewhat more aspirational. I have my work at the Witherspoon Way to thank for that, I suppose. I'm sure that the right career for me is out there somewhere, waiting for me to find it."

Julius studied the basket. "Am I to assume that in exchange for assisting you in finding your dream job the consultant gets whatever is in that basket?"

"Right," she said briskly. "Do we have a deal?"

"You want me to agree to the deal before I see the nature of the bribe?"

"I suppose I could give you a peek."

She raised the lid of the basket very briefly to reveal the items neatly packed inside—two hard-boiled eggs, an orange, two chunky slices of multi-grain bread, a little plastic canister filled with peanut butter, a bottle of spring water and a thermos.

"It's a picnic breakfast," she explained. She snapped the lid of the basket closed to keep out the rain. "There's coffee in the thermos."

"Huh. I don't know about this. With the exception of the coffee and the peanut butter, it all looked sort of healthy."

"It's *all* very healthy. The coffee is fair-trade organic and the peanut butter is not only organic, it is unadulterated with sweeteners or stabilizers."

"That picnic also appeared to be very vegetarian."

"Is that a problem?" she challenged.

"Nope. Food is food." He plucked the picnic basket from her arm with a quick, deft motion. "You've got yourself a consultant. When do you want to start?"

"How about this morning?"

"Let's make it lunch. Your morning is already booked."

"It is?"

"You're having your little chat with Dev about those stalker emails, remember?"

"Oh, yeah, right."

"See you for lunch."

Julius loped off with the picnic basket. She stood there in the falling rain and watched him until he vanished from sight around a wooded bend. He made a very interesting Big Bad Wolf.

It's just a business arrangement, she told herself.

But it was possible that wasn't the whole truth. It was, in fact, conceivable that an objective observer would describe the situation in an entirely different way.

Some people—the unenlightened type—might say that she was flirting with the Big Bad Wolf.

Ten

Satisfied with her first serious move toward finding her calling, Grace went back inside the house. She took off her coat and hung it on a hook in the small closet off the kitchen that served as a mudroom. It was a good time to practice her third ritual. She needed to fortify herself for the coming interview with Chief Nakamura. It was hard to think of him as Devlin when he was in uniform.

She locked the doors, changed into her workout clothes and unrolled the exercise mat. She stood at the end of the mat for a time, composing herself from head to toe—mind and body—as she had been taught.

When she was ready she took the first step in the fluid moves of the ancient system of physical meditation that, together with the evening house-check and the breathing exercises, kept the nightmares and panic attacks under some semblance of control.

Eleven

"You should have told Devlin about those emails you've been receiving from Witherspoon's account," Irene said.

"There didn't seem to be much point," Grace said. "There isn't anything he can do. Besides, there have only been a few of them."

She spoke mostly into her mug of coffee because she knew what was coming next. Talk about easy predictions, she thought. Maybe she should consider a career as a psychic.

"You've only received a *few* emails from some demented stalker?" Irene yelped. "Listen to yourself, woman. Someone is harassing you and all you can say is, well, there have only been a few scary emails."

"Okay, okay, maybe I'm feeling a tad defensive because everyone is on my case this morning about those emails. I don't think I'm being stalked. Not exactly. And would you please keep your voice down? It's bad enough that my friends, family and Julius Arkwright think I'm a naive idiot. I would appreciate it if you didn't broadcast the news to your customers as well."

They were sitting at a table in Irene's office. Grace had headed straight to Cloud Lake Kitchenware as soon as she finished talking to Devlin at the Cloud Lake Police Department headquarters two blocks away. Julius had insisted on accompanying her to the tense interview. By the time it was over she had felt utterly drained and in need of a friendly ear. But all she had gotten from Irene thus far was more lecturing.

The door between the office and the sales floor of the gourmet cookware store was closed but there was a long window. Grace could see most of the front of the shop. It was not yet noon but Cloud Lake Kitchenware was bustling with customers who were browsing the cookbook collection, admiring bouquets of colorful silicon spatulas and examining the gleaming pots and pans.

The employees, dressed in dark green aprons stamped with the shop's logo, were busy but that did not mean they could not overhear a private conversation in the office—not if Irene's voice rose any higher.

Irene cleared her throat and lowered her voice. "I can't help but notice that you put Julius into a third category."

Grace frowned. "What?"

"You said friends, family and Julius Arkwright thought you were a naive idiot," Irene reminded her. "You placed Julius in a special category."

"Well, he's not family and he's not exactly a friend."

"What is he, then?"

"I'm not sure how to describe him," Grace admitted.

"But you're sure he thinks you're a naive idiot?" Irene asked, evidently intrigued by the possibility. "He actually said that?"

Grace slumped back in her chair. "He didn't use those exact words but it's not hard to tell that's what he's thinking. It appears to be a commonly held assumption."

"That's not true. Your friends and family and, I'm sure, Julius, as well, are just worried about you, that's all."

"Yes, I know. And deep down I appreciate it, really I do. But in spite of appearances, I'm not entirely incapable of taking care of myself."

"We know that."

"Yeah, sure you do." Grace drank some of her coffee. "Be honest. You think I'm a naive idiot."

Irene's eyes narrowed in sudden comprehension. "You know who is sending those emails, don't you?"

"I'm not positive but I suspect that the sender is probably Nyla Witherspoon." Grace set the mug down on the desk. "I'll bet she came across the password for Sprague's email account. It's not like Sprague treated it as top secret."

"Now she's pissed and sending you those emails because she thinks you embezzled money from Sprague Witherspoon that should have come to her."

"Assuming Nyla is behind the emails, I need to remind everyone that she started sending them *before* it was discovered that a lot of money was missing. She was jealous of Sprague's office staff because we worked so closely with her father. But she fixated on me."

"Because you were the one who did the most to elevate his career," Irene said calmly.

"People keep saying that, but it's not true."

"There's no maybe about it. Your cookbook and the blog are what put Witherspoon into the big time."

"I keep trying to explain that it was Sprague Witherspoon, himself, who was the force behind his own success. I just helped him market his concepts."

"Bull," Irene said. "It was the cookbook and the related blog with all those dippy daily affirmations that made him famous in the motivational guru business. You're the one who wrote all of that stuff."

Grace raised her brows. "Dippy daily affirmations?"

"Sorry." Irene winced. "As a branding technique those affirmations were nothing short of brilliant. But getting back to the emails, who else might have the password to Witherspoon's account?"

"Any number of people, including me," Grace said morosely.

"I'll bet Nyla or whoever is behind the emails is hoping the cops will assume that you are sending those emails to yourself."

"That possibility has occurred to me," Grace said. "Why do you think I didn't mention them to Devlin? I figured he would jump to that conclusion."

"No," Irene said. She said it very firmly.

"Whoever is emailing me from Sprague's account has been very careful to make sure the contents are not overtly threatening. I think that indicates that the sender doesn't want the cops to look too hard in that direction."

"But the emails are definitely intended to rattle your nerves," Irene said.

"Oh, sure." Grace drank some more coffee and lowered the mug. "I must admit the sender has had some success in that regard. I'm not sleeping well these days."

"I wouldn't be sleeping well, either, under the circumstances," Irene said. She paused a beat and then softened her tone. "Do you really believe that Julius thinks you're naive and maybe not too bright?"

Grace started to say yes but she hesitated and then shrugged. "Maybe. But he's hard to read. I also have to face the fact that there is another possibility."

"What's that?"

"He might still be wondering if I did kill Sprague Witherspoon."

Irene set her mug down with a bang that reverberated through the office. "I'm sure he doesn't believe that."

"Do you know him well enough to be able to tell what he's thinking?"

"Well, no. As you just said, he's hard to read. But Julius and Dev have been friends for years. I'm sure Dev would never have gone along with the dinner date last night if he wasn't convinced that you and Julius made a good match."

Grace managed a grim smile. "And everyone thinks I'm naive."

Irene glared. "I beg your pardon?"

"Get real. You know me well enough to trust me but Devlin doesn't. Furthermore he's a cop—one who happens to have an old pal in town, someone whose instincts he probably does trust. So he goes along with your little matchmaking scheme because he figures it will give him the perfect opportunity to get Julius's take on me."

Irene opened her mouth to protest but after a few seconds she closed it again. She drummed her fingers on the desktop.

"Hmm," she said.

"Don't worry, I'm not taking Devlin's distrust personally," Grace said.

Irene's brows rose. "That's very gracious of you."

"I'm serious. Dev's first priority is to protect you. I can see it in his eyes every time he looks at you. The possibility that your best friend might be a murderer—and/or an embezzler—is naturally of considerable interest to him."

"I'm sure he doesn't believe that you killed Witherspoon or stole the money."

"I didn't say he believed all that stuff. I just said he's concerned—in part because I'm now living in his town but mostly because of you. He's a good cop. He's also a good husband. He'll do what he thinks he has to do to protect you."

"Yes, but I still can't believe that he went so far as to ask Julius for his take on you," Irene said.

"Seems like a logical move, when you think about it."

Irene eyed her keenly. "You know, some people might be quite annoyed upon discovering that what they thought was an innocent blind date was actually an undercover sting operation."

"Turns out I've got bigger problems," Grace said. "As we at the Witherspoon Way would say, *Today I will focus on priorities and ignore the unimportant crap.*"

Irene looked pained. "You just made up that affirmation on the spot, didn't you?"

"Yep. Has a certain ring to it, don't you think?"

They drank their coffee quietly for a time. The silence between them was the kind that could be generated only by a long friendship. After a while Irene stirred in her chair.

"Let's reverse this process," she said. "What's your take on Julius Arkwright?"

"He's bored," Grace said.

"What?" Irene stared at her, startled. "Devlin and I have been wondering if Julius is sinking into some kind of low-grade depression. He hasn't even dated very much since his divorce a couple of years ago."

Grace shrugged. "He's drifting. With some people, boredom can look a lot like depression."

"When did you get a degree in psychology?"

"Okay, you've got me there. But if you will recall, Mom made me spend a lot of time with a shrink after the crap that happened up at the old asylum. I learned a lot. What made you and Devlin think that Julius was depressed?"

"Dev told me that Julius is thinking very seriously about selling his venture capital company," Irene said slowly.

"So? A lot of people build companies and then sell them. It's a dream come true for most businesspeople."

"Dev says he doesn't think that's the case with Julius."

"Why not?"

"Julius built Arkwright Ventures from scratch," Irene said. "He poured his heart and soul into it, according to Dev. Julius loves the venture capital business or at least he did at one time. He's made a fortune because he's very good at what he does. But about two years ago his wife left him for another man."

Grace squared her shoulders. "I repeat, so?"

"Wow." Irene blinked. "Aren't you the hard-hearted woman today?"

Grace tightened her grip on her mug. "Don't look at me like that. Divorce happens."

"Well, yes, but you're usually a little more sympathetic about such things."

"Maybe Julius poured a little too much of his heart and soul into his business," Grace said. "Maybe he should have saved some for his wife."

Irene nodded slowly. "You may be right. Dev did say that Julius was married to his company. It's entirely possible that the wife felt neglected. But, really, she didn't have to run off with Julius's vice president and trusted friend."

Grace thought about that. "Okay, you're right, that's cold."

"Dev says Julius has seemed sort of numb since then, like he's running on autopilot. He keeps making money but the thrill is gone."

"There are problems in the world and then there are problems," Grace said evenly. "Frankly, the ability to make money without even trying doesn't strike me as a huge burden to bear."

Irene smiled briefly. "You really are not inclined to be sympathetic to Julius Arkwright today, are you?"

"He doesn't need sympathy. But if it makes you feel better, I can tell you that this morning I hired him to consult for me."

Irene's mouth fell open. "You *what*?"

"Last night when he took me home he told me that I needed to draw up a strategy designed to help me find a new career. This morning I hired him to show me how to go about making the plan."

"You hired him?" Irene said. Now she looked blank.

"Technically speaking, it was a bribe."

"Either way, you're joking. You can't afford Julius Arkwright."

"I already gave him the bribe. He took it. We have a deal."

Irene's eyes widened. "Please don't tell me you're sleeping with him. At least not yet. I like Julius, yes. I think the two of you would make an interesting couple. But it's way too soon—especially for you. We both know that jumping into bed with a man on the first date is not your style."

"No, of course I'm not sleeping with Julius Arkwright." Grace brushed that aside with a wide, sweeping motion of her hand and beetled her brows at Irene—making it clear that she had no intention of hopping into bed with Julius. Unfortunately she could not be sure if she was trying to reassure Irene or herself. "But I think he's got a point about me needing some kind of career path plan," she continued hastily.

"You do?"

"I'm certainly not getting anywhere on my own. I can't seem to focus. He appears to be an expert on planning and strategy. So, when he ran by my house this morning I intercepted him with a picnic basket full of breakfast goodies and told him it was a bribe for his services as a consultant. He accepted."

"Did he?" Irene tapped the pen lightly on the desktop. "So the blind date was not a complete disaster."

"Not if it keeps me from ending up as a street mime out in front of Nordstrom."

Irene looked at her. "Well, at least you'd be working in front of Nordstrom. You wouldn't be just any street mime."

"You know what I mean. I want to find out what it is that I am meant to do in life, Irene. My calling. My passion. I haven't had any luck with the online questionnaires that are supposed to guide you to an appropriate career path. So I figure I have nothing left to lose by getting some planning advice from an expert."

"In other words, you do like Julius," Irene said with a smug air. "At least enough to ask for his advice."

Grace smiled a crafty smile. "Some people would say I'm using him."

Amusement lit Irene's eyes. "I seriously doubt that Julius would let anyone use him. He has been known to do the occasional favor, however."

"Really?"

"Who do you think arranged the financing I needed to start Cloud Lake Kitchenware? Who do you think helped me find a website designer to take the business online? Who do you think guided me through the tax and accounting issues and taught me how to do a profit-and-loss statement?"

"Ah," Grace said. "I see."

Irene's expression turned serious. "Like I said, I'm rather fond of Julius and grateful to him. Furthermore, I know that Dev would trust him with his life. In fact, that is what happened when they served together in a war zone a few years ago. Dev also trusts Julius with our retirement fund investments. But if you're going to get involved with Julius Arkwright, I think there is something you should know about him."

"I'm listening."

"The vice president who married Julius's ex is Edward Hastings. He's one of the Seattle-real-estate-empire Hastingses. Fourth-generation land developers. His family's company owns a huge chunk of downtown Seattle real estate, including a few office towers."

Grace considered the information briefly and then raised one shoulder in a dismissive little shrug.

"Why does that matter to me?" she asked.

"Shortly after Edward Hastings left Arkwright Ventures he not only married Julius's ex, he also became the president and CEO of the Hastings family empire."

"Still waiting for the other shoe to drop, Irene."

"There are rumors that under Edward Hastings's control the firm has stumbled a few times in the past eighteen months. Major deals have slipped away to competitors."

Grace watched Irene over the rim of the coffee mug. "What does that have to do with Julius?"

"I'm a small-business person who swims in a very small pond here in Cloud Lake. I admit that I don't know a lot about the shark pool in which Julius does his hunting. But I try to keep up with the Pacific Northwest business news, and because of Dev's friendship with Julius, I sometimes hear bits and pieces of gossip."

"What have you heard that is worrying you?" Grace asked.

Irene leaned forward and folded her arms on the desk. "Hastings is in real trouble. Some people are predicting that under Edward Hastings's leadership we will see the downfall of a family-held company that has been around for nearly a century. The business world is like a small town—once a rumor starts, it can easily become a self-fulfilling prophecy."

Grace reflected briefly. "What does this have to do with Julius?"

"The gossip is that the downward slide of the Hastings family empire has been caused by one man—Julius Arkwright."

"They think he's out for revenge? That he's somehow sabotaging Hastings?"

"Yes."

Grace gave that some thought. "And this has been going on for how long?"

"Nearly two years. The timing is significant."

"Because it coincides with the timing of Julius's divorce?"

"People are saying that Julius intends to destroy Hastings. Dev tells me that when Julius sets his sights on a goal, he doesn't quit. Like a heat-seeking missile, he just keeps going until he reaches his target."

"I can't believe you set me up on a blind date with a man you feel compelled to describe in military terms."

"That's Dev's description," Irene said. "I just wanted you to know about the rumors before you got any more involved with Julius. If it's true that he's plotting revenge, there may be collateral damage."

"You're the one who set up the blind date. Now you're trying to warn me about Julius?"

"I really do think that you and Julius would be good together. But I will admit that Dev and I were also hoping that if you two hit it off, Julius might be . . . distracted from whatever it is he's doing to Hastings."

"Stop trying to make me feel sorry for Julius Arkwright."

Irene blinked. "That is not exactly what I'm trying to accomplish here."

"Yes, it is. You're trying to make me think that he's depressed and obsessed with revenge and in need of fixing. But as far as I can tell, Julius is more than capable of taking care of himself. I just told you, I have other priorities at the moment. I'm trying to get a life, remember?"

"Right. A life." Irene sat back in her chair. "And you've hired Julius Arkwright to help you come up with a plan to get said life."

"That's it," Grace said smoothly. "Just a business transaction. You can move along. Nothing to see here."

"Don't give me that. What happened when Julius took you home last night?"

Grace pursed her lips. "Among other things, he asked me flat-out if I murdered Witherspoon."

"Oh, jeez," Irene groaned. "Not exactly a great conversation-starter."

"Nope. But it sure was a fine way to end one, which is what happened. Sort of. I kicked him out of the house. On his way out the door he assured me that he believed me."

"But you kicked him out, anyway."

"Of course." Grace swallowed some coffee and lowered the mug. "But then he called me."

"Did he, now?" Irene said very softly.

"I ended up telling him about the weird emails and the next thing I knew, he was ordering me to tell Devlin about the emails, which is why I went to Devlin's office today, et cetera, et cetera. And there you have it. A complete portrait of a blind date gone bad but possibly a good sign for the future of my career planning."

Irene tapped the pen on the desk again, very thoughtful now. "Is there any way that call last night could be described as phone sex?"

"Absolutely not."

Talking to Julius on the phone had been a strangely intimate experience, Grace thought. But she refused to describe it as phone sex. Not that she'd ever had phone sex. It was simply that, after getting hit with the latest email from the stalker, she had felt a need to confide in someone. It just so happened that Julius had been the one to call her at that moment. Serendipity. Or coincidence. Or chaos theory. Something like that probably explained everything.

"I'm not sure what to say." Irene shook her head. "Like Dev, Julius is a little deep in places."

"Now there's a startling revelation."

Irene ignored her. "I guess it comes down to the fact that I think you can trust him. And, like I said, he's the kind of man who will do favors for friends. He took a chance on me when no one else would."

"Any investment is a risk but you and Cloud Lake Kitchenware are as close as it gets to a sure thing."

"Cloud Lake Kitchenware is working," Irene said. Pride and satisfaction brightened her expression. "It's actually going to turn a nice profit this year. But it will never make the kind of money that Julius is accustomed to raking in with his big investments. This particular project is petty cash for him."

"As it happens, Julius told me that he's got enough money."

Surprise lit Irene's eyes. Then she smiled. "Did he say that?"

"Yes."

"Don't think I've ever heard anyone actually say that before."

"I told you, what Julius Arkwright is looking for these days is a way to escape boredom."

"Considering the fact that you met Julius less than twenty-four hours ago, you sure seem to know a lot about him."

"He's hard to read but not impossible." Grace drank the rest of her coffee and set the mug down. "I know you meant well, but promise me you won't set me up with any more blind dates, at least not until I get my life together." She rose to her feet. "I'd better be on my way. I have to do some grocery shopping and then I am scheduled to meet my consultant for a luncheon meeting. We are supposed to start building my business plan."

"What will you do if you don't come up with a strategy that leads you to your personal calling?"

"Fire my consultant."

Twelve

T he rain had stopped by the time Grace finished her shopping and got behind the wheel to drive back to the lake house. The high cloud cover remained, however, infusing the atmosphere with the peculiar glary gray light that made sunglasses a necessity, even in winter.

She did not recognize the expensive-looking silver sedan parked in front of the lake house but she knew the blonde in the front seat all too well. Nyla Witherspoon.

First a visit with the local chief of police and now Nyla had decided to pay a call on her. The day was not improving markedly, Grace decided. She tried to come up with an affirmation that applied to the situation. Nothing sprang to mind.

She brought her car to a halt and mentally braced herself for the encounter. Nyla erupted from the front seat of the sedan.

She was a thin, sharp-faced woman who, if she smiled more, would have been quite attractive in a chic, elfin way. But when she was not smiling—which was most of the time as far as Grace could tell—she looked like all she needed was a broomstick and a pointed hat to complete her ensemble. The bitterness and anger that simmered in her eyes seemed to bubble up from someplace deep inside.

She stalked over to the compact, arriving just as Grace got the door open.

"Did you think you could hide here in Cloud Lake?" Nyla's sunglasses made it impossible to read her eyes but her voice was tight with rage. "Did you think I wouldn't find you?"

"I didn't know you were looking for me," Grace said. She took off her own shades. "You could have called. What do you want, Nyla?"

"You know why I'm here. I want my father's money—the money that should have come to me."

"I've told you before, I don't have it."

"You're lying. You embezzled it from my father's corporation. You've probably got it hidden in some offshore account."

Grace closed her eyes for a couple of seconds and reminded herself that Nyla had some serious issues.

"I don't know anything about the missing money," she said. She tried to pitch her voice to a soothing level. "By the way, I told the police about those emails you've been sending to me from your father's account. It amounts to stalking, you know."

"What are you talking about? What emails?"

"Nyla, if you're the one who has been emailing me, it has got to stop. The cops are trying to catch your father's killer. They need your help. Focusing your rage on me won't do any good."

Nyla's sharp features tightened. "A lot of people, including the police, think that you might be the one who murdered my father."

Grace spread her hands. "Why would I kill my employer and cut off the cash flow? Think about it, Nyla. Sprague was the one who brought in the money, not me. It was his name on the blog and on the cookbook. I was just his assistant. Trust me, with your father gone, the cash flow will dry up fast."

"You shot him because he found out that you were stealing his money. He probably confronted you, maybe threatened to report you to the police. You had to get rid of him."

"That simply is not true," Grace said. "I was home the night your father was murdered."

"Your so-called alibi won't hold water. Yes, I know they say the security video shows your car parked in the apartment garage that night but that doesn't mean you didn't leave the building. You could have slipped out and taken a cab to my father's house on Queen Anne."

"You can't prove that. No one can prove it, because it never happened."

"Your prints were at the scene." But Nyla sounded less certain now.

"My prints were at the scene because I'm the one who found the body," Grace said, struggling to hold on to her patience. "Get real, Nyla. That's not proof."

"Someone must have seen you leave your apartment that night," Nyla wailed.

"I'm not lying," Grace said, trying to de-escalate the situation. "When the cops find your father's killer, I'm sure they'll find the money, too."

But Nyla was no longer looking at her. She was staring past Grace's shoulder. Uncertainty flashed across her face. She switched her attention back to Grace.

"I'm willing to negotiate," Nyla said quickly. "I'll give you a percentage. We can call it a finder's fee or a commission. I swear you won't walk away empty-handed. Return the money and I won't press embezzlement charges. Think about it. I'll give you forty-eight hours."

Without waiting for a response, she swung around and went swiftly toward her car.

Curious to see who or what had distracted Nyla and inspired her to quit the scene, Grace turned and saw Julius coming around the side of the house. She realized he had used the footpath to walk from his place to hers.

He did not appear to be in a rush but he was covering a lot of ground in an efficient manner. He was dressed in jeans, a khaki shirt, low boots and a black leather bomber jacket. A pair of wraparound sunglasses glinted ominously in the grayish light. The overall effect was rather menacing. Grace understood why Nyla had decided to depart in a hurry.

Julius reached Grace's side seconds before Nyla sped past, tires spitting out gravel. He seized Grace's arm and hauled her out of the way of the small bits of flying rock.

"Was that, by any chance, Witherspoon's daughter?" Julius asked.

"Good guess. Nyla Witherspoon." Grace tried to gently extricate her arm from Julius's hand. He seemed to have forgotten that he was holding on to her. "She's convinced I stole her father's money and murdered him. But the interesting thing is that she offered me a deal."

Julius finally noticed that she was attempting to wriggle free of his fingers. He released her. "What kind of deal?"

Grace pondered her answer while she opened the rear door of the compact and took out a sack of groceries. "She wants the money so badly she offered to give me a finder's fee if I return it. No questions asked. She promised she wouldn't press embezzlement charges."

Julius took the groceries from her, holding the heavy sack easily in one arm.

"Did she say anything else?" he asked.

"She seems to think that my alibi for the night of Sprague's murder is weak. She reminded me that my prints are at the scene of the crime."

"But all she cares about is getting her hands on the money?"

"It's all she has left of her father," Grace explained. "I think she's grieving the loss of a relationship she never had. She thinks the money will somehow compensate."

"Do you know the source of her issues?"

"Oh, yes. All of us who worked in the office were aware that Nyla blamed her father for her mother's suicide years ago."

Grace opened the front door. Julius followed her inside and into the kitchen.

"It feels chilly in here, doesn't it?" Grace said.

She went to the thermostat on the wall and checked the setting. The controls were set to the usual daytime temperature.

"This is not good," she said. "Looks like there may be a problem with the heating system. I'll give the repair company a call after lunch. Luckily I've got the fireplace for backup."

"Try rebooting the system first," Julius said.

"Oh, yeah, like I know how to reboot an HVAC system."

"I'll take a look at the controls after lunch."

She glanced at him. "Thanks."

"No guarantees."

He set the groceries on the kitchen table and took off his sunglasses. Dropping the glasses into the pocket of his jacket, he watched Grace remove the free-range eggs and a bag of organically grown red peppers from the sack. She set them on the counter next to the refrigerator and returned to the table.

"Back to Nyla Witherspoon," he said. "Your theory is that she is more interested in the money now than in finding her father's killer?"

"I think the money is important to her for emotional as well as financial reasons. But I wouldn't be surprised if she's also being pressured to get her hands on her inheritance."

"What kind of pressure?" Julius's eyes sharpened. "Is she in debt?"

"Not that I know of," Grace said. She reached into the sack and took out the almonds, sunflower seeds and hazelnuts she planned to use for a batch of homemade granola. "Got a hunch her fiancé may be pushing her to find the money."

"Dev mentioned a fiancé."

"His name is Burke Marrick. Sprague did not approve of him. Kristy, Millicent and I had our doubts about him, too. Marrick showed up in Nyla's life a few months ago and swept her off her feet. It was a whirlwind courtship. They got engaged within weeks. She thinks he's Mr. Perfect."

Julius got a knowing look in his eyes. "But you and your friends think that Marrick wants to marry Nyla for the traditional reason— her money."

Grace opened a cupboard and stored the nuts and seeds on a shelf. "You're not much of a romantic, are you?"

"I'm a realist."

"Whatever." Grace removed the Brussels sprouts from the sack and set them on the counter next to the other items she was going to store in the refrigerator. She paused for a moment and met Julius's eyes. "Here's what I think—Nyla is afraid that if she loses the money, she'll lose Mr. Perfect, too. That possibility, coming on the heels of her father's murder, it's just too much for her. She's falling apart—consumed with anger, resentment and a deep sense of loss. Internally she's probably a cauldron of seething emotion so she's lashing out."

"People who are lashing out are dangerous, Grace."

"I know."

Julius went silent for a moment. She studied him covertly while she removed the last items from the grocery sack. She could almost see the computer in his head doing its thing, processing a lot of ones and zeroes. Arkwright the Alchemist was calculating; probably working on a strategy. She wasn't sure that was a good thing. True, she had invited him into her life with the breakfast picnic bribe but she knew that she had to tread cautiously. Men like Julius tended to take charge in a hurry. It was their nature.

Out of nowhere, one of the Witherspoon affirmations brightened with the intensity of a halogen bulb in her mind. *Embrace the unknown. It is the only certainty.*

"What are you thinking?" she asked.

"About the missing Witherspoon money." Julius looked out the window at the gray surface of the lake as if it were a divining mirror that reflected answers. "It seems to be one of the keys to whatever is going on here. You're the expert on pithy sayings. I'll bet you know the one that applies in this instance."

"Follow the money?"

"That's one affirmation I do believe in," he said. He met her eyes. "It never lets me down."

"I'm sure the cops believe in it, too," Grace said. "They probably watch television, just like the rest of us."

"They may be looking into the money angle but it won't hurt to have someone from our side take a look as well."

She stilled. "Someone from our side?"

His brows rose. His eyes glittered with dark amusement. "If there's one thing Arkwright Ventures can provide here, it's financial expertise. There are people on my staff who are very, very good at following the money."

"I see," she said. She was not certain where to go with that.

"Now, about lunch and your business plan," he said.

"Whoa." Grace held up a hand, palm out. "Stop. Just a second, here. I need to think about your offer."

Julius somehow managed to look bewildered and possibly a bit hurt. "You don't want me to look into the money angle?"

"It's not that." She paused, trying to come up with a reasonable explanation for her objections. The reality was that her impulsive reaction had been emotional, not logical.

"What is the problem?" Julius asked.

It was a reasonable question.

"I know you mean well and I appreciate your good intentions," she said carefully. "Really I do."

"This isn't a matter of good intentions. It's a simple, logical approach to a problem." He looked around the kitchen. "What were you planning for lunch?"

"Forget lunch," she said, putting a little steel into the words.

If he had appeared bewildered and a little hurt a moment ago, he was downright crushed now.

"I thought there would be lunch," he said.

"Pay attention, Arkwright. This isn't a corporation I'm running here and no one elected you CEO. This is my life, my future. If you're going to do stuff that impacts one or both of those things, you need to discuss it with me first. You do not just waltz into my house and announce that you're going to appoint someone I've never even met to examine the finances of a man some people think I may have murdered. It may be a good idea or it may not. The point is, I need to be involved in the conversation. Is that clear?"

There was a charged silence in the kitchen while Julius considered her declaration of independence. Then he evidently came to a conclusion.

"Okay," he said.

She eyed him with deep suspicion. "Okay? That's it? Just okay?"

Julius's expression was one of polite bewilderment. "Should there be more?"

"No, I guess not."

"So," Julius said. "What do you think about having one of the Arkwright financial wizards try to trace the embezzled Witherspoon money?"

She raised her eyes to the ceiling. "There are privacy issues, for heaven's sake. Not to mention legal issues."

"Not a problem," Julius said.

"I beg your pardon?"

"It won't be the first time that Arkwright Ventures has offered its professional expertise to the police for the purposes of some forensic accounting work. I'll talk to Dev. He'll coordinate with his contacts at the Seattle PD. He's worked with them before on cases that spilled over the city limits."

"I see." She thought about that for a moment. "Well, okay, then."

"Excellent. I'll get right on it after lunch." Julius cleared his throat. "I would remind you that I did not waltz into your kitchen. I just walked in. Carrying the groceries for you."

"Whatever." She pushed herself away from the counter. "All right, we have an understanding. *New day, new opportunities to shape the future.*"

"Is that one of the Witherspoon affirmations?"

"Yes, it is, as a matter of fact. It accompanied the recipe for granola in the Witherspoon Way cookbook." She paused, trying to decide what to do next. Julius was standing in the middle of her kitchen and showing no signs of going anywhere. She needed to do something with him. "Where were we?"

"Lunch," he said, looking hopeful.

"Right. Lunch." She headed toward the refrigerator, grateful for something concrete to do. "And then my career plan."

"We'll start by making a detailed list of your skill set. But first I have another, off-topic question for you."

"What's that?" she asked. She reached for the handle of the refrigerator door.

"I need a date for tomorrow night," Julius said. He did not take his eyes off her. "I have to attend that thoroughly boring business dinner and charity auction that I mentioned to you. I also have to deliver the thoroughly boring after-dinner talk on the thoroughly boring subject of the Pacific Northwest investment climate. Would you consider going with me so that I don't have to sit at the head table alone? You might be able to keep me from dozing off."

She opened the refrigerator, trying to process the invitation.

All rational thought winked out of existence when she saw the things sitting on the center shelf.

For a few seconds she just stood there. Her mind refused to accept the reality of what she was seeing. It had to be a hallucination.

But it was not a dream.

She screamed, dropped the carton of eggs and slammed the door closed.

"Not exactly the response I was hoping for," Julius said.

He was at her side in the blink of an eye. He opened the refrigerator door. Together they both looked at the dead rat lying on the serving platter. It was surrounded by sprigs of parsley. There was a slice of lemon in its mouth. Next to the platter stood an unopened bottle of vodka.

"That settles it," Julius said. "Someone really is stalking you."

Thirteen

A t least it wasn't cooked," Grace said. She shuddered. "Although whoever put it in my refrigerator went to the trouble of making that poor rat look like it was ready to serve for dinner."

Devlin looked up from his notebook. "Poor rat?"

"I'm no more fond of rats than anyone else," Grace said. "But it's really bad karma to kill an innocent creature just so that it can be used to stage some kind of sick revenge fantasy."

"Something tells me whoever left that thing in your refrigerator is not overly concerned with karma," Julius said.

The three of them were in the kitchen. Julius had called Devlin immediately after the discovery of the dead rat. Devlin and one of his officers, a sympathetic, competent woman named Linda Brown, had done the usual cop workup, including photographs of the rat and the bottle of vodka, but it was clear no one expected to find any clues.

As Officer Brown had pointed out, even if the perp hadn't had the presence of mind to think about fingerprints, most people possessed enough common sense to use gloves to handle a dead rat. She had taken the vodka, the rat, the platter and the culinary trimmings away in evidence bags.

Watching the process from the far side of the kitchen, Grace had decided to cross off a career in law enforcement. Handling dead rats was probably one of the less unpleasant jobs a police officer confronted.

She was now seated in a chair at the kitchen table, her hands folded tightly in her lap. She was unnerved. She could think of no other word to describe the shaky, edgy sensation that sent icy chills through her at intermittent intervals.

Breathe.

The refrigerator would have to be cleaned and disinfected from top to bottom, she decided. All the food inside would have to be tossed out. She couldn't bear the thought of eating anything that had shared the same space with the dead rat.

No, she concluded, simply sanitizing the refrigerator would not be enough. It would have to be replaced. She wondered how much new refrigerators cost.

And then there was the issue of the broken window in the guest bedroom. There had been nothing high-tech about the intruder's technique. Whoever it was had simply smashed the glass and climbed through the opening. That explained why the house had felt so chilly when she and Julius walked in, Grace thought.

Julius had told her that he would pick up some plywood at the hardware store and cover the opening. Ralph Johnson at the glass shop had assured her he could have a replacement ready the following day.

Buying a new refrigerator and replacing the window would put a serious dent in her savings but there was no other option. She had drawn the stalker into her mother's house. She had caused this mess. She would clean it up.

Devlin stood in the center of the room, legs braced slightly apart, and continued making notes.

"Earlier today when we discussed the emails, you told me that the stalking has been going on since the day that Witherspoon was found murdered, right?" he said.

"The emails started that night but I hadn't really considered it stalking until today," Grace said. She wrapped her arms around herself. "Until now it's just been the emails. As I explained, they were not actually threatening. I thought perhaps Sprague Witherspoon's daughter was sending them. But I honestly can't see her dealing with a dead rat."

Julius, who was lounging against a counter, arms folded across his chest, shook his head. He didn't actually say anything but, then, he didn't have to say anything, she thought. She was pretty sure she knew what he was thinking. And maybe he had cause. Maybe she had been a little naive.

"Julius is right, this incident officially makes it stalking," Devlin said in his flat cop voice. "Tell me about your relationship with Witherspoon's daughter."

Grace went through it again, even though she had given him most of it that morning.

"That's all I can tell you," she said when she was finished. "She showed up at my door today, demanding that I give her the money she thinks I embezzled from the Witherspoon Way. She accused me of scamming her father and murdering him. She offered to keep quiet if I returned the money. She left when Julius arrived. Next thing I know there's a dead rat in my refrigerator."

"And the bottle of vodka," Julius reminded her quietly.

Her mouth tightened. "Yes. And, yes, before you ask, Devlin, it's the same brand of vodka that I found in Sprague's bedroom."

Devlin watched her for a long moment. "What's with the vodka?"

"I don't know," Grace said. "But there was a liquor bottle in the basement of the old asylum the day I found Mrs. Trager's body. I remember that it was a bottle of vodka. I didn't notice the brand but I think the label was green and gold like the label on the bottle in Sprague's bedroom and the one that was left in my refrigerator. That day, when I found Mrs. Trager and Mark, I used the bottle to—"

She broke off. No one tried to fill in the missing blanks.

Devlin frowned. "You mean you found the bottle in the basement of the Cloud Lake Inn, don't you?"

"Irene and I and everyone else back then usually referred to the place as the asylum," she said. "It was a hospital for the mentally ill at one time."

"You stumbled onto that murder when you were in your teens, according to Irene," Devlin said.

"I was sixteen," Grace said.

Another bad night coming up, she thought. No escaping this one. Might as well not even go to bed. Crap.

"According to the file, Trager had gone home for lunch that day." Devlin glanced down at his notes. "There was evidently an argument. Trager murdered his wife sometime around noon. The boy was a witness. The kid told the police that Trager wrapped up the body before loading it into his truck. He needed to hide it until he could dispose of it. And then there was the problem of the boy. Trager transported the body and Mark to the inn—the asylum—and left both in the basement. He didn't dare dump the bodies until after dark."

"Meanwhile, he had to go back to work," Grace said.

"He would have needed a boat to take the bodies out onto the lake," Julius said.

Devlin looked up again. "Trager owned a small outboard that he used for fishing. He had stored it in his garage for the winter. He probably planned to get it after dark and haul it down to the lake. He could have put it into the water at the asylum. There's an old dock there."

"But he got nervous waiting for nightfall," Grace said.

"It's a common problem for killers," Devlin explained. "Lot of truth in that old saying about the bad guys returning to the scene of the crime. They can't help themselves."

Julius nodded. "They go back to make sure they haven't made any mistakes."

"In this case Trager returned to the scene of the crime that afternoon and found Grace and the boy," Devlin said.

"Mark Ramshaw," Grace said. She squeezed her hands tighter in her lap. "Mrs. Trager sometimes looked after him while his mother worked. Mr. Trager wouldn't allow his wife to go out of the house to work but he let her make a little money watching the Ramshaw boy. Mark was just six years old."

"Why did Trager leave the kid alive in the basement?" Julius asked.

"Presumably Trager didn't murder Mark right away because he wanted the boy's death to look like an accident," Devlin said. "If he had strangled the kid or crushed the boy's skull, the autopsy would have shown results not consistent with death by drowning."

"How did he plan to explain Mrs. Trager's death?" Julius asked.

"The investigators concluded that, given the vodka and the meds at the scene, Trager intended to make it appear that his wife was a suicide. She downed some pills and a lot of booze and took the family boat out on the lake and went overboard. It happens."

"What about the injuries from the beating he gave her that day?" Julius asked.

Devlin shrugged. "I'm guessing here, but I've heard more than one bastard tell me with a straight face that his wife got banged up when she fell down a flight of stairs."

Grace looked at him. "You did some research into the Trager case, didn't you?"

"Right after the Witherspoon murder," Devlin said. He did not sound apologetic. "Sorry, Grace. You're Irene's best friend. I had to look into your past."

Grace sighed. "I understand."

Julius moved to stand behind her chair. He rested one hand lightly on her shoulder. It felt good to have him touching her, she thought; comforting.

Devlin went back to his notes. "Trager confronted you when you tried to escape with the boy. There was a struggle. Trager fell down the basement steps and broke his neck. You and little Mark ran for help. Your mom and sister weren't home that day so you went to Agnes Gilroy's house for help. She took you in and called the police. According to her statement, there was a lot of blood on your clothes. At first she thought it was yours."

"It was Trager's blood." Grace looked down at her clasped hands. "I used the vodka bottle, you see. When I tried to follow Mark up the basement steps, Trager came after me. He grabbed the back of my jacket. I smashed the bottle on the railing, turned and . . . and slashed at him with the jagged edges of glass. There was . . . a lot of blood."

Julius's hand tightened on her shoulder. She fell silent. For a moment no one spoke.

It would definitely be a very bad night.

Julius studied Devlin. "I want to talk to you before you contact the Seattle police. Arkwright Ventures would like to offer its forensic accounting services to the authorities."

Devlin considered that briefly and then nodded. "Tell me what you want to do. I'll clear it with Seattle." He turned back to Grace. For the first time the mask of his professional demeanor slipped. "Damn it, Grace. I'm sorry to have to take you through it all again. But we need to figure out what the hell is going on here. Your boss was murdered. Someone is stalking you. There's a lot of money missing. This is a big puzzle and none of the pieces fit together."

She nodded wearily. "I know. It's okay. You need information."

For a moment no one spoke.

"Got any ideas?" Devlin asked eventually. "I could use some guidance here."

Grace looked at the refrigerator. A dark tide of revulsion rose inside her. She looked away.

"As far as the rat is concerned, I suppose Nyla is the obvious suspect," she said. "But as I told you, I can't imagine her handling a dead animal of any kind, let alone a rat. But then, I have a hard time imagining anyone deliberately putting a dead rat on a platter and sticking it inside a refrigerator." She paused. "Well, maybe in a lab setting. A lot of rats are used in scientific experiments."

"That was no lab rat," Julius said. "That one came straight out of an alley."

Grace looked up at him. "Guess that means we can cross off any scientists or lab techs on the suspect list. Unfortunately, there weren't any there in the first place."

"Plenty of suspects left on that list," Julius said quietly.

"Too many." Devlin closed his notebook. "I'm going to call the Seattle police and talk to the investigator in charge of your case. Maybe if we compare notes we can sort out some of the people involved in this thing."

"Thanks," Grace said. She tried hard to project some positive energy and enthusiasm but judging by the look on the faces of the two men she didn't think she was succeeding.

"You never know." Devlin stuffed the notebook back into his jacket. "What are you going to do now?"

She gazed dolefully at the offending appliance. "Throw out all the food in the refrigerator and then go shop for a new one."

Devlin eyed the refrigerator. "This one looks almost new."

"Mom bought it less than a year ago," Grace said. "It's probably still under warranty. But I could never again eat anything that came out of that refrigerator."

"I understand that you want to clean it out," Devlin said. "But there's nothing wrong with the appliance."

Julius squeezed Grace's shoulder. "I'll help you dump the food. When we're finished we'll shop for a new one."

Fourteen

Julius studied the ranks of gleaming appliances arrayed on the sales floor. It was a bit like walking into an arms dealer's show-room. All the polished hard surface reminded him of so much high-tech military armor.

"Who knew there were so many different kinds of refrigerators?" he said.

For the first time since the discovery of the dead rat and the vodka bottle, Grace looked wanly amused. He was surprised by the wave of relief that whispered through him when she smiled.

Watching her stoically respond to Dev's interrogation had been one of the harder things he'd done in his life. He had wanted to carry her away to someplace safe where no one could ask her any more questions; a place where she could forget the past. He was still dealing with the mental image of her as a teenager covered in the blood of the man who had tried to murder her.

"I take it you haven't done this kind of shopping before?" Grace asked.

"No," he admitted. "The interior designer selected the appliances for my condo in Seattle. The house I bought from Harley came with all the stuff I needed, including the refrigerator."

Shopping for a refrigerator now topped his list of Most Unusual Second Dates, he decided.

"You didn't have to come with me," Grace said. "It wasn't necessary, really."

"Yeah, it was," he said. He watched the salesman approach. "But I admit I'm out of my depth here. Do you have any idea of what you want in a refrigerator?"

"We'll just ask for the latest version of the same model that Mom bought." Grace drew a deep breath. "Although it's going to put a very big hole in my bank account."

He thought about offering to buy the refrigerator for her but he kept his mouth shut. He knew she would refuse.

Grace gave him a sidelong glance. "Thanks."

"For what?"

"For understanding why I have to replace the refrigerator."

"I get it," he said.

No amount of scrubbing or disinfectant would remove the memory of the dead rat.

"I know you get it," she said. "I appreciate that."

"Doesn't mean you can't sell the old one, though. You could probably recover a few hundred bucks."

She smiled again. "Good point. I'll have it moved out onto the back porch until I can sell it."

"I doubt if this store is going to be able to deliver your new refrigerator today," Julius said. "It's nearly five now. What do you say we go out to dinner?"

She hesitated. "Thanks, but I really don't feel like going out. I'll just grab some takeout on the way home."

JAYNE ANN KRENTZ

"Takeout sounds good," he said.

She eyed him. "Did you just invite yourself over for dinner?"

"I never got lunch, remember?"

"I never got my first consulting appointment."

"You're not going to want to be alone this evening, not after what happened today," he said. "Do you mind if I join you for takeout?"

"I'm pretty much vegetarian," she warned.

"I'm sure I'll survive."

She gave that a moment's close thought and then nodded once. "Okay. Thanks. It's very kind of you to offer to keep me company."

"I'm not known for my kindness."

"What are you known for?"

Julius watched the salesman start to circle. "Making money."

"That's a very cool gift," Grace said. Her eyes warmed with amusement again. "Most people would give anything to possess it."

The salesman was closing in now.

"Look," Julius said, "I'm good at investing but what I know about buying refrigerators wouldn't even fill a small shot glass."

"Don't worry," Grace said. She moved forward to intercept the salesman. "I've got this."

Fifteen

They were back in Grace's kitchen by six-thirty. The salesman had promised to expedite the delivery of the new refrigerator. Julius occupied himself with opening the bottle of Columbia Valley Syrah that he had selected while Grace was making her takeout selections at the gourmet grocery store in town.

The little domestic scene in the kitchen would have been very comfortable and cozy, he concluded, if not for the edgy heat of the smoldering arousal that kept him restless and semi-erect. It was as if he was walking a tightrope without a net. *Don't screw this up again, Arkwright.*

He was old enough and sufficiently experienced to be able to control the sexual side of the situation. But what he was feeling around Grace was different in ways he could not explain. He wasn't sure what to do about the sensation but he did know one thing—he wanted to stay as close to her as possible until he figured out what the hell was going on between the two of them.

He poured the wine into two glasses and turned around just in time to see Grace bend over to close the oven door. She was still wearing the jeans and the deep blue, loose-fitting pullover she'd had on that morning. He took a moment to admire the way the denim hugged her nicely rounded rear.

She closed the door and straightened, using one hand to push her whiskey-brown hair back behind her ear. He knew from the faint tilt of her eyebrows that she'd caught him watching her.

"What?" she asked.

"Nothing." He handed her one of the glasses. "Here you go. Medicinal purposes only."

"Definitely," she said. She took a healthy swallow of wine and dropped into one of the wooden chairs. "Thanks. I needed that."

Julius lowered himself into the chair across from her. "You live an eventful life, Miss Elland."

"I will admit that lately my life has been somewhat out of the ordinary." She drank some more wine.

"No Witherspoon affirmation for the current state of affairs?"

She reflected briefly and then shook her head. "No, but I'm sure one will come to me."

"So, in spite of all that power-of-positive-thinking stuff and those Witherspoon affirmations, you do see a role for the occasional dose of reality?"

"Hell, yes."

"Good to know." He saluted her with the wineglass. "What's for dinner?"

"Tofu satay and seaweed salad." She leaned back in her chair, stretched out her legs and closed her eyes. "I'll bet you're excited about the menu, aren't you?"

"My favorites," he assured her.

She opened her eyes, amused. "I did warn you."

"I don't have any problem with the menu. But what with one thing and another, I don't believe you ever got around to answering my question this afternoon."

He waited to see if she would pretend to have forgotten. But this was Grace, who was probably too honest for her own good.

"Do you really need a date for tomorrow night?" she asked.

He moved one hand slightly. "I can handle it on my own. Wouldn't be the first time. But I'd rather have you sitting at my side at the head table. I hate making conversation at those kinds of events. No one ever has anything interesting to say, including me. Not that you could have a meaningful conversation with ten people sitting at a table under those circumstances. And then there is the entertainment for the evening, courtesy of yours truly, who will deliver what is known far and wide as the Speech from Hell."

Grace erupted in laughter. The wine sloshed precariously in her glass.

"Are you certain it will be that bad?" she asked when she got the laughter under control.

"My after-dinner talk? I know it will be bad."

She searched his face. "How can you be so sure?"

"Because I am not without experience."

Grace watched him thoughtfully now. "This is a talk you've given before?"

"I've given variations of it so many times during the past few years, I've lost count. I get asked to speak to investor groups, business associations and the occasional MBA class. I have no idea why anyone invites me back a second time. Public speaking is not my forte, believe me."

She put down her glass and folded her arms on the table. "Let's hear it."

"What?"

"Your speech. Give me the talk that you plan to deliver tomorrow evening."

He realized she was serious.

"Forget it," he said. "Delivering the Speech from Hell is the very last thing I want to do tonight."

"Here's the deal I'm willing to make, Arkwright. If you want me to attend that business and charity affair with you tomorrow night, I insist that you preview your after-dinner talk for me now."

He watched her closely, trying to decide whether or not she was joking. But there was no amusement in her eyes.

"Why do you want to hear the SFH?" he asked.

"Plain old curiosity, I guess."

He thought about it. "I'll let you read it, will that do? I've got twenty bucks says you won't be able to make it more than halfway through."

"Twenty bucks?" She grinned. "And here I thought you were a big-time player."

"Twenty bucks—twenty thousand bucks." He shrugged. "What difference does it make?"

"You really are bored with the subject of money, aren't you? But you're right. A wager is a wager. And since I can't put up twenty grand, I'll go with the twenty bucks. Where's the SFH?"

"I store it online. If you really want to do this, I can pull it up on your computer."

"I really want to do this," she said.

He groaned. "Fine. It won't take long for your eyes to glaze over. Fire up your laptop. And get ready to pay me twenty dollars. No IOUs, by the way. Cash only."

"Understood."

She got up from the table and disappeared into the front room.

When she returned she had her laptop as well as a notepad and a pen. She set the computer down on the table in front of him.

Reluctantly he went online and downloaded the Speech from Hell. Without a word he turned the computer around so that she could see the document.

She whistled. "Lot of data here."

"It's a business talk, remember?"

She started reading with an alarming degree of concentration.

"It's not the Great American Novel," he warned.

"There is no Great American Novel," she said absently. "This nation is too big and too diverse to produce only one great book. We've got lots of them and there will be more written in the future. Art doesn't stand still."

He decided there was no good response to that so he poured himself another glass of wine and sat back to await the settling of the wager.

At some point in the process Grace reached for her notepad and pen. A sense of doom settled on him. Just how bad was the Speech from Hell? On the bright side, she would be going to the reception with him. Cheered at the thought, he lounged deeper in the chair. He entertained himself with a pleasant little fantasy that involved Grace spending the night with him in his Seattle condo. After all, the event would not be over until quite late and it would be an hour's drive back to Cloud Lake. It only made sense to stay the night at his place and drive back the following morning.

The more Grace read of the SFH, the more he immersed himself in his daydream. He was strategizing ways to broach the subject to her when she finally looked up from the screen. She reached for her glass of wine.

"Okay," she said. "Somewhere in this speech there's a very good after-dinner talk."

He raised his brows. "Think so?"

"It's too long and loaded with way too many facts and figures. That might work for a formal business presentation but you said this was an after-dinner talk."

"So?"

"You told me that business decisions are usually made on the basis of emotion. Well, after-dinner talks are all about emotion. Heck, every speech is about emotion."

He went blank. "Emotion."

"Right. But I do see a thread in here that will work. If we refocus on the emotional takeaway buried below all the details, you'll be brilliant tomorrow night."

"I know my limitations. I'm brilliant at making money. I am not brilliant at giving after-dinner talks." He glanced at her notepad. "What the hell do you mean about an emotional takeaway?"

"Studies show that audiences never remember the facts and figures of a talk—they remember the emotions the speech generated," she said. "You can't infuse too many emotions into an after-dinner talk about the current business climate so we will concentrate on one."

He narrowed his eyes. "I double-dare you to find a single emotional element in that talk."

She gave him a smug smile and aimed the tip of her pen at one of her notes. "It's right here, the reference to your mentor."

"What mentor?" He stopped. "You mean the guy who gave me my first job after I left the Marines?"

"You said that individual gave you a break and taught you how to read a spreadsheet and a profit-and-loss statement."

Julius smiled slowly, amused for the first time since the discussion had turned to the topic of the Speech from Hell.

"My first employer was a Marine," he said. "He knew that it wasn't easy starting a new life in a civilian career, especially if, like me, you had a very limited skill set. He hired me as his driver. I learned a lot listening to him talk business in the back of the car. Eventually I became his fixer."

Grace's eyes lit with curiosity. "What did you fix?"

"Anything and everything that was a problem for him. The job covered a lot of territory."

She tapped a finger on the table and gave the subject a moment's thought.

"I think we'll change that job title for this talk," she said. "Fixer sounds a bit shady. Mob bosses and sleazy government officials have fixers."

He studied her over the rim of his glass. "Got a better word for fixer?"

"Executive administrative assistant works. Like fixer, it covers a lot of territory." She smiled a little, satisfied. "Out of curiosity, how did you apply for that first job?"

"I sent my résumé to the HR department of the company. Got no response. So I went to the president's office and sat there all day, every day, for a week until he got tired of walking past me and agreed to give me an interview."

Grace glowed with approval.

"That's it," she said. Her eyes were bright with enthusiasm. "That's your story. I love it. You're going to inspire everyone in your audience."

"I am?"

"You're going to tell them to look around and find at least one person who won't be able to get a foot in the door the traditional way and help that individual do what your mentor did—open the door a little wider."

An icy chill shot down his spine. "You want me to give a motivational talk?"

"You can think of it that way."

"You are out of your mind," he said, enunciating each word with great precision. "The audience tomorrow night will be composed of businesspeople and their significant others. It is not, I repeat, not a motivational seminar."

"An audience is an audience. You're going for an emotional hit. Your job is to make people leave feeling good about themselves. You want them to be inspired by their better angels."

"If you gathered up all the better angels in the audience tomorrow night, you wouldn't have to worry about how many of them could dance on the head of a pin because you wouldn't have a single dancing angel. Trust me on this."

"I disagree," Grace said. "I'm sure there will be a sprinkling of self-absorbed narcissists in the crowd. And statistically speaking there will be a few sociopaths—hopefully the nonviolent type. But I think most will be folks who at least want to think of themselves as good people. Your job is to remind them to heed the call of their better natures."

"So that they can feel good about themselves?"

"No, because it's a matter of personal honor for each individual in that crowd. Your job is to remind them of that fact."

"We're talking about businesspeople, Grace. All they care about is the bottom line."

"I understand that's important to them." Grace assumed a patient air. "And there is nothing wrong with making money. You evidently do that rather well. But I also know that honor matters to you. It will matter to a lot of those in your audience. If nothing else you can remind them that they have a golden opportunity to leave a legacy. That legacy will be in the form of the people they mentored along the way."

"What makes you think that I care all that much about honor?"

She smiled. "You're a Marine. Everyone knows there are no ex-Marines."

He could not think of a response to that so he looked at the notepad.

"You're living in fantasy land. I wouldn't even know where to begin to write a talk like the one you're suggesting."

"We'll start with your own personal story. Tell them how you got that first job with the man who became your mentor. Trust me on this. I helped Sprague write his motivational talks. I know what I'm doing here. I guarantee you that you'll have the audience eating out of the palm of your hand."

"So I give them a feel-good story," he said. "How the hell do I end it?"

"Think like a Marine. Give your audience a mission and send them out to fulfill it. They'll feel great about themselves after you finish, and that's the whole point here."

He contemplated her in silence for a moment.

"How did you learn about Marines?" he asked finally.

"My father was a Marine." She smiled a misty smile. "He was killed in a helicopter crash when I was a baby. I never got the chance to know him. But Mom told me a lot about him. That's how I know what I know."

Julius considered that for a while.

"Okay," he said, "I'll try the speech your way. But I'm warning you, it will probably be an even bigger disaster than my old Speech from Hell. I'm not into this motivational crap."

"That's the spirit. Think positive."

"Actually, there is a silver lining in this situation," he said.

"What's that?"

He smiled slowly. "You'll be there to witness the fiasco. Later I will get to say *I told you so*. Everyone likes to say that, right?"

"The new version of your speech will work." She got to her feet and crossed the room to open the oven door. "By the way, you never told me the name of your first employer—the man who became your mentor."

"Harley Montoya."

"Harley?" Grace turned around quickly, shocked. "Your next-door neighbor? The man who sold you the house here in Cloud Lake?"

"That Harley."

Grace smiled, pleased. "That is sort of sweet."

"Sweet is generally not the first word that comes to mind when people describe Harley."

Sixteen

They worked on the Speech from Hell until sometime after nine with a break along the way to eat the tofu satay and seaweed salad. Julius decided that tofu and seaweed tasted surprisingly good, at least as long as Grace was sitting on the other side of the table.

"That should do it," Grace said. She hit save on the computer. "Your audience will love it."

He studied the notes he had made on the notepad. "I don't know that anyone will love it, but it certainly won't be the speech they'll be expecting from me."

"There's nothing like the element of surprise to wake up an audience." She got to her feet. "I need some exercise. The rain has stopped. Want to go for a walk?"

He looked out the window. "It's cold out there."

"It's not that bad."

"And dark."

"The moon is out, there are lamps along the footpath and we can take flashlights for backup."

A moonlight walk with Grace suddenly sounded like an excellent plan, Julius thought. It would give him an excuse to stick around a little longer, maybe come up with a way to present his grand plan for staying the night in the city at his place.

He felt better already. Maybe there was something to the positive-thinking nonsense.

"You're right," he said. "After all that speech writing, I could use some exercise, too."

She bundled herself up in the jacket that he would always think of as her Little Red Riding Hood coat. He took his leather jacket off the back of the chair and pulled it on. Together they went out onto the back porch. Grace paused to lock the door.

The night air was well chilled. They went down to the water's edge. He waited to see which way she would go. Turning right was the route into town. It ended at the public marina. Left would take them past his house. Beyond that, at the top of the lake, heavily shrouded in trees and night, was the old asylum.

He was not surprised when Grace chose to walk toward the lights of town. He fell into step beside her. Neither of them spoke for a while but the silence felt comfortable, at least it did to him. Silver moonlight gleamed on the surface of the lake. The low footpath lamps created a string of fairy lights. They did not need the flashlights.

"Thanks for the help with the SFH tonight," he said after a while.

"You're welcome. By the way, you owe me twenty bucks."

"I always pay my debts."

"Thanks for understanding why I had to buy a new refrigerator." She paused. "We're even, right?"

"Even?"

"You know, a favor for a favor."

"Oh, yeah. Got it." He came to a halt. "Do you have a problem with owing someone a favor? Or is it just me?"

Grace stopped, too. "Not exactly. Okay. Maybe it's just you. I'm not sure yet."

"You're not making things any more clear."

"It's just that I don't want you to think of me as some kind of hobby," she said.

He tried to wrap his brain around that. And failed.

"What?" he asked.

"You heard me." She turned her head slightly to look at him. The hood of the jacket shadowed her face, making it impossible to read her eyes. "I think you're just bored. I don't want you to get the idea that involving yourself in my current problems would be an interesting way to . . . distract yourself."

He stared at her, a slow-burning anger heating his blood.

"That is the dumbest reasoning I've ever heard," he rasped. "No wonder your track record with relationships is so bad."

"My track record?" Her voice rose in outrage. "You're the one with a failed marriage behind you and no visible signs of a serious interest in dating since your divorce."

"Who told you that?" he demanded.

"Irene is my friend, remember? I told her the blind date hadn't gone well but that I had hired you to consult for me. I think she panicked. She thought I ought to know a little more about you."

"We're a real pair, aren't we?" He gripped her shoulders with both hands. "Just to clarify, I am not getting involved in your problems because I'm looking for a way to distract myself."

"No? Why, then?"

"Damned if I know."

He pulled her close and crushed her mouth beneath his own before she could say anything else.

He wasn't looking for a distraction but he was looking for something, and since he could not put a name to it, he was willing to settle for sex—as long as it was sex with Grace.

As far as he was concerned the kiss had been waiting to happen since she walked through Devlin and Irene's front door the previous night. But it seemed to catch Grace by surprise. She went still.

For three of the longest seconds of his life he wondered if he had made a terrible mistake by misreading the heat in the atmosphere between them.

But on the fourth beat of his heart he felt a shudder go through Grace's supple body. She braced her gloved hands against the front of his leather jacket.

And then she was kissing him back. It was a tentative response at first, as if she wasn't sure it would be a good thing to go down this road with him. He moved his mouth across hers, trying to persuade her that he was worth the risk.

She pressed closer and made a soft, urgent little sound in the back of her throat. In the next moment she was responding with a hungry, sexy energy that sent lightning through him.

He moved his hands from her shoulders down to the front of her coat. He got the garment unfastened and slipped inside, settling his palms on the lush, feminine curve of her hip. He was tight, hard, intensely aroused and intensely aware of everything about Grace. Her scent dazzled him. Her gentle curves made him desperate to touch her more intimately.

No wonder he hadn't been interested in dating anyone else for so long. He'd been waiting for this woman. He just hadn't realized it until now.

Grace's arms moved up to circle his neck. She leaned into him and opened her mouth a little. He was suddenly lost in the sweet, hot, aching need.

The muffled sound of a cell phone ping shattered the crystalline atmosphere. Grace froze. So did he.

"Damn it to hell," he said softly.

Grace pulled away and took a sharp breath.

They both looked down at the pocket of her jacket. Slowly Grace took out her phone and studied the screen.

"An email from Sprague Witherspoon's account," she whispered. "Nyla is not giving up easily."

"Assuming the crazy emailer is Nyla Witherspoon." A cold fury splashed through him. "What does it say this time?"

Grace opened the email and read it aloud in a flat, emotionless voice. *"Savor the present because it is all that is certain."*

"One of those damned Witherspoon affirmations?" Julius asked, knowing the answer.

"Yes, but there's more this time." There was a faint shiver in Grace's words now. *"Thirty-nine hours and counting."*

"Sounds like Nyla's counting down the forty-eight hours she gave you earlier today," Julius said. "Let me see your phone."

Grace handed it to him without a word. He studied the email, searching for any clue in the format but to all appearances it had come from Sprague Witherspoon.

"That settles it," he said. "Looks like I'll be spending the night with you."

"What?"

The shock in the single word was not particularly heartening but he told himself that he had handled tougher negotiations.

"Nyla Witherspoon, or someone posing as her dead father, seems to be determined to scare the hell out of you. I don't think it's a good idea for you to be alone—not at night."

"Julius, I appreciate the offer," she said, very earnest now. "But there are some things you don't know about me. I'm not a sound sleeper, especially when I'm stressed. And I have problems with nightmares, especially lately. Sometimes I get up and walk around the house in the middle of the night. People find it . . . unsettling."

"What people?"

"Look, I'd rather not go into the details, all right?"

"Sure. But just so you know, I'm okay with you walking around the house in the middle of the night. I do that, myself, on occasion."

She stared at him, uncomprehending. "You do?"

"Yes," he said. "I do. We'll stop by my place first. I need to pick up a few things."

She held up a finger. "Just to be clear, if you stay at my house, you're sleeping in the guest bedroom."

"Understood."

He waited but she did not seem to know where to go after that so he took her arm and piloted her back along the footpath.

Seventeen

T hey walked past her house, past Agnes Gilroy's place and on around the little cove to Julius's house.

Julius went up the back porch steps and opened the kitchen door. He flipped on the lights and stood aside, waiting for her to enter first. She got an odd, tingly feeling when she stepped into his kitchen. A deep sense of curiosity infused her senses.

Kitchens were very personal, in her opinion. They said a lot about an individual. This one had a retro vibe. The old appliances, cupboards and tile countertops had been caught in a time warp. But everything, from the old-fashioned gas range and the chrome toaster to the ancient coffeemaker, appeared to be clean, in good repair and ready for action.

A Marine lived here, she thought, biting back a smile. Electrical cords were neatly secured. Canisters were lined up against the backsplash in strict order—short to tall. Even the saltshaker and the pepper mill seemed to be standing at attention. She suspected that Julius's office and his condo in Seattle probably radiated the same sense of order and discipline.

"I'll throw some things in a bag and get my shaving gear," Julius said. "Wait here. This won't take long."

She walked slowly around the kitchen, taking in the feel of the space. Everything whispered Julius's secret to her—he was a man who had long ago learned to live alone.

He reappeared at the entrance to the kitchen, a black leather duffel in one hand.

"Ready," he said.

She looked at him. "You really don't have to babysit me tonight. I mean, it's very nice of you and I appreciate it but—"

He crossed the distance between them in two long strides and silenced her with a straight-to-the-point, no-nonsense kiss. When he raised his head, his eyes were dark and intent.

"Yes," he said. "I do have to do this. Think of it as part of the consulting services that you hired me to provide."

"That's a stretch. How many times have you spent the night with one of your clients?"

He smiled the slow, wicked smile that made her pulse kick up, but in a good way. Arkwright the Alchemist.

"Every job has unique requirements," he said. "I try to be flexible and adaptable."

Neither of them should be thinking about sex, she told herself. But she knew that the subject was burning in the background, a smoldering fire that would flash out of control if she wasn't very careful. Too soon. Too many unknowns.

They went out onto the back porch. Julius locked up. The back door of the neighboring house banged open as they went down the steps. Harley Montoya's bald head gleamed in the porch light. He was wearing a pair of khaki pants and a faded sweater. He moved to the edge of the porch and gripped the railing.

"Thought I heard someone out here," he roared. "'Evenin', Grace. What are you two doing? Little late for a stroll around the lake, isn't it?"

"It's never too late for a walk around the lake," Julius said.

"Don't give me that bullshit," Harley said. "Pardon my language, Grace. That's a duffel bag you're carryin', Julius. You two are fixin' to spend the night together at the Elland house."

"That's the plan," Julius said. "You've probably heard by now that someone is stalking Grace."

"Yep." Harley peered at Grace. "Agnes told me about the rat in your refrigerator. Some real sick people out there. But don't worry, Julius will take good care of you."

"Julius very kindly offered to stay with me tonight so that I won't have to be alone in the house," she said.

"It's gonna be all over town tomorrow, you know," Harley warned.

Grace opened her mouth to say *He's going to sleep in the guest bedroom*, but that sounded defensive so she decided to shut up. Harley probably wouldn't believe it, anyway. Tomorrow morning no one in town would believe it, either.

"I'm planning to put in an alarm system and maybe get a dog," she said instead.

Harley snorted. "You'll be fine with Julius. In my experience, he's about as good as an alarm system and a dog."

"Thanks," Julius said. "I'll treasure your words of high praise."

"You do that," Harley said. "Take good care of Grace. See you tomorrow."

Harley went back inside his house. The door banged shut behind him.

Julius took Grace's arm. They walked through the garden to the gate that opened onto the path.

Grace glanced around at the lush landscaping. "Is this your work?"

"Of course not," Julius said. "Harley takes care of my garden and his own."

They started back toward Grace's house.

"Harley was right," Grace said after a moment. "The fact that you spent the night at my place will be all over Cloud Lake by noon tomorrow."

"Got a problem with that?"

She gave it some thought. "No, I don't have a problem with it. I've got a problem with finding dead rats and bottles of vodka in my refrigerator, and I've got a problem with someone sending me creepy emails but, no, I don't have a problem with you spending the night in my spare bedroom."

"I like a woman who knows how to keep her priorities straight."

When they reached her house, Grace pulled some fresh linens out of a closet. Together she and Julius made up the bed in the guest bedroom.

Earlier Julius had tacked up a sheet of plywood to cover the opening left by the smashed pane of glass. The second pane was still in place so the room was not completely shuttered. Grace could see clouds moving across the night sky, obscuring the moon. Another storm was on the way.

Getting the bed ready proved to be an unnervingly intimate process, at least on her side. By the time she had finished stuffing the pillow into the pillowcase she could have sworn that the atmosphere in the room was charged with electricity.

Julius made himself at home with the ease of a stray cat—or a man who was accustomed to living out of a suitcase. She looked at him across the expanse of the freshly made bed.

"The guest bath is just down the hall," she said, determined to adopt the same casual attitude toward the situation that Julius was exhibiting. "There are some sesame seed crackers if you get hungry."

"Thanks," he said.

She went toward the door. "I'll say good night, then."

Julius followed her as far as the doorway.

"Good night," he said.

She hesitated, aware that something more needed to be said. But she did not know how to bring up the subject of the hot kiss in the icy moonlight.

She turned away and went down the hall. She could feel Julius's eyes on her until she escaped into the relative safety of her bedroom.

She undressed, changed into her nightgown, robe and slippers and went into the master bath to brush her teeth.

When she emerged a short time later the door to Julius's room stood slightly open but the lights were off. She waited a moment. When she heard no sound from the guest bedroom, she hurried through the ritual of securing the house.

At least it was only a partial ritual that night, she thought. She did not have to check the closets or look under the bed in Julius's room. Something told her that if there was a monster hiding there, Julius could deal with the problem.

Eventually she turned off the lamps. The night-lights that she had placed strategically throughout the house came up, infusing each space with the exception of Julius's room with a reassuring glow. Julius must have unplugged the little night-light in his room.

She went back to her room and sat on the edge of the bed for a while, doing her breathing exercises. During the meditation process thoughts always swirled and intruded. The trick was to return the focus again and again to the breath.

When she was finished she crawled under the covers and gazed up at the shadowy ceiling and brooded on her decision to allow Julius to spend the night in the guest bedroom. One moment she managed to convince herself that there was no harm in letting him stay; the next moment she was forced to conclude that it might not have been one of her brighter ideas. She was violating one of her own rules.

But it was good to know that tonight she would not be alone if the monster came out from the darkness.

In the end she opted to go with a Witherspoon affirmation: *Meet challenges with creativity.* She had no idea what that meant in regard to Julius but it sounded reassuring.

Julius stretched out on the bed, his hands folded behind his head, and contemplated the ceiling of the guest bedroom. He thought about how Grace had walked through the house, not only double-checking all the locks that he had secured earlier, but opening and closing cupboards and closets. It all sounded methodical, as if it were a nightly routine.

Some people might have considered the detailed security check a tad obsessive but he understood. The enemy could be anywhere.

Eighteen

A soft rustling sound brought her out of a restless sleep and vaguely menacing dreams. She woke up breathless, her pulse skittering. It took her a few seconds to center herself.

You are the eye of the storm—you are calm and in control.

She had left the bedroom door partway open. As she watched, a dark shadow moved along the hallway. Panic shivered through her. She sat up quickly and pushed the covers aside, instinct warning her to get on her feet so that she could choose fight or flight.

Reason took over. It was Julius out there in the hall. It had to be Julius. Perhaps something had awakened him.

Her pulse rate steadied and her breathing calmed. The problem was that she was not accustomed to having a man in the house—not at this hour, at any rate. She reached for her robe, slid her feet into the slippers and went out into the hall.

The front room lay in unexpectedly deep shadows. It took her a few seconds to realize that the night-light in that room was no longer illuminated. The bulb must have burned out, she thought. She made a note to change it in the morning.

Then she saw Julius. He stood at the window watching the night through a crack in the curtains. He was wearing a dark crew-necked T-shirt and the khakis he'd had on earlier in the evening. His feet were bare.

"What is it?" she asked quietly. She moved farther into the room. "Do you see something?"

"No," Julius said. He turned back to the window. "I just had a feeling—"

"That someone was watching?"

Julius shrugged. "Something woke me. Probably a car going past on the road. It's pretty damn quiet out here at night."

"You turned off the night-light in this room, didn't you?"

"Didn't want to be silhouetted against it. I'll switch it on when I go back to bed." He glanced at her. "Is that okay?"

"Yes, certainly." Grace hugged herself. "I've had a creepy feeling that someone was watching every night since I started receiving those damned emails. I've been telling myself it's just my imagination."

"Someone *is* watching you—we just don't know if that person is here in Cloud Lake or at some other location. When we find out why, we'll know the identity of the watcher."

Julius walked across the room and came to a halt in front of her. He kissed her forehead.

"Go back to bed," he said. "You're not alone tonight."

"I know. Thanks."

The atmosphere was once again charged with edgy tendrils of anticipation. It was as if she was standing on a high cliff above a crashing sea, she thought. She longed to take the dive into the deep, mysterious waters but she was very sure now that becoming involved in an affair with Julius would be a high-risk endeavor.

The silence between them lengthened. It was as if they were both waiting for something momentous to happen.

It was then she realized that she was the one who would have to make the first move. Julius was leaving the decision up to her. He knew how to wait for what he wanted. He possessed the patience of a hunter.

This man is different. Not another stray. You need to think about this.

She pulled herself together.

"I'll see you in the morning," she said.

"I'll be here."

It was a promise.

Grace made herself go back down the hall to her bedroom. This time when she climbed into bed she fell into a dreamless sleep. Julius was standing guard against the monsters tonight.

Nineteen

I t was cold and the dampness in the night air warned of rain but the watcher in the shadows was not quite ready to leave the cover of the trees.

The night-lights in the lake house had shifted a few minutes ago. Someone had gotten out of bed—Grace, probably. She was finally becoming aware that she was being stalked. It had been fun watching her dash out to buy a new refrigerator today. Bonus points for that move. Talk about an overreaction. The woman's nerves must be shredded now.

The hunt had gone according to plan until recently. Who knew that the game would prove to be so addictive?

Julius Arkwright was an unforeseen complication, but a minor one. He was what the military described as a soft target.

Grace would be an even softer target.

Twenty

The muffled crunch of gravel announced the arrival of a car in the drive. Grace hit save on the keyboard. Following the instructions of her new consultant, she had been attempting to create a skill-set list. She had been working diligently ever since Julius had left that morning but she had not made much progress. She was afraid that there were not many employers who would leap at the opportunity to hire someone whose chief skill was the ability to write affirmation-themed cookbooks and blogs.

There had been other obstacles to productivity that morning as well. Memories of breakfast with Julius kept interrupting her attempts to focus on her project.

She had found the experience of waking up to a man in her kitchen—one who was making coffee, no less—disconcerting. She had always told herself that when the right man came along, she would reconsider her policy of not allowing a man to spend the night but somehow that had never happened.

That morning, however, she had been confronted with the reality of Julius, and she still could not decide if he was the right man or the wrong one.

For his part, Julius had not exhibited any such uncertainties. He had settled in as if he got up and made coffee for the two of them every day of his life. Due to the empty refrigerator, breakfast had consisted of toast and peanut butter and a couple of oranges. Eating the meal with Julius had been an unexpectedly gratifying experience. She wondered if she ought to be worried about that.

There had been no way to handle his departure discreetly. Agnes was an early riser. She had come out onto her back porch to wave cheerfully at Julius when he left to take the footpath to his place. Grace had watched from the kitchen window as he stopped and chatted briefly with Agnes. Everyone involved had acted as if it was all very routine.

Grace had known then that Harley Montoya was right. The news that Julius had spent the night at the Elland house would be all over town by noon. Sure enough, shortly after nine, Agnes had departed in her tiny, fuel-efficient car. She liked to run her errands early in the day.

She had returned from her mission an hour ago.

Grace got to her feet and went to the window. It had rained early that morning but the storm front had passed and the clouds had broken up. The forecast promised more rain that afternoon but for now there was some winter sunlight.

She watched the BMW come to a halt in the drive. She did not recognize the vehicle but when she saw the man who climbed out from behind the wheel, a frisson of uncertainty made her catch her breath.

"Crap," she said aloud to the empty room.

No, she thought in the next breath, she ought to take a much more positive attitude toward her visitor. He was probably the only potential employer she knew who might be interested in her unique skill set.

Larson Rayner was also a suspect in Sprague's murder.

She opened the door just as he reached out to stab the doorbell with one elegantly buffed nail.

Larson smiled at her with his patented I-can-make-your-life-better-in-ten-easy-steps smile. Blue-eyed and dark-haired, with a lean, athletic build, a square-jawed profile, very white teeth, a touch of gray at the temples and a sincere, straightforward manner, he was perfectly cast for the role he played in real life. He had been born to be a motivational speaker.

"Hello, Grace," he said.

Sprague had mentioned that Larson had taken elocution lessons at the start of his career. The results had paid off in a warm, resonant voice that worked as well in person as it did with a microphone.

"I wasn't expecting you, Larson," she said.

"Great to see you again." His eyes warmed with deep concern. "How are you holding up? I've been very concerned. You went through a traumatic experience."

"I'm doing fine, thanks," she said. She infused her voice with all the perky, upbeat energy she could summon.

The front door of Agnes's house opened. Agnes stepped out onto her porch with a pair of pruning shears in hand. Grace made a point of waving at her enthusiastically. Agnes returned the greeting, the big shears gleaming in the sunlight. She smiled cheerfully and went down the steps to go about her gardening tasks.

Grace had a hunch that Agnes would be heading back into town that afternoon to run a few more errands. Two male visitors at the Elland house in less than twenty-four hours was bound to stir up interest.

JAYNE ANN KRENTZ

It occurred to Grace that she might as well take advantage of Agnes's curiosity. It was hard to imagine Larson as a killer but one thing was certain, there had been no love lost between Larson and Sprague. The rivalry between the two men was long-standing. It was not inconceivable that Larson might have been driven to murder. The idea of being alone with him raised a few red flags. Agnes made a very convenient witness.

Grace went out onto the porch, allowing the door to close behind her. She moved to the railing.

"Agnes," she called, "I'd like you to meet Larson Rayner. You may have heard of him. He's a very popular motivational speaker. Larson, this is Agnes Gilroy."

"How exciting," Agnes said. She bustled through the garden to the hedge that served as a fence. "I've seen you on TV, Mr. Rayner. Such a nice-looking man. You are just as handsome in real life. A pleasure to meet you."

Impatience glittered in Larson's eyes but there was no hint of it in his warm voice.

"The pleasure is all mine, Ms. Gilroy," he said.

"Oh, do call me Agnes. How nice of you to come all this way to see our Grace."

"I consider Grace a colleague," Larson said. "She's had a terrible shock, as I'm sure you're aware. I wanted to see how she was getting on."

"That is so thoughtful of you," Agnes said. She chuckled and winked at Grace. "So many interesting gentlemen looking after you these days, dear. Take advantage of it while you can. The older you get, the leaner the pickings."

Grace felt the heat rise in her cheeks.

"Thanks for the advice, Agnes," she said. She turned to Larson and lowered her voice. "Just to clarify, I think that if you had been deeply

TRUST NO ONE

concerned about me, you would have shown up here sooner. So why don't you come inside and tell me the real reason for your visit today?"

Larson blinked, evidently both surprised and deeply hurt by the casual manner in which she had brushed aside the possibility that his intentions were of a friendly nature. Tiny creases appeared briefly at the corners of his eyes and his jaw tightened but he followed her into the house.

She led the way into the kitchen and set about making coffee.

"Have a seat," she said.

Larson hesitated and then lowered himself into a chair on the far side of the table.

"Coffee?" she asked.

"Thanks," he said. "I could use a cup. Long drive from Seattle. Traffic was bad this morning. There was an accident on the inter-state."

"I hope you don't take cream in your coffee," she said. She watched his face while she ran water into the glass pot. "The refrigerator is no longer functioning. I've got a new one coming this afternoon. Mean-while, I had to toss out all of the food that was inside this one."

"I don't use cream or sugar," Larson said. He glanced at the refrig-erator. "It looks fairly new."

"I'm going to sell it," she said, avoiding the question of warranties.

She paid close attention but as far as she could tell, Larson immedi-ately lost interest in the refrigerator. Dead rats didn't seem like his thing, anyway, she thought. She poured the water into the machine, measured the coffee and hit the on switch.

"I'll come straight to the point," Larson said. "I'm here because I want to offer you a position on my staff."

Her first real job offer and she hadn't even finished her business plan. She couldn't wait to tell Julius.

"I see," she said. "I'm flattered, of course, but I've been doing a lot of thinking and I'm not sure I want to stay in the motivational field. It might be time to move on to something different."

"I agree," Larson said.

"You do?"

Determination gleamed in his eyes. "Look, I had my differences with Witherspoon but I have nothing but admiration for you and your abilities. You were an invaluable asset to the operation but Sprague didn't give you the credit you deserved. Furthermore, I'm sure he also underpaid you. I guarantee you that I'll double your salary."

It was Larson's air of desperation more than the offer of a better salary that piqued her curiosity. In her experience, he had always been supremely confident and sure of his own charisma.

"That's very generous of you," she said. "But the thing is, I'm considering another career path entirely. I really don't think that I'm cut out to be an assistant to a motivational coach for the rest of my life. *Life is enhanced when we seek fresh challenges*, as we in the Witherspoon Way like to say."

That clearly irritated Larson but he kept the sincerity vibe going.

"It's natural that you would want to consider all your options," he said. "But I disagree with your negative analysis of your own potential."

"I wasn't being negative." She folded her arms and lounged against the counter next to the coffeepot. "I said I'm looking for fresh challenges."

"Your talents lie in the motivational field. The problem is that you haven't had a chance to fully explore the opportunities. That was Witherspoon's fault. I knew him better than anyone else did. He was slick, I'll give him that. But he used people. What's more, he did it so well, most of them never realized how they had been used until it was too late."

"That sounds personal," she said coolly.

Larson grimaced. "I admit that I'm one of the people he used on his way up. Look, I know that you and everyone else in the Witherspoon office heard that last argument I had with Witherspoon. Losing the McCormick seminar was the final straw. It was the fifth time in six months that I'd had a call from a client informing me that a certain firm would not be doing any more business with my company. On each occasion I found out that the Witherspoon Way was booked, instead."

"You think Sprague somehow stole those contracts from you?" Grace asked.

Larson's right hand clamped into a fist on the kitchen table. He seemed unaware of the small action.

"I *know* he stole those seminars from me," he said.

Footsteps sounded on the back porch, startling Grace. She glanced out the window and saw Julius. He opened the door and entered the kitchen with the air of a man who had every right to be there. He crossed the floor to where Grace stood, gave her a quick, proprietary kiss and then turned to Larson.

"You've got company," he said to Grace.

But Larson was already on his feet, smiling broadly. The hand that had been curled into a fist was now extended in greeting. "Larson Rayner. Grace and I are colleagues."

"Not quite," Grace said.

But she could tell that neither man was listening to her. They were too busy circling each other, metaphorically speaking. There was a lot of testosterone in the atmosphere. Julius and Larson were assessing each other the way men did when there was only one woman in the vicinity and they both wanted to lay claim to her.

It would have been more flattering, she thought, if Julius and Larson had been vying to carry her off into a hidden bower to ravish her. But she knew that each man had a somewhat different agenda. Larson wanted to take advantage of her rather eclectic skill set. As for Julius, she was pretty sure his protective instincts had been aroused.

"Julius Arkwright," Julius said.

The men shook hands briefly. The gesture was short and brusque.

A gleam of interest sharpened Larson's expression. "Arkwright Ventures?"

"That's right," Julius said.

He said it easily, as if everyone owned a thriving venture capital business that raked in millions. But there was something else infused into the words—a quiet possessiveness that made it clear he could and would protect what was his. He might be a bored lion but he was, nevertheless, a lion.

Larson's smile widened and his eyes brightened with what was probably intended to look like admiration. Grace thought the expression bore a striking resemblance to that of a shrewd salesman who has spotted a potential client.

"I'm very pleased to meet you," he said. "I'm a fan. I admire what you've done with your company. You've got a major talent for spotting up-and-coming markets and trends."

"I've got good people working with me," Julius said.

Larson nodded sagely. "A good leader gives credit to his people." He switched his polished smile to Grace. "I'm here today because I fully respect Grace's abilities. I'm hoping to add her to my own staff."

Julius's eyes went a couple of degrees below freezing. "Is that so?"

She shot him a warning frown. "Larson came to see me today to offer me a job."

"Doing what?" Julius asked.

"I was in the process of describing the position to Grace when you arrived," Larson said. He smiled at Grace. "I hope you will consider joining Team Rayner."

"I'm really not much of a team player," Grace said.

"You'll have your own office and all the freedom and support you need to give free rein to your creativity," Larson said. He was very earnest now. "I repeat, I will double whatever Witherspoon paid you. What's more, if you guarantee me a minimum of one year of service, I'll give you a commission on all of the seminars that you book."

"That's a very generous offer," Grace said. "But I really do need to think about it. I've got a lot of things going on in my life at the moment and I have this feeling that it's time for me to move on to another career."

Larson's smile lost some of its sparkle. "I understand that you're ready for a new challenge. I'm in a position to make that happen for you. If you aren't ready to join my team as a full-time member of my staff, will you consider consulting for me?"

"What kind of consulting?" she asked. "You're a leader in your field. Actually, now that Sprague is gone, you'll probably become the premier motivational speaker in the Pacific Northwest—maybe the whole West Coast. I don't think you need me."

"Ah, now there you are mistaken." Larson held up a hand, palm out. "No need to be modest. I know for a fact that you were the one who wrote that cookbook and the Witherspoon Way blog. You made Sprague a media sensation. But he never gave you any of the credit, did he? I'll bet he didn't give you a percentage of the take on those seminars, either."

Grace stilled. Julius regarded her with a thoughtful expression. She was learning to interpret that particular look and she was fairly certain it never boded well. But she gave him credit for having the good sense not to say anything.

"Where are you going with this, Larson?" she asked quietly.

Larson shoved his fingers through his hair. "Isn't it obvious? I want you to take over my social media. In addition, I'd like to take that cookbook idea of yours and expand it into a full lifestyle series based on the theme of positive thinking and your affirmations. Yes, I know you were the one who came up with those, too."

"In other words, you are offering me a position as a ghostwriter for both your blog and your books."

"Well, yes," he said. "We both know that it's the Rayner Seminars brand that will sell the blog and the books. But I promise you that you will be well paid, and I will see to it that your contribution is acknowledged at every step of the way."

"Like I said, I'll think about it," she said.

"What's holding you back?" Larson glanced skeptically at Julius and then turned back to Grace. "Has someone made you a better offer?"

"No," she admitted. "I'm still trying to find my path forward."

"Might as well earn some good money while you work on finding that path," Larson said. He paused for emphasis. "One more thing you should know."

"Yes?"

"I'm making similar offers to your former coworkers, Kristy Forsyth and Millicent Chartwell. I want the whole team. I guarantee that all of you will be able to name your own price."

Grace looked at him. "Aren't you afraid that one of us might be an embezzler?"

To her amazement, Larson chuckled. "Haven't you heard the latest news on the case? Sprague was the embezzler."

Grace stared at him, dumbfounded. "I don't understand."

Julius went to the coffee machine. "Rayner may be right. I came here to give you the news. According to the investigators who are examining the financial records, it appears that Sprague Witherspoon may have been skimming off the money."

"But it was Sprague's money," Grace said. "Why would he hide the theft?"

"Could have been a couple of reasons," Larson offered. "One was that he was using the money for purposes he wanted to keep secret."

"Such as?" Grace challenged.

Larson shrugged. "There are rumors that he may have had a gambling addiction."

"That's . . . almost impossible to believe," Grace said, stunned.

Julius poured himself a cup of coffee. "There are other reasons why a successful entrepreneur would want to hide a lot of cash. The experts are still looking into the records."

She shot him a curious glance. They both knew that by "experts" he meant his wizards at Arkwright Ventures.

"The embezzlement issue has gone away," Larson said. He took out a card and handed it to Grace. "I think it's safe to say that when the police finally solve Witherspoon's murder, the killer will turn out to be someone connected to his gambling addiction. It's a dangerous world. Here's my private line. Call me with any questions, night or day. I'll check back with you soon."

"Okay," Grace said. She didn't know what else to say. She was still grappling with the news of Sprague's gaming addiction.

"You were born for the motivational world, Grace." Larson smiled. "You just need a chance to shine." He glanced at his watch. "I'd better get going. I've got an appointment back in Seattle."

"You never got your coffee," Grace said.

"Some other time, thanks," Larson said. "A pleasure to meet you, Julius. I would be happy to sit down with you at your convenience to discuss what Rayner Seminars can do for you. Good-bye, Grace. Call soon. I don't know how long I can keep this offer open."

He walked out of the kitchen and across the living room. Grace trailed after him and opened the door.

Larson went down the porch steps and got into his car. Julius came to stand behind Grace. Together they watched Larson drive out to the main road and disappear.

"He seems a little desperate," Julius said.

"I think he's just very enthusiastic about moving his company forward," Grace said.

"No, that was desperation I saw in Larson Rayner. He wants you very, very badly. You must have been damn good at the positive-thinking business."

"I did have a flair for affirmations, and the cookbook was one of my better ideas," Grace said. "But I'm not sure that I can work for Larson."

"Why not?"

"Because I don't think he's sincere about the power of positive thinking," she said. "I'm not saying he's a phony but he's not committed the way Sprague was committed. Sprague genuinely wanted to help people. His belief in positive energy was real. He inspired me."

Julius's brows rose. "Larson doesn't inspire you?"

"Nope."

"Here's a little inside job-hunting tip—if you're only willing to work for people who inspire you, you're going to discover that you're looking at a very small group of potential employers."

She sighed. "That has occurred to me."

Twenty-One

She led the way back into the kitchen and turned to face Julius.

"Are the investigators really convinced that Sprague may have used company money to cover up his gambling losses?" she asked.

"It's still a theory at this point. I'm told that there are some strong indications that may be the case. But I'm not buying that story, not yet. I told the wizards to look deeper."

"It's almost impossible to believe that Sprague was a gambler. But if it's true, it changes a lot of things, including the pool of suspects in the murder."

"No," Julius said. "It doesn't affect the suspect pool. There is still the little matter of the vodka bottle. No professional assassin employed by a mob boss would have gone to the trouble of researching your past to come up with that little bit of incriminating information. There was no need to do that. Pros almost always get away with murder, literally. I think the murder was a lot more personal. And there's still the issue of the stalker."

"This is getting more confusing by the day."

"No, I think we're finally starting to see a pattern. But meanwhile, I'm glad you're not jumping on Rayner's offer of a job because I'm not enthusiastic about the idea of you going to work for him."

"Why not?"

"Something about that guy feels off."

"He's a professional motivational speaker," she said. "We know how you feel about the business."

"What he's got is a talent for sales," Julius said. "And as far as I'm concerned, he's still on the suspect list when it comes to Witherspoon's murder."

"Sprague and Larson argued furiously shortly before Sprague was killed," Grace said. "The quarrel happened in Sprague's private office but Millicent and Kristy and I were working in the outer office at the time. We heard the shouting."

"What were they fighting about?" Julius asked.

"Sprague had just received a contract for a major speaking engagement in Los Angeles. Larson felt the contract should have been his. He accused Sprague of sabotaging him. He was sure that Sprague had used his connections to tell the client that Rayner Seminars was in trouble financially."

"Why would that have mattered to the people who wanted to hire a motivational speaker?" Julius asked. "Seems like financial troubles would just make a motivational guru all the more motivated."

She gave him a quelling look. "That is not funny. As I recall, the topic of the seminar was 'A Positive-Thinking Approach to Wealth Management.'"

Julius grinned briefly. "Okay, I can see the problem there."

"You wouldn't want to book a motivational seminar on that subject with a speaker whose own company was heading for bankruptcy."

Julius turned thoughtful. "Is it true that Rayner is having financial troubles?"

"The rumors started circulating a few months ago. Whether or not they are true, I can't say."

"I take it Rayner and Witherspoon had a history?" Julius said.

"Oh, yeah," Grace said. She led the way back into the kitchen. "They started out as partners and there was some kind of blowup. Rumors of the feud have circulated in the motivational world ever since the breakup."

Julius was briefly distracted. "There's a motivational world?"

"Yep and it's a small one—at least it is at the level Sprague and Larson occupied."

"Any idea what caused the falling-out between the two?"

"There was a woman involved," Grace said. "Sprague's second wife, not Nyla's mother. I'm told the second Mrs. Witherspoon was about thirty years younger and quite attractive. Evidently Larson had an affair with her. I've heard that—for men—there are only two things worth fighting over—money and women."

"I've heard that old saying, too," Julius said. "I wouldn't put too much stock in it, though."

"No?" She watched him closely. "Why not?"

"I'm not saying men don't fight over money and women. I'm just saying that there's not much point fighting over a woman who doesn't want you, and when it comes to money, there's always more out there. Why risk prison for either reason?"

"Beats me," Grace said, amused. "But people seem willing to do just that all the time. Prison is full of people who shot other people for cold hard cash or drugs. And there are also a lot of people in prison who murdered other people in a jealous rage."

"Can't argue with that," Julius said. "I'm just saying those aren't good reasons to kill."

She watched him drink his coffee.

"That's very Zen," she said.

"More like common sense." Julius went to stand at the window. "The other problem with that old saying is that it leaves out a couple of other viable motives for murder."

She filled her own mug. "Such as?"

"Power and revenge."

She leaned back against the counter. "Okay. But both of those motives could have been at work in a scenario that features Larson killing Sprague."

Julius tried a sip of his coffee. "When did Larson Rayner have the affair with Sprague Witherspoon's wife?"

"Long before I was hired. Maybe four or five years ago."

"Did Rayner marry Witherspoon's ex?"

"No. I gather she did well out of the divorce but as far as I know she moved on."

"That probably makes jealousy an even more unlikely motive," Julius said. "So we're back to money. Did Witherspoon steal some of Rayner's clients?"

She raised her chin. "I honestly don't think Sprague did anything underhanded. But some of Larson's clients did switch their business to Witherspoon."

Julius nodded thoughtfully. "Thanks to you."

"I was able to leverage some ideas that worked out well for the firm," she said, going for modesty. "My skill set is somewhat limited but I do have a few tools in the box."

"And now Larson Rayner wants you and your skills," Julius said. "No surprise there. When an ambitious politician loses a race, one of the first things he does is try to hire the winner's campaign manager. Same holds true in the business world."

Grace waved one hand. "Good grief, I am not some sort of motivational gun for hire."

"You've got to admit it would look interesting on a business card: *Positive Thinking Gun for Hire. Affirmations for the up-and-coming motivational guru.*"

"Sometimes I think you go out of your way to try to impress me with your cynicism," Grace said.

"I'm a pragmatic man."

"Bullshit."

Julius's brows rose. "Bullshit?"

"What? You didn't think I knew the word?"

He smiled. "I hadn't considered the question until now. The subject hasn't arisen."

"I assure you I have a wide-ranging vocabulary, but generally speaking I reserve it for the appropriate occasions."

"Me calling myself a pragmatist qualifies as an occasion that requires the use of the word bullshit?" Julius asked. He didn't sound offended, merely curious.

"Yes, I do believe bullshit is the appropriate word here," Grace said firmly. "You probably think of yourself as pragmatic because you can make the hard decisions when necessary. You get to the bottom line before anyone else and you see no point dwelling on the emotions involved in arriving at your destination."

Julius nodded thoughtfully. "I'd say that's a fair summary of my personal philosophy."

"Here's the thing, Julius—you wouldn't throw an innocent person under the bus just to close a deal or achieve your goals. You may be cynical, but you have your own code and you stick to it."

He shook his head, clearly perplexed by her naiveté. "What makes you so sure of that?"

She smiled. "If you had chosen to be a bad guy, you would do a much better job of playing the role."

Twenty-Two

The new refrigerator arrived forty-five minutes after Larson Rayner left. The deliverymen obligingly disconnected the old one and moved it out onto the sheltered back porch. They wrapped it in heavy sheets of plastic to protect it from the elements until Grace could sell it.

Julius could see the relief in her eyes when the offending appliance was finally gone from the kitchen. He understood.

The new window was installed an hour later. Following that, Grace insisted on going grocery shopping to restock her gleaming new appliance.

What with one thing and another, it was nearly one o'clock before Julius was able to settle down to the business of explaining a few of the facts of business life to his new client.

"Let's get this straight," he said. "A talent for writing cheery little feel-good affirmations is not considered a useful skill in most high-powered, high-paying industries."

"Maybe I need a low-powered industry," Grace said.

"Not a lot of those left," Julius said. "And what about the low pay that usually goes with the few that might still be out there?"

"Good point," she said.

"We need to find a different way to describe your skills."

"How many ways are there to say that I can write optimistic affirmations?" Grace asked.

"I don't know yet," Julius said. "But let's try to think positive, shall we?"

She glared at him. "That is not amusing."

"Right. Back to work, then."

The rain returned but there was a fire in the fireplace and Julius thought that the little house felt cozy and comfortable. The work on Grace's résumé was not going well but he had already concluded that he would be content to labor over it for a very long time if it meant he could remain close to Grace.

The phone rang just as she got up to make a pot of tea. Julius saw her flinch a little, even though it was a regular call, not an email alert.

Grace took the call. The conversation was brief.

"Yes," she said. "Yes, of course." She glanced at the clock. "I can be there by two-thirty or three if the traffic isn't bad."

She ended the call and looked at Julius.

"That was someone from the Seattle Police Department," she said. "Evidently there was a break-in at the Witherspoon Way office. The police aren't sure when the burglary occurred and they can't tell if anything of value was stolen. But because the incident may be linked to Sprague's death, we've been asked to go to the office and see if we can figure out what was taken."

"We?" Julius repeated.

"The three of us who worked for Sprague," Grace explained. "Millicent and Kristy have also been asked to come in and take a look."

"Well, it's not like we weren't planning on driving into the city this afternoon for that damn dinner and charity auction tonight," Julius said. "I'll take care of a few things at my office while you and your friends talk to the police."

"Okay," she said.

"So, about tonight," he said.

Everything inside her tightened a couple more notches. "Yes?"

"Looks like I'm more or less going to be keeping you company in the evenings until this stalker problem is resolved."

"Yes?" she said again.

"What do you say we spend the night in the city? I'm thinking there's no point making the long drive back here at midnight. I've got a guest bedroom at my condo."

She gave that some thought. He was right. One way or another they would be spending the evening under the same roof. What did it matter if they drove back to Cloud Lake or stayed in Seattle?

"I'll pack a bag," she said.

Julius smiled and for a moment she once again pondered the risks of flirting with the Big Bad Wolf.

Twenty-Three

T he bastard wrecked the place," Millicent announced. "Whoever did this must have been really pissed off when he couldn't find whatever it was he thought Sprague had hidden here."

"The cops aren't sure the intruder had any connection with the murder," Grace reminded her. "You heard the officer. They think this may have been random. They said it's quite possible that someone looking for drug money realized the office had been empty for a while."

"The only things missing are the laptops," Kristy said. "They're always prime targets in this kind of thing."

The three of them were standing in the reception area of the Witherspoon offices. A police officer had taken the inventory of missing items and left a short time ago. Afterward, the management firm that leased the space to the Witherspoon Way had authorized all former employees to pick up any personal possessions they had left behind. A representative of the management company was waiting outside in the hallway to lock up when they were finished.

It was the first time any of them had been allowed back into the office since the day Grace discovered Sprague's body. Kristy and Grace had brought small cardboard boxes to collect the few things they had left behind in their desks. Millicent had brought along a shiny, hard-sided roll-aboard suitcase.

The yellow crime scene tape had been removed but the office looked as if it had been hit by a whirlwind. Millicent was right, Grace thought. Whoever had ransacked the place must have been furious that there wasn't more worth stealing.

Sprague had overseen the interior design of his office environment. He had insisted that the space reflect the serene and harmonious inner balance that he urged others to seek. To that end he had hired a designer who had gone all in on a minimalist approach. The palette ran the gamut from gray to off-white. The only touches of color had been the brilliant flowers in the glass vases. Kristy had been assigned the task of replacing the blooms as needed. Sprague had often noted that she had a way with greenery.

The desks in the individual offices were state of the art, designed to conceal the high-tech necessities of the modern corporate world. One swipe at the small control screen on each desktop and the computer, phones and other machines vanished beneath a Zen-smooth surface.

To finish the look, Sprague had brought in a feng shui expert to arrange the furniture so that it was properly oriented. The all-important grounding touches like the little fountain in the corner had also been installed by the expert. The fountain no longer gurgled.

"I wonder why Nyla Witherspoon didn't remove the laptops, herself," Millicent said.

"What would she do with them?" Kristy asked. "I can't see her selling them on eBay."

"I've got a feeling that Nyla has been focused on other things lately," Grace said.

Kristy hugged herself and shook her head. "I think the cops are right. There probably isn't a connection between this break-in and what happened to poor Sprague. Grace, I remember you said that there was no sign that the killer took anything from Sprague's home the night the murder was committed."

"That's true," Grace said. "Although I have to tell you, I did not take the time to look around. I got out of the house as quickly as possible."

Millicent sniffed. "A very wise move."

"Still, I don't recall that anything appeared to have been disturbed," Grace said. "And there was nothing in the papers about robbery having been a possible motive. If the killer was the same person who ransacked this place, you'd think he would have stolen some of Sprague's personal valuables, too."

"As far as I'm concerned, the missing laptops are Nyla's problem," Millicent announced. "I assume you heard the rumors about Witherspoon's little gambling problem?"

"Yes," Grace said. "But it's hard to believe he was paying off gambling debts."

"I can't believe it, either," Kristy said.

"Well, I do believe it and it explains a lot," Millicent said. "It's also a huge relief to me, I can tell you that. As the company bookkeeper, I was afraid I was at the top of the suspect list when it came to the embezzlement thing. My issues now revolve around job-hunting. I assume you both got the call from Larson Rayner?"

"Yes," Kristy said. "I'm thinking about it but I'm going to stall until we find out for certain that Larson is cleared of any connection with the murder of Sprague."

"Larson drove to Cloud Lake to talk to me about a position at Rayner Seminars," Grace said. "I'm not sure what I'm going to do. Kristy's right, it will be easier to make a decision once we know who killed Sprague."

Millicent laughed. "Unlike you two, I'm not nearly so fussy when it comes to employers. I need a job and Rayner Seminars is set to take over the motivational business in our region. I'm going to grab Larson's offer."

Kristy looked down at a heap of dead flowers that had been yanked out of the vase on her desk and dumped on the floor. "What, exactly, are we supposed to do besides collect our own belongings? I hope they don't expect us to clean up the place."

The reception desk had once been Kristy's command post and she had occupied it brilliantly, handling the media as well as the Witherspoon bookings.

"Don't know about you two," Millicent said, heading toward her office with the little suitcase, "but if anyone thinks I'm going to tidy up here, they've got a surprise coming. The burglar was responsible for the damage, not me. I'm going to clean out my desk."

She disappeared into her office.

"This is all just so sad," Kristy said.

She sank into the high-tech office chair and picked up the framed photo of her family that had been knocked facedown on top of the desk. Very carefully she put the picture into her cardboard box.

"Got an affirmation for us, Grace?" Millicent called from the other room.

"How about *Today I will be open to new possibilities*?" Grace suggested. "I used it with the roasted fennel recipe in the cookbook."

"I hate fennel," Millicent yelled back.

More drawers banged.

Kristy made a face and angled her head in the general direction of Millicent's office.

"She'll do all right," Kristy said very softly.

Grace smiled. "Probably. Meanwhile, you and I need to remember that, thanks to Sprague, we've got a lot of unique skills to sell to our next employer."

"Please don't recite any more Witherspoon affirmations. I want to savor my gloom."

"Okay," Grace said.

She went to the doorway of her office and contemplated the chaotic scene. Files had been yanked out of drawers and dumped on the floor. There wasn't a lot to retrieve, she thought. She had never kept much in the way of personal items in her workplace. There wasn't room for that sort of thing in a minimalist environment.

She set the cardboard box on the desk and started to pack up her few personal possessions—the large coffee mug emblazoned with the Witherspoon Way logo, the blue wrap that she kept in the bottom desk drawer for those days when the building HVAC system wasn't working well, a pair of sneakers that she wore on her lunch break when she went to the nearby dog park to eat her lunch and watch city canines frolic.

She was in the process of putting her selection of herbal tea bags into the box when she heard the familiar brittle voice in the outer office.

"Don't touch anything," Nyla Witherspoon said fiercely. "Not a damn thing. This was my father's office. If any of you take so much as a pen, I'll report you to the police."

"Take it easy, honey. I'm sure they just came back for their personal things. You heard the security guard out in the hall. He's keeping an eye on the office."

Grace recognized Burke Marrick's voice. Rich and resonant, it would have taken him far in the motivational speaking world.

She went back to the doorway of her office. Nyla was standing in the center of the reception area, vibrating with rage. Her sharp features were twisted with anger. She looked more than ever like the Wicked Witch of the West.

Burke put one hand on her shoulder as if he thought he might need to restrain her from taking a swing at Kristy.

There was no question but that Nyla had landed herself an impressive trophy fiancé. Burke had certainly hit the genetic lottery when it came to his looks. And he knew how to dress to make the most of his startling green eyes, gleaming dark hair and well-toned physique. Somehow a woman knew just by looking at him that he would be very skilled in bed.

"Get out of here, all of you," Nyla hissed. "You have no right to be here."

"The police called us in today and the building manager told us that we were free to pick up our personal things," Kristy said calmly. "Don't worry, there's nothing of value left to steal except the chairs and the desks. Good luck selling them on the used-office-furniture market."

Nyla clenched her fingers around the strap of her designer purse. "I said get out. Now. Everything in here—everything that belonged to my father—is mine now. I'm the sole heir, in case you weren't paying attention. Leave now or I will call the police and have all three of you arrested for theft."

Millicent appeared in the doorway of her office. "Don't worry, Nyla, we were just leaving." She looked at Kristy and Grace. "Right?"

Kristy sighed and picked up her cardboard box. "Right."

Grace went back to her desk, grabbed her box and carried it into the outer office. The three of them marched toward the door.

"Wait," Nyla yelped. "Let me see what you've got in those boxes."

Burke touched her shoulder again, a little more firmly this time. "Don't worry about it, Nyla. I'm sure they are just taking the things that belonged to them."

"Damn it, I don't trust any of them," Nyla wailed. "Don't you understand? One of them murdered my father."

There was a hushed silence. Grace moved first. She walked toward Nyla and held out the box.

"Take a good look," she said. "A lovely mug and some herbal tea. You're welcome to both. You can't have the wrap, though. My sister gave it to me for my birthday."

Nyla glanced into the box. Her mouth tightened.

Kristy followed with her box. "Here you go, Nyla. Help yourself. A box of tissues and a photo of my family."

"I can't believe we're doing this," Millicent grumbled. She crouched in her stilettos and opened the roll-aboard to reveal a couple of designer scarves, another pair of stilettos and a coffee mug. "I don't think the scarves are your color, Nyla. You're better in black, don't you think?"

"Leave," Nyla whispered. "All of you. And don't come back."

"Good idea," Millicent said.

She straightened and rolled her suitcase toward the door. Grace and Kristy followed. The three of them walked to the elevator in silence. Millicent stabbed the button.

"That woman is a real case," she said.

"We all know that she harbored a lot of resentment toward her father," Grace reminded them. "Now that he's gone, she's dealing with the fact that she won't ever be able fix that relationship. She's grieving."

Kristy snorted softly. "Give me a break. She never tried to reconcile with her father. Heaven knows he wanted to bond with her. But I swear she enjoyed nursing her so-called grievances. I'm telling you, she's the one who murdered Sprague."

"I wouldn't be surprised," Millicent said. She stabbed the elevator button again and glanced back down the hall toward the office. "She is the sole heir, isn't she?"

Grace followed her gaze. "Got a feeling Mr. Perfect has other ideas."

Millicent's smile was cold. "I agree with Kristy. I wouldn't be surprised if they planned the murder together."

"Serves them right that the money disappeared," Kristy said.

Twenty-Four

T hat was my journey. I would not be here tonight if not for the things Harley Montoya taught me. Many of us can look back and name the people who gave us not only a chance but the guidance and direction that we needed at a crucial moment in our lives . . ."

Grace finally allowed herself to breathe. Julius was doing well on the podium. Granted, he might not make it in the motivational speakers' world or on the campaign trail. But he was delivering the new version of the Speech from Hell with a conviction that was resonating with the audience.

Nothing grabbed people's attention like a strong dose of passion and Julius had communicated more than enough to rivet the crowd. The darkened ballroom had been hushed from the outset when it became clear that the after-dinner talk was not going to involve a lot of dull facts and figures. There hadn't been so much as a clinked glass or the clatter of a spoon on a dish since Julius had launched into the speech. Even the waiters had stopped to listen at the back of the room.

"... Those of us who have achieved success in the business world now

*find ourselves with an opportunity to wield some real power—the kind
that leaves a lasting legacy, the kind that can change lives.*

*"Look around and find at least one other person who reminds you of
yourself when you were starting out. Figure out what you did right and
what you did wrong along the way. Focus on the things that you can reflect back on with a sense of pride because you know you did the right
thing, the honorable thing, even if it cost you some money or a contract at
the time. Offer those lessons to that individual who reminds you of yourself, the one who is still trying to decide what kind of person he or she
wants to be. Your mission is to help shape the future."*

Julius swept up the notecards, turned and walked across the raised
dais. It took a couple of beats for the audience to realize that the
speech had ended. A good sign, Grace thought, satisfied. Always leave
them wanting more.

The applause exploded across the banquet room just as Julius
started down the steps. By the time he got to the floor, half the people were on their feet. By the time he reached the round table where
Grace stood with the others, clapping madly, the rest of the audience
was standing.

Grace knew that she was practically glowing. She smiled at Julius.

"That was wonderful," she said beneath the roar of applause. "You
were brilliant."

"Don't know about brilliant," he said. "But at least they didn't fall
asleep this time."

Without warning, he pulled her into his arms and kissed her. It
wasn't a long, involved embrace—just a short, sure, triumphant kiss
that sent the unmistakable impression of intimacy. It was the sort of
kiss lovers exchanged.

The crowd loved it. Possibly even more than they loved the speech,
Grace thought.

By the time the kiss was over she was flushed and breathless and intensely aware that everyone around her was smiling.

Julius held her chair for her.

"Thanks," he said so that only she could hear. "I owe you."

"No," she said quickly.

"Yes," he whispered. He gripped the back of her chair. "Sit down. Please. No one else can sit until you do."

"Oh, right." She looked around the room. People were still on their feet but the clapping was fading. Definitely time to sit.

She dropped into her chair. Julius guided it back into position and sat down beside her. Everyone else sank back into their seats.

A murmur of congratulations broke out around the head table. A banker sitting two place settings away wanted to know Julius's opinion of some pending financial regulations. Grace reached for her water glass—and nearly dropped it when she felt Julius's hand close over hers under the table.

He squeezed her fingers gently. The small action seemed as intimate as the kiss, perhaps more so. *He's just thanking you for saving him from the Speech from Hell. He's relieved it's over. He's grateful for your suggestions. Don't read too much into a little squeeze of the hand.*

The master of ceremonies resumed control of the audience, thanked Julius for the talk and moved on to the next item on the evening's agenda, the closing remarks and the reminder that the auction would start in twenty minutes in the main wing of the museum. Last-minute bids were being accepted.

Once again everyone stood. A group quickly gathered around Julius. It seemed as if half the room was eager to engage him in conversation. Many of the people looked vaguely familiar. Grace knew she had seen their faces in the newspapers and on local television.

She started to ease out of the way so that the others could get closer to Julius. He did not look around but he reached back and captured her wrist.

She stopped and leaned in close so that she could speak directly into his ear.

"Ladies' room," she whispered.

At that he broke off a discussion on the subject of the lack of government funding for high-tech research and looked at her.

"I'll wait for you in the lobby," he said. He released her.

"I won't be long," she promised.

She slipped off through the crowd, aware of a few curious gazes cast her way before she escaped into the calm of an empty hallway. She paused to get her bearings, spotted the *Ladies* sign at the end of the hall and headed in that direction.

There were three other women at the long row of sinks when she entered. They nodded as if they knew her and smiled. She was quite sure she had never met any of them in her life but she smiled back and headed for a stall. This was what came of being attached to Julius's side that evening, she thought. Back in Cloud Lake it was easy to forget his position in the Pacific Northwest business community.

By the time she exited the stall the other women had left. She breathed a sigh of relief at finding herself alone and opened her clutch to take out a lipstick. The door swung open again just as she was using a tissue to blot the extra color off her mouth.

The newcomer was a striking woman in her early thirties. Her blond hair was pulled back in an elegant chignon. She wore a sleek, black-and-white cocktail dress and a pair of black heels.

There was recognition in her eyes, just as there had been in the eyes of the three women Grace had encountered when she entered the room. But this woman was not smiling.

"You're with Julius tonight," the newcomer said. There was a thread of grim determination in her voice, as if she was confronting an enemy and was prepared to fight.

"He invited me to accompany him this evening," Grace said.

The tension in the atmosphere was disturbing. She waited, uncertain what to do next. The woman was blocking the route to the door, perhaps by accident but maybe by design.

"I'm Diana Hastings," Diana said. There was a husky edge on the words, as if she was trying to suppress some fierce emotion. "Julius's ex-wife."

"I see." Grace looked at the door. The uneasy sensation was transitioning to red-alert status. She needed to escape as quickly as possible. Whatever this was about, she was sure it was not going to end well. "I'm Grace Elland. A pleasure to meet you. If you don't mind, I need to get back to the lobby. Someone is waiting."

"Julius. You're going to meet Julius."

"Well, yes."

"So you're the new girlfriend." Diana looked bemused. "You're not exactly his type, are you?

"I have no idea and you're mistaken. Julius and I are just friends. He's advising me on how to build a business plan."

That was sort of true, Grace thought. Kisses had been exchanged but she and Julius were not sleeping together. And the part about the business plan was fairly accurate.

"Julius doesn't kiss his friends the way he kissed you in front of the audience tonight," Diana said. "No man kisses a woman like that unless he wants to make sure that everyone around him knows that he's sleeping with her."

"Oh, for pity's sake, Mrs. Hastings—Diana. Julius and I only met recently. It was a blind date arranged through friends. I'm just doing

Julius a favor tonight. He needed a companion for this event and I was—uh—convenient."

"No." Diana shook her head with great certainty and moved farther into the room. "Oh, I don't doubt that he finds you convenient. Julius is very good at manipulating people to get what he wants. But I know that you two are sleeping together. That was obvious tonight."

Grace felt her temper start to flare. "Not true, but even if it was, it wouldn't be any of your business, now, would it?"

Diana's fingers tightened around her gold leather evening purse. "I don't give a damn if you're sleeping with him. I suppose I should feel some sympathy. You must be as naive as I was when I married him. But do you know something? I can't even feel sorry for you. I just don't *care* if you two are having an affair. Is that clear?"

The situation was escalating. Diana's face was flushed, her eyes a little wild. Instinctively Grace softened her own voice.

"Very clear," she said. "You've made your point, so if you don't mind, I'll be leaving now."

She started forward, intending to circle around Diana and make a break for the door.

"No, I haven't made my point." Diana did not move. "You're welcome to him, as far as I'm concerned. Julius is cold, ruthless and calculating but that's your problem, not mine. I want you to take a message to him."

"If you've got something to say to him, I suggest you speak to him, yourself. You can do it right now. He's waiting in the lobby. Do you mind getting out of the way?"

Diana did not budge. She was gripping her little purse so tightly her knuckles were white.

"Tell that bastard that I know what he's doing," she said. "Tell him everyone in Seattle knows."

Grace debated her chances of getting past Diana without physical contact. They didn't look good. She felt her temper start to slip again.

"Do I look like a messenger pigeon?" she asked.

"Tell Julius that I know he wants revenge. I get that. But he should take it out on me—not my husband and my husband's family. They are innocent. What Julius is doing is so unfair. And pointless. It's not as if I ever meant anything to him. I was just one more transaction, an entry in his portfolio. I know he never truly loved me. Tell him that even in my nightmares I never believed that he would be this cruel."

"What?" Grace was so shocked she could not think of how to follow up so she just stared at Diana.

The door of the ladies' room swung open without warning, forcing Diana to move aside. She did so but she seemed unaware of the two women who walked into the room behind her. She was focused utterly on Grace.

"Julius is deliberately trying to destroy my husband's company," Diana said, her voice tight with fury and frustration. "It's common knowledge. Julius wants to exact vengeance on me because I left him. He can't abide losing. He's Arkwright the Alchemist. He always wins."

The two women who had just entered the room watched the scene with hushed fascination. Diana ignored them.

Grace assessed her options. There were now three people blocking the room's only escape route. A Witherspoon Way affirmation flashed through her mind. *Be the eye of the storm. It is the only way to control the chaos around you.*

It took everything she had to smile at Diana but she managed the feat.

"It's all a huge misunderstanding, Mrs. Hastings," she said. "The rumors are wrong. I can assure you that Julius is not out to destroy your husband's company."

Tears sparked in Diana's eyes. "Tonight that son of a bitch gave a very nice, very noble speech about the importance of legacies and honor and making a difference. But what he's doing to Edward and the Hastings family makes Julius a complete hypocrite. You tell him that, damn it."

"If you know Julius as well as you think you do," Grace said, "then there is something else you should know."

Diana frowned. "What?"

"Julius is very, very good when it comes to business. You said it yourself. They call him Arkwright the Alchemist."

"You don't have to tell me." Diana dashed the back of her hand across her eyes, smearing her makeup. "Believe me, I'm well aware that he's a legend in the business world."

"Then stop and think about this for a minute," Grace said. "If Julius Arkwright actually had set out to destroy your husband's company, Hastings would have filed for bankruptcy months ago. The firm would be in smoking ruins. Julius doesn't mess around. I would have thought you would remember that aspect of his character."

It was Diana's turn to stare. She did not say a word. The other two women were still frozen in place. For a moment no one moved.

Grace couldn't think of anything else to say so she turned and yanked a towel out of the dispenser. She marched toward the trio who stood in her way.

"Excuse me," she said.

She did not stop. Abruptly the three scattered. Grace kept going. She obeyed the little sign on the wall that advised her to use the paper towel to open the door. Tossing the towel aside, she escaped into the hall.

The door closed softly on the still-life-with-bathroom-fixtures in the ladies' room.

Twenty-Five

When he saw Grace coming toward him through the crowd, he knew that something had happened in the short span of time that she had been gone—something unpleasant.

She wore a simple, sleek black gown with a demure neckline, long sleeves and a narrow skirt. Her hair was pulled up in a severe twist. He suspected that she had gone for a look suited to an up-and-coming businesswoman. But he thought she looked more like a sexy little cat burglar weaving her way through the knots of people. When she drew closer he saw the mix of relief and wariness in her eyes.

He took her arm and instinctively checked her back trail. He saw no one who appeared alarming.

"What's wrong?" he asked, keeping his voice low.

She wrinkled her nose. "I'm afraid there was a small scene in the ladies' room a few minutes ago."

That stopped him for a moment.

"What the hell kind of scene could occur in a restroom?" he finally asked.

"I ran into your ex-wife. Or, rather, she ran into me. I think she followed me into the ladies' room."

"Damn."

Grace's mouth tightened. "Brace yourself. It gets worse. There were witnesses."

"All right, let's take this step by step. First, define scene."

"Diana Hastings cornered me and made some accusations. It was awkward. She's very upset, Julius. Angry and scared. That is not a good mix."

He tried and failed to come up with a reason why Diana might be angry with Grace.

"She can't be jealous of you," he said. He stated that as the blunt fact that he knew it was. "She's the one who left me, remember? So why would she confront you?"

"She's not mad at me," Grace said. Her tone made it clear that she was doing her level best to exert patience. "I was just a placeholder."

"For what?"

He was starting to feel as if he was falling down the rabbit hole. Every man knew that what happened in the ladies' room was supposed to stay in the ladies' room. He was pretty sure there was a rule about it somewhere.

"Diana is harboring a great deal of fear and frustration toward you," Grace said quietly. "She took it out on me—probably because she's terrified to confront you directly. She thinks you're trying to get revenge against her and Edward Hastings by destroying the Hastings family empire."

The pieces of the puzzle finally slipped into place. He allowed himself to relax a few notches.

"I see," he said. "That business."

"An unfortunate turn of phrase, as it happens." Grace narrowed her eyes. "Yes, that business. She wanted me to deliver a message. She said she was aware of what you're doing and that she thinks it's . . . not very nice."

He blinked. "Those were her words?"

"Well, no," Grace said stiffly. "More forceful language was employed. But that's neither here nor there."

"Don't worry. What's going on at Hastings has nothing to do with me. Hastings has been digging its own grave for the past eighteen months."

"I assured Diana that you were not responsible for the company's troubles."

He was strangely gratified by that news.

"You said that?" he asked. "You told her that I wasn't the one undermining Hastings?"

"Naturally. But I don't think that's going to be enough to defuse the situation."

He thought about that for a moment. "No offense, but what the hell do you know about Hastings's financial problems?"

"Nothing," Grace admitted. "I just pointed out the obvious to Diana."

"What, exactly, is the obvious?"

"I reminded her that you are very good at what you do. I told her that if you had been trying to destroy the company for going on eighteen months, Hastings would have crashed and burned by now."

"Huh."

He couldn't think of anything to say to that so he steered her into the auction room. He was aware that almost every eye in the place followed them to their seats. He could feel the tension vibrating through Grace.

"Ignore them," he said into her ear as he sat down beside her.

"Easy for you to say."

"All we have to do is buy that overpriced chunk of art glass that you picked out earlier and then we're out of here."

"Right. And I would remind you that you were the one who said we had to buy that beautiful piece of art glass."

"I said we had to buy something. I didn't give a damn what we bought."

"It's a really beautiful piece of glass," she said, very earnest now. "I'm sure it will look lovely in your condo."

He started to tell her that the bowl was going to be hers. He had seen the way her eyes glowed with appreciation when she looked at it earlier. But before he could say anything he realized she had gone very quiet. Alarmed, he gave her a quick head-to-toe appraisal.

"Are you okay?" he asked.

"I'm fine," she said softly.

She was focused on the stage. Her calm, serene expression made him suspicious.

"You're doing some kind of breathing thing, aren't you?" he said.

"I'm using one of the Witherspoon affirmations as a mantra, if that's what you mean, yes."

"Which affirmation?"

"Let's just say that I am in my peaceful place where negative energy cannot touch me."

"How is that working for you?"

"Shut up and get ready to bid."

Twenty-Six

Burke Marrick was tall, sexy and gorgeous in the dark, dangerous ways of fictional vampires—all sharp cheekbones and mesmerizing green eyes. Mr. Perfect was too good to be true, Millicent thought, but he was certainly interesting.

She watched him slide gracefully into the booth across from her. She was halfway through her martini but she might as well have been drinking liquid excitement with a twist of nerves. She was, after all, about to make a business proposition to the man who had, in all likelihood, murdered Sprague Witherspoon.

Somehow, knowing that Burke was probably a killer just made the whole thing all the more thrilling.

"I got your message," Burke said. "What is this about?"

His voice suited the rest of him, vampire-soft and seductive. Everything inside her tightened with anticipation. This was the feeling a woman got when she decided to have sex with a devastating stranger, she thought. But Burke wasn't any random pickup. He had a major part in the play she had been scripting for the past few months—ever since he had arrived, unannounced, on the stage. True, the story line had changed from the original version but she was nothing if not adaptable. She had learned the trick early on in life when she had concluded that nothing on the streets could possibly be as bad as life with a violent stepfather and a drug-addicted mother. Her theory had proven correct.

The trendy South Lake Union bar was crowded, just as she had known it would be at this hour. The din of conversation, laughter and background music would provide privacy for the discussion she intended to conduct with Burke.

"Thank you for agreeing to meet me here," she said.

She was about to do something very daring, something she had never done before. But as the Witherspoon affirmation said, *We grow only when we dare to move out of our comfort zone.* She had always considered the affirmations to be downright silly, albeit great marketing tools. But she was willing to admit that this particular affirmation had some truth in it.

One thing was certain, if there was ever a time to take risks, this was it.

"Your message said that you wanted to talk about something that was of mutual interest," Burke said. "What is it?"

She smiled, satisfied. "Good to know I was right about you, Burke. I pegged you as the sort of man who likes to go straight to the bottom line."

"What is the bottom line in this case?"

"Money," she said. "A lot of it." She paused for emphasis and lowered her voice. "Not as much as you would have had if your own plans had worked out the way you had hoped, but still, a lot of money. And an opportunity to make more."

Wariness sparked in Burke's eyes but his smile was polished and perfect.

"I have absolutely no idea what you're talking about," he said.

"Then you must think I'm as naive as Grace Elland."

The waitress appeared at the table and looked expectantly at Burke.

"What can I get for you?" she asked.

Burke glanced at Millicent's glass and raised a brow.

"Vodka martini," Millicent said. "Dry. Straight up. With an olive."

Burke smiled. "Sounds good."

"Got it," the waitress said. "I'll be right back with your cocktail."

Millicent waited until the woman had vanished into the crowd. Then she idly stirred her drink with the little plastic spear on which the olive was impaled.

"Let me give you some background," she said. "I don't have a CPA degree. I never went to college. But I am very, very good when it comes to juggling money, and I'm very, very good with computers. I handled Witherspoon's taxes and his investments. I had access to Witherspoon's personal as well as his business accounts. He didn't like to be bothered with the small stuff of daily life. He was a Big Picture guy. I paid his bills—all of them, including those related to Nyla. I'm the one who transferred her allowance into her account on the first of every month."

Mild surprise and a hint of respect gleamed in Burke's eyes but he seemed more amused than alarmed.

"Interesting," he said. "But now you're out of a job."

"Not for long. Witherspoon's chief competition was Larson Rayner."

"So?"

"Larson has concluded that the easiest way to take Witherspoon's place in the motivational guru business is to recruit the very people who turned the Witherspoon Way into a powerhouse operation."

Burke nodded. "Hiring his competitor's people makes sense. I assume Rayner has made you an offer?"

"Yes. I told him I would be delighted to accept a position at Rayner Seminars. And then I thought about you."

"I'm listening."

"I know you were blackmailing Witherspoon for the last few months of his life because I was the one who transferred the money into a certain account earmarked *medical expenses* on the last day of every month."

"I repeat—I have no idea what you're talking about," Burke said.

But there was an edge on the words.

She ignored the interruption. "Witherspoon was very clever about it. When he created the account he told me that the money was being used to pay the costs of hospice care for an elderly relative. I wasn't suspicious at first. Witherspoon, being Witherspoon, wanted the very best private care for his dying aunt and he could afford to pay for it."

"You should consider writing fiction for your next career, Miss Chartwell."

"Please, call me Millicent. You and I are going to be very close friends soon. To continue with my story, you were smart enough to keep the payments reasonable—just a few thousand dollars a month. Everyone knows that it's easy to spend that kind of money on private nursing care."

Burke's face remained impassive for a few seconds. In the shadowy light his eyes went gem-hard. But before he could say anything the waitress appeared with the martini.

When they were once again alone, Millicent took a sip of her cocktail and lowered the glass. She smiled.

"Let me give you the next chapter," she said. "The money you made with the blackmail scheme was just penny-ante stuff, wasn't it? You were after a much bigger prize—Nyla's inheritance. But that seems to be slipping away, doesn't it? If things don't work out the way you hoped, you may have to pull the plug on your current business plan and move on to another opportunity."

Burke considered that while he drank some of his martini.

"What do you know about my current business objective?" he asked.

"I'm aware of the real value of Witherspoon's estate. But aside from the nice house on Queen Anne, the car and some artwork, the bulk of his fortune has vanished into thin air." Millicent smiled. "The authorities suspect embezzlement but they'll never find the money."

Burke went very still. "Are you going to tell me that you were the one who made it disappear?"

She took another sip of the martini and lowered the glass. "I'm brilliant with money. Just ask Witherspoon. Oh, wait, you can't because he's dead, isn't he? Who knew that he had a secret addiction problem—gambling, to be precise."

"Thanks to you fiddling with his online accounts?"

"Yes." She tried to assume an air of modesty but she was fairly sure she did not succeed.

"You set it up so that it would look like Witherspoon was embezzling from his own company to pay his gambling debts." Burke whistled softly. "You're good, Miss Chartwell. Impressive."

"Thank you. But let me assure you that Sprague left a great deal of money behind, and that money is safe in an offshore account. What's more, I'm good enough to pull off the same operation a second time."

Comprehension lit Burke's eyes. "With Larson Rayner?"

She smiled and munched the olive.

"How?" Burke asked, suddenly intent.

Euphoria zinged through her. The dance of seduction was working. Now the real conversation could take place. She and Burke were two pros talking shop. This was so much more thrilling than seducing a random bar hookup.

"You'd be amazed at the kind of money that starts sloshing around when a successful motivational guru gets real traction," she said. "And there are so many ways to skim off the extra cash."

Burke frowned. "You're saying that Rayner is getting traction?"

"He has been successful all along but now, with Witherspoon out of the picture, he's set to go into the big time. He's got the looks and the charisma. All he needs is a little fairy dust from Witherspoon's secret source. If everything works out, you and I can ride the gravy train until we decide to get off."

"Who supplies the fairy dust?"

She chuckled. "Grace Elland, of course. She's the one with the magic touch. She took Witherspoon to the top. There's no reason to think she can't perform the same trick again with Larson Rayner. What's more, Larson knows that. When he offered me a job today, he told me he was also making offers to Grace and Kristy. He wants Witherspoon's team."

"But Grace is the one he needs the most. What if she declines the offer?"

"Why would she do that? She needs a job. Larson will pay her double what she earned at Witherspoon and probably include a slice of the pie. She'll take the offer, believe me."

Burke swallowed some more of his martini and lounged into the corner of the booth.

She had him now. The one thing a professional con artist could not resist was the prospect of another big score. Running a successful con created a rush unlike any other.

"One question springs to mind," Burke said. "Why invite me to join you on the new gravy train? What do you want from me?"

"I know how to skim money off the top of any organization," she said. "But laundering the kind of cash that's sitting in that offshore account is more complicated. I need a partner."

"You want me to help you wash that money?"

"And the money we will acquire from Rayner's operation," she said. "He's set to go even higher than Witherspoon. I see our partnership as an ongoing enterprise for the two of us."

"Where does Nyla fit into this plan?"

Millicent waved that aside. "She doesn't."

Burke looked thoughtful. "You're saying I don't need her any longer."

"I know you planned to marry her for the money. Hell, the whole office, including Witherspoon, figured that out. But Nyla's inheritance has vanished, hasn't it? I'm the only one who knows where it is and how to get it. All we have to do is figure out how to bring it home and scrub it clean without making Nyla or the cops suspicious."

"You're stuck, aren't you?" Burke was amused. "You really do need someone to launder the money."

"Either that or I have to go live on some no-name island for the rest of my life. I like it here. Not much in the way of shopping on those no-name islands."

"I'd want a guarantee of a fifty-fifty split."

"Of course." Millicent raised her glass. "Like I said, partners."

Burke tapped one finger on the table. "What makes you think you can trust me?"

"Isn't it obvious? We need each other."

He drank some more of his martini while he considered that. It was time to tighten the leash, she thought.

"Here's the thing, Burke. I've got proof that you were blackmailing Witherspoon because I'm the one who made those monthly payments. I traced them to that account in New York months ago. That evidence will be sent to the police if I were to, say, suffer an unfortunate accident." Millicent used her fingers to make a very precise triangle around the base of her martini glass. "Proof of blackmail will put you right at the top of the suspect list in the Witherspoon murder."

Burke looked impressed. "I do believe that we have a partnership."

"Excellent." She pushed her empty glass aside and reached for her purse. "Would you care to go somewhere more private to celebrate?"

"Where do you suggest?"

"My apartment is within walking distance."

Burke smiled slowly. "That sounds very convenient."

Twenty-Seven

Y ou can't just give me this gorgeous bowl," Grace said. "It's too much."

"Too much what?" Julius asked.

"Too much of a gift," she shot back.

He drove into the parking space in the condo garage, shut down the engine and turned to look at her.

She sat in the passenger seat, cradling the carefully wrapped art glass with both hands as if it was a priceless gem. It wasn't priceless. Granted, he had just paid far too much for a glass bowl that couldn't even be used to serve salad, but it wasn't priceless.

What was priceless was the look on Grace's face when he handed the art glass to her and told her that it was hers. She was still arguing.

"What am I going to do with that bowl?" he asked patiently. "I'm not into art glass. You're the one who picked out the damn thing so I'm assuming you like it."

"I love it. It's gorgeous. I can see it now displayed under the right light in the right place in a room. It will glow like a big, multicolored diamond."

"Fine. Go ahead and display it any way you want."

She stared at him, shocked. "You mean you don't like it? You should have said something when we were looking at the auction items before the event. I would never have chosen a piece this pricey."

"It's not like there was any cheap art there to bid on. Look, it's a glass bowl. It's nice. But art is not my thing."

"Art is good for you. It stimulates the senses."

He looked at her for a long moment, savoring the sight of her sitting there in his car. In a few minutes she would be standing in the front hall of his condo. It was after midnight and neither of them had wanted to make the hour-long drive back to Cloud Lake. The only question was whether Grace would be sleeping in the guest bedroom or in his bed.

The low-grade fever that had been heating his blood since the night he met her rose a couple more degrees.

"Trust me," he said, "my senses are already running in overload condition. Not sure I could handle any more stimulation."

Her brows snapped together. "What are you talking about?"

He decided not to answer that question. Instead, he got out of the SUV, circled behind the vehicle and opened the door on the passenger side.

Grace handed the package to him with both hands.

"Hold this while I get out," she instructed. "And for goodness' sake, be careful with it."

He tucked the package under one arm. The bowl was surprisingly heavy. He reminded himself that large hunks of thick glass were always weighty objects.

With his free hand, he assisted Grace out of the high front seat. He was learning to enjoy watching her bail out of the vehicle. She never did it the same way twice but it was always interesting. Tonight her stiletto heels made the disembarkation process something of a high-wire balancing act. She negotiated the exit with her customary fluid grace, bouncing a little on the toe of her right foot before she got both feet on the ground.

"You need a ladder for this sucker," she said.

He smiled. "I've been meaning to ask you if you ever studied dance."

"Not unless you count aerobic exercise classes," she said. "Why?"

He closed the door of the SUV. "Just wondered. You move like someone who's had some training."

"Here, give me that bowl." She took the package from him.

He pocketed the keys. "I wasn't going to drop it."

"Maybe not but it's clear that you are not going to treat this work of art with the proper respect." She held the package in both hands. "Besides, someone has to handle the suitcases."

"This is true."

He opened the cargo bay of the vehicle and smiled a little at the sight of the two bags inside. He liked the way his duffel looked sitting next to Grace's little roll-aboard suitcase. It was as if they belonged together, he decided.

He hauled both bags out of the SUV and closed the rear door.

"Elevator's that way," he said. He angled his jaw to indicate the center of the garage.

She started toward the stairwell and elevator lobby, clutching the package with great care.

"You know, if you really don't want to keep this bowl you could give it to one of your relatives," she said. "Or a close friend."

Her refusal to accept the bowl as a gift was starting to annoy him. "It's yours."

"Okay, okay, you don't have to bite my head off."

"I didn't bite your head off," he said. "I'm just stating a fact. The damn bowl is yours."

"Thank you."

Her excruciatingly polite tone was even more irritating.

"I can't believe we're arguing over a damn bowl," he said.

"It is a little weird, isn't it? The thing is, I've never owned an expensive piece of art."

"Neither have I, at least not as far as I know. The interior designer who did my condo spent a fortune on what she called finishing touches but I don't think any of it qualifies as art. Just expensive stuff."

"You're rich," Grace said. "If you don't collect art, what do you collect?"

"Money, I guess. I've never had the urge to collect anything else."

"Like I said, you're bored."

He was about to tell her that the one thing he had not been lately was bored—not around her—but the sound of rushing footsteps echoing in the stillness of the garage stopped him cold. Shadows shifted in the yellow glare of the fluorescents.

Two men dressed in black clothing exploded out of the dark valley between a car and the concrete wall. One moved toward Grace. The second attacker gripped a length of pipe in both hands. He lunged at Julius.

Julius dropped the duffel and the suitcase and sidestepped the swinging pipe. The length of heavy metal sliced harmlessly through the air at the place his rib cage had been a heartbeat earlier.

The attacker staggered back a step, caught his balance and tried for

another swing. Julius rolled once across the floor, slamming into his
assailant's legs. There was a solid thud and a grunt when the man hit
the ground.

Julius got to his feet, grabbed the pipe and wrenched it out of the
attacker's hand. The man on the ground barely noticed. He was too
busy clutching at his midsection and trying to get some air into his
lungs.

Julius whirled around and saw that the first man had Grace backed
up against the wall. He held the point of a knife at her throat.

"Don't move, bitch," the knife man hissed. "We just want to have a
little quality time with your boyfriend. It'll all be over real quick."

"It's over now," Grace said. She looked at Julius.

The knife man automatically glanced over his shoulder. He looked
stunned when he realized that his companion was groaning on the
floor of the garage.

"Don't move another inch," he snarled at Julius. "I'll cut the bitch's
throat. I swear I'll do it."

Julius knew that panic and adrenaline were driving the bastard
now. The situation on the ground had shifted on him. He and his
partner were rapidly losing control.

Grace was still clutching the package that contained the art glass.
She rammed it straight up in front of herself, raising it high. The force
of the upward momentum pushed the attacker's arm aside, briefly de-
flecting the blade.

She kicked the knife man in the groin, the toe of her stiletto striking its target with a speed and accuracy that told Julius it was not the
first time she had practiced the maneuver.

But she could not keep her balance in the heels. She dropped the
package on the concrete floor and went down hard next to it.

The knife man staggered backward, clutching at his privates. Julius kicked his legs out from under him and grabbed his arm, twisting hard.

The knife man screamed. His blade clattered on the concrete floor.

Grace kicked off her shoes, scrambled to her feet and sprinted toward the fire alarm on the wall. She pulled it hard, filling the garage with screeching noise.

The door of the stairwell burst open. Julius saw the familiar face of the night-shift doorman, Steve.

"The cops are on the way," Steve yelled above the shrill sound of the alarm.

The combination of that news and the unrelenting shrieks acted like a tonic on the two assailants. The one who had wielded the pipe staggered to his feet with astonishing alacrity and charged toward the alley door.

The knife man tried to follow but Julius grabbed him and swung him around.

"You pulled a knife on her," Julius said. "That's not allowed."

He delivered two quick, hard chops. The knife man went down again. This time he stayed down.

Julius briefly considered trying to snag the one who had brought the pipe to the party but gave it up as a lost cause. The bastard had a head start.

"We've got the security camera video to give to the cops," Steve shouted over the alarm. "I saw them attack you but it took me a few minutes to get down here."

Julius nodded and looked at Grace. She was bending down to examine the package that contained what was left of the art glass. The lumpy condition of the wrapping paper was mute testimony to the fact that the bowl had not survived in one piece.

She straightened and turned around. Julius opened his arms. She walked straight to him. He hugged her close.

"It was so beautiful," she said against his chest.

"Yes, it was," he said. "I was wrong about it."

"How is that?"

"I thought that it would never serve any useful purpose."

Sirens sounded in the distance.

Twenty-Eight

"You know," Julius said, "I was hoping this evening would end somewhat differently."

Grace met his eyes in the mirror, aware that her emotions were all over the place. Among other things she was experiencing an irrational urge to laugh. It was the adrenaline, she thought, or, rather, the aftereffects. The fierce rush of biochemicals that had flooded her bloodstream during the course of the assault in the garage was fading, leaving her shaky and unnerved.

She was pretty sure that Julius had to be buzzed on similar discordant sensations but if that was true, he was doing a much better job of concealing it. More practice, maybe.

The camouflage of calm control was not quite perfect, however. She was sure she could detect a little ice and fire in his eyes.

They were standing side by side at the twin sinks in the master bath of Julius's condo. The police had taken their statements, arrested the knife man and departed. They had promised to call with any updates.

She contemplated Julius's reflection in the mirror and wondered why he looked so disturbingly sexy. The last thing she ought to be thinking about at that moment was sex. But she found herself fascinated, not just by the heat in his eyes, but by small details—his rumpled hair and the careless way his black tie hung loose around his neck.

En route to the huge bathroom he had removed his tux jacket and tossed it over the back of a chair. His ebony-and-gold cuff links were sitting on the black granite countertop, gleaming in the glow of the bathroom light fixtures. The collar of his crisp white shirt was open, revealing a hint of dark, curling chest hair. There were some smudges here and there but on the whole he reminded her of James Bond after a tussle with one of the bad guys.

Breathe.

Not that she was having an anxiety attack, not yet, at any rate. That would probably come later, in the middle of the night. Stupid damn nerves. She reminded herself that she had packed her emergency meds.

One decision had just been made—the big decision of the day— the issue of where she would spend the night. She would have to sleep in Julius's guest bedroom. She could not abide the thought of waking up in his bed in the midst of a full-blown panic attack. Not the most romantic scenario. If she was going to succumb to a case of what the Victorians had called shattered nerves, she wanted to be alone when it happened.

But in the meantime, she could not seem to stop thinking about sex. She wanted to hurl herself into Julius's arms again, just as she had following the assault downstairs. But this time she wanted to carry him off into his bedroom and throw herself on top of him.

Breathe.

She exhaled slowly, with some control, and took stock of her own image in the mirror. She did not look at all sexy. She looked like she'd been dragged through a couple of alleys and dumped on a back step.

The hair she had so carefully pinned up into a sophisticated knot had come down in the course of the short, violent struggle in the garage. Her dress was ruined. The skirt had ripped open at the seam and split halfway up one thigh. She figured that had probably happened when she kicked the knife-wielding attacker between the legs. The sides and back of the garment were torn and stained with garage floor dirt. She knew that when she took the dress off she would find bruises on her hip and shoulder. She had scraped one knee on the concrete. It oozed a little blood. The heel of her left palm was raw. The soles of her bare feet were covered in grime.

She was uncomfortable but the real pain from her bruises and scrapes hadn't struck yet. That would probably come later, like the nightmare and the anxiety attack.

In addition to sex, she longed for a shower. She understood the latter. She needed a shower. It was the desire to ravish Julius that she could not wrap her head around. She had never wanted to be in a man's arms the way she wanted to be in Julius's arms tonight.

Breathe.

She gripped the front of the sink with both hands to steady herself.

"How, exactly, did you expect the evening to end?" she asked.

"Hell, I don't know," Julius said. He considered the question briefly. "Maybe with a nightcap to celebrate the fact that for the first time ever no one fell asleep during the Speech from Hell."

"A nightcap," she repeated without inflection.

She focused on that thought, keenly aware that Julius was watching her in the mirror. His mask of cool control slipped a little more, revealing the stark hunger in his eyes. The stirring sensation deep inside was becoming intense. The atmosphere crackled with tension. She tightened her grip on the sink.

"Don't tell me you couldn't use a drink," Julius said. "I sure as hell need one."

She nodded slowly. "A drink is an excellent suggestion. But I think I need a shower first." She shuddered. "That creep in the garage touched me."

Julius's eyes went stone-cold.

"They were waiting for us," he said. "We were not just a couple of random victims. They were there because of us."

She shivered. "The one with the knife said something about spending a little quality time with my boyfriend."

"Unfortunately, that leaves a lot of room for interpretation. You've got a stalker but I've got a few old enemies of my own." Julius frowned in thought and then shook his head. "Can't see any of them resorting to low-end street talent like that pair in the garage, though. The people I've left on the ground can afford better." He paused. "Or they would do the job themselves."

"I'm sure neither of those two men was my stalker. I've never met either of them."

"Doesn't mean someone didn't hire them to take me out of the picture," Julius said somewhat absently.

She stared at his reflection, shock and horror shifting through her as his meaning sunk in.

"Because of me," she whispered. "I'm the one who brought those two down on us."

He met her stunned eyes in the mirror.

"No," he said. "Not another damn word about being responsible. Those two thugs and whoever hired them—if it turns out that they were hired—are responsible. No one else. Understood?"

The words held the implacable force of a command.

She looked at his reflection. "Julius."

He put his hands on her shoulders and turned her toward him. His mouth came down on hers. He kissed her with a ruthless, driving need that acted like an accelerant on a flame.

She did not try to resist. She did not want to resist.

"Yes," she said against his mouth. "Yes."

She clutched at him, trying to wrap herself around him. She heard the torn seam of her dress rip farther up her thigh.

Julius took the kiss to a deeper, even more explosive level. She felt his hands at her waist and then they went lower. He found the ripped seam, gripped delicate fabric and tore it all the way to the top of her thigh. He pushed the tattered hem of the garment up to her waist, exposing the thin triangle of lace and silk.

The next thing she knew he was cupping her bottom and lifting her up against his erection. She could feel the hard length of him beneath the fabric of his trousers.

She was breathing faster now, in the grip of a rush that was unlike anything she had ever experienced. She needed the release that she knew Julius could give her. A part of her was shocked by her volatile reaction but another part—the part that was in the ascendant at that moment—was thrilled. This was a new side of herself, a side she had always suspected existed, one she had searched for from time to time in the past but never found. This was real passion, the kind that made lovers do mad, crazy, over-the-top stuff in the heat of the moment.

She struggled with the front of Julius's shirt and finally got it open.

Fascinated, she spread her fingers across his chest, savoring the warmth of his skin and the contours of the muscles beneath. He held her easily, as if she was weightless.

He set her on her feet again just long enough to lower the zipper at the back of her dress. He peeled the front of the gown down to her waist and tugged the long, narrow sleeves off her arms.

He had her bra unhooked before she realized his intention. His hands closed around her breasts, his palms deliciously rough on her nipples.

She was intensely aware of everything about him. She could tell from the harsh rasp of his breathing that he was fighting for control and she gloried in her own feminine power. But at the same time she was lost in the waves of excitement. She could not wait to see what awaited her at the end of the wild ride.

He got his fingers inside the bikini panties and moved his palms down over her hips, sweeping away the lacy scrap of fabric. He tossed the panties aside and wrapped his hands around her waist.

He lifted her up again and set her on the edge of the counter. The shock of the cool granite against her backside made her take a sharp breath.

"Cold," she said.

"Not for long," he promised.

She heard the whisper of leather against brass and knew that he had just unfastened his belt. The next thing she heard was the slide of his zipper. When she looked down she saw the hard, heavy length of him. For the first time she experienced something that might have constituted a qualm.

"Oh, my," she said.

He opened a nearby drawer and took out a small foil packet. He got the packet open and quickly sheathed himself.

He put his hands on her knees, parted her legs and moved between her thighs. When he found her melting core she shuddered and clutched his shoulders. He stroked slowly, deliberately against her clitoris. She strained toward him, trying to capture his fingers inside her. She needed him inside her. He teased her unmercifully until she was so desperate, so sensitized that she could scarcely breathe.

"You are so wet," he said against her throat. "So ready for me."

"Now," she ordered. She used her grip on his shoulders to urge him closer. "Inside me. Do it now."

She made it an order, not a plea.

He guided himself into her, taking his time so that she was aware of every inch of him. Never had she felt so stretched, so full. She hovered on the brink of a release that she knew would change everything. All the questions she'd had about this secret side of herself were about to be answered.

She tightened around him. Her head tipped back. She closed her eyes against the glare of the bathroom lights and dug her ruined nails into the muscles of his shoulders.

Julius groaned, anchored her rear with his hands and began to piston within her. She fought him when he retreated, closing herself ever more tightly around him in an effort to make him stay deep inside her.

But he was as determined to control the cadence as she was and he was so much stronger.

Stronger—yes—but she knew that he was also vulnerable. She could feel the rigid tension in the muscles of his shoulders. She knew that every time she strained to hold him he was forced to use more control to master himself.

A moment later the wildfire of her release flashed through her. Julius was pulled into the vortex. She held him close as he drove into her one last time.

The hoarse growl of his exultant satisfaction echoed against the tiled walls. He throbbed heavily inside her for an endless moment.

When it was over he sagged over her, bracing his hands on the counter on either side of her hips. He sucked in deep breaths for a moment. Then he raised his head.

"That," he said, "was how I had hoped the evening would end."

Twenty-Nine

Julius eased out of her body. She winced a little because she was still so sensitive and he was so big. He searched her face and then lifted her gently down off the counter. Her legs felt weak. She grabbed the edge of the sink to steady herself.

"Are you all right?" he asked.

She managed a weak smile. "Aside from the fact that I look like I've been run over by a truck, do you mean? Absolutely."

"Got an affirmation for this?"

"How about *The truck that doesn't kill you only makes you stronger*?"

He nodded with a sage air. "A very uplifting thought." He checked his own reflection, grimaced and started to peel off his rumpled and stained shirt.

"You may have been hit by a truck," he said, "but I look like I was standing on the tracks when the train went past."

The crazy urge to laugh rose up inside her again. She managed to control it but she could not help smiling at Julius's reflection.

"You don't look so bad for a man who caught a bad guy this evening," she said.

"Only after you took him down with that shot to his balls. And in stilettos, no less." For the first time, Julius smiled with icy satisfaction. "I hate to say this because I sure as hell don't want to encourage that kind of exercise, but we made a damn good team tonight."

She smiled, too. "Yes, we did."

Julius's smile vanished. He watched her intently. "Where did you learn those self-defense moves?"

"It was part of the therapy that Mom prescribed after I stumbled into the Trager murder. I was having trouble sleeping. Nightmares."

"Sure," he said, as if sleep that was ripped apart by images of blood and panic were commonplace and only to be expected.

"I saw a shrink for a while but Mom thought the self-defense classes would give me a sense of control. I've kept up with the training."

"It shows," Julius said. "You move like someone who has studied dance or gymnastics or martial arts."

"I'm not the only one who has had some training," she said. "You're good. Very good. The Marines?"

"That's where it started. Afterward I did some martial arts to stay in shape. Like you, I keep up with the exercises." Julius paused. "Back in the day when I was Harley's fixer—"

"You mean when you were his executive administrative assistant," she put in smoothly.

That surprised a short, harsh laugh out of Julius.

"Right," he said. "What I was about to say is that fixing things for Harley Montoya occasionally got complicated. Some of his development projects were located in regions around the world where you could not always count on the support of local law enforcement. In addition, whenever Harley traveled to foreign job sites he was a target for kidnappers. Grabbing foreign executives and holding them for ransom is a big business in a number of places around the globe."

She nodded. "You were Harley's fixer and his bodyguard. That explains a lot."

"First time I've gotten into a fight here in Seattle, though." Julius glanced down at his crumpled shirt. "Can't remember the last time I had trouble in a parking garage."

She smiled faintly. "They do say that parking garages are dangerous places."

"Yeah, I've heard that." He studied her. "Are you sure you're okay?"

She turned back to her image in the mirror. "I need a shower."

"So do I." He glanced at the big, elegantly tiled shower with its array of gleaming faucets, hand sprayers and water jets. "I think there's room enough for two."

"You *think* there's room for two?"

"Never actually conducted an experiment."

She smiled, pleased. "No time like the present."

Thirty

Millicent pulled the tumbled sheets up around her waist and watched the vampire dress. The sex had been every bit as good as she had known it would be, fueled by the knowledge that, even though she controlled him for now, he was still dangerous.

Burke finished fastening his belt and came to stand at the side of the bed.

"That was definitely interesting," he said.

"Yes, it was." She stretched her arms high over her head and yawned. "Maybe we'll do it again sometime."

He smiled. "I'll look forward to it."

She settled herself more comfortably on the pillows, not bothering to cover her breasts. She had, after all, paid a lot of money for them. They were works of art and she liked to display them in the best possible light.

"One last question," she said.

He paused at the door of the bedroom. "What is it?"

"I know that you were blackmailing Witherspoon but I wasn't able to find out what you had on him. Care to satisfy my curiosity? I must admit he always struck me as squeaky clean."

"No one is squeaky clean." Burke smiled. "Least of all Sprague Witherspoon. Shortly before I started dating Nyla, I did my research. I stumbled into the family secret almost by accident."

"Well? What is the Witherspoon family secret?"

"Long before he reinvented himself as Sprague Witherspoon, rising star of the motivational seminar world, Witherspoon was someone else—Nelson Clydemore—small-time con and, eventually, ex-con."

It took a second before the penny dropped. Then she started to laugh.

"Oh, that's rich," she said. "That's just so entertaining. If only Kristy and Grace knew. They both believed that he was the real deal—a true believer in the positive-thinking crap."

"Clydemore did three years for fraud," Burke said. "According to the court records, he ran a pyramid scheme. It all fell apart when some of his clients got suspicious of results that were too good to be true and contacted the Feds. Clydemore went to prison and served his time. When he got out he assumed a new identity. He became Sprague Witherspoon."

"Amazing. Does Nyla know about her father's past?"

"No. She was born after he metamorphosed into Witherspoon, Motivational Guru. There's no indication that Nyla's mother or Sprague's second wife knew the truth, either."

"That explains why Witherspoon paid blackmail," Millicent said. "You threatened to reveal his past. It would have destroyed his business."

"Sure. But that's not why he paid off on time every month."

Millicent smiled. "He wanted to keep the secret from Nyla."

"He knew that if he was exposed as an ex-con who had once run pyramid schemes, she would have been devastated and publicly humiliated. Their relationship was already tense. He didn't want her to become any more bitter and resentful toward him."

"I see." Millicent made a face. "Family dynamics can get very weird."

"Yes," Burke said, "they can. But sometimes they can be quite profitable."

He disappeared into the living room. A moment later she heard the door close behind him.

Definitely dangerous, she thought. But then, it wouldn't be nearly as much fun if there was not some risk involved.

She pushed aside the covers, rose and went into the bathroom to clean up. When she was finished she put on a robe and slippers and settled down with her laptop. Managing a lot of money in various fake accounts designed to throw the authorities off track was hard work.

The security intercom buzzed some time later. She smiled. He had come back for more. No surprise there. She was very good at sex and men got addicted very quickly to good sex.

She closed down the laptop, got to her feet and crossed the room to welcome back the vampire.

Thirty-One

Julius stood beneath one of the showers and watched Grace enjoy the blasts of hot water that were striking her from all directions. She looked sleek and sexy with rivulets running off the points of her delicate breasts and disappearing into the crease that divided her buttocks. Her hair was plastered to her head and her eyes were closed against the force of the water.

He wanted to brace her against the wall and lose himself in her again but he knew that she was exhausted. He should have been exhausted, too. And he would be, eventually, he assured himself. The hard, fast, amazing sex had taken off some of the edge but it would be a while before he could sleep.

He was coming down from the wildfire high generated by the combination of the brutal encounter in the garage and the primal mating act that had followed. But now he was aware of another sensation, one that was equally elemental.

"I'm hungry," he said. "And I'm ready for that drink. What about you?"

Grace opened her eyes. He could see her taking stock of her current status. A trace of surprise crossed her face.

"I'm hungry, too," she said. She wrinkled her nose. "Weird."

"Not when you consider how much energy we expended this evening." He moved out of the shower, allowing himself one last survey of his private mermaid. She looked so good standing there, nude, in the artificial waterfall.

He made himself turn away and finish toweling off. When he was done he wrapped the towel around his waist. Absently, he used his fingers to rake his hair straight back from his forehead. A sense of unfinished business made him pause.

Grace turned off the shower. He handed her a fresh towel and watched while she hastily wrapped it around herself. When she realized he was still looking at her she raised her brows.

"Something wrong?" she asked. "Aside from the fact that we got mugged tonight, that is."

"Not sure yet." He opened a nearby closet and took out the brown, freshly laundered robe inside. "Here, you can use this." He eyed her left knee, which was still oozing blood. "We'd better cover that. Have a seat."

She tugged on the robe. "Thanks, but I can deal with the bandaging."

He was not in a mood to argue. He picked her up and set her on the edge of the counter. She sighed but did not protest.

He eased aside the flap of the robe and examined the raw scrape on her knee.

"It doesn't look too bad," he said. "But I'll bet it hurts like hell."

"A little," she admitted. "But there's no permanent damage."

He opened a drawer and removed a tube of antibiotic cream. She stiffened when he used a cotton swab to dab the cream on her injured knee but she didn't say anything.

He took out a box containing several sizes of bandages and selected one that looked like it would cover the scrape. He plastered it neatly in place.

When he looked up from the task he found her watching him with a very intent expression. The soft, seductive intimacy of the situation stirred his senses. He tried to shake off the rising tide of desire. She had been in a fight. She was hurt and would soon be feeling a lot more pain. She had to be exhausted. The sex would have to wait.

"That should take care of the wound," he said. "You'll probably be bruised tomorrow but I can't do much about that."

"Thank you," she said. There was a husky rasp to her voice and a sultry heat in her eyes.

He had to be strong for both of them, he decided.

He lifted her down off the counter and set her on her feet. "I'm going to make a couple of sandwiches and dig out the whiskey bottle while you're finishing up in here."

"Okay." She fiddled with the sash of the robe, managing to briefly expose one dainty breast. "This robe is . . . big."

"It's mine," he said. "Sorry, I don't have one your size."

She appeared pleased by that information.

"Good," she said.

"Good?"

She smiled and looked a little smug. "Never mind."

Women. Sometimes a man needed a translator.

"I'll go make the sandwiches," he said.

When in doubt, talk about food.

He left the bathroom and crossed the bedroom to the big walk-in closet. He opened a drawer and pulled out a clean black crewneck T-shirt, briefs and a pair of well-worn jeans. He did not bother with a belt.

Barefooted, he went down the hall to the kitchen, turned on some lights and opened the refrigerator. He had alerted his housekeeper that he would be spending the night in town. The Remarkable Renee, who came in once a week to clean, had gone grocery shopping for him. In addition to the wedge of cheddar cheese, dill pickles, bread and mayonnaise there was also a carton of eggs and a few other items.

Making the cheddar-and-dill-pickle sandwiches gave him time to think about something other than the fact that Grace was with him and that they had just had the best sex he'd had in a very long time, possibly in forever. Definitely in forever, he concluded.

By the time Grace came down the hall enveloped in his robe, her feet bare, he had the sandwiches and the whiskey waiting on the long, gleaming sweep of black granite countertop that served as his kitchen table. It also did duty as a lunch and dinner table when he was in the city. He never used the polished teak dining table and chairs in the dining room.

"Check your email," he said.

She stopped, bewildered, for a beat. And then her eyes narrowed a little as understanding hit her.

"Crap," she said. "Do you think . . . ?"

"Check it."

"I had my phone off for your speech and forgot to turn it back on afterward, what with all the excitement."

She went to the table where she had left her evening bag and took out her phone. She powered up the device and studied her messages. When she raised her eyes she looked bemused.

"No email from the stalker," she said. "But what does that tell us?"

"It tells us that the stalker tried to send another kind of message tonight. He or she might not know yet that it didn't get delivered as planned. I doubt if the guy with the pipe called his client to report that there had been a few problems and that his pal is sitting in jail."

Grace took a deep breath and climbed up onto one of the high stools. She watched him pour the whiskey as if she was mesmerized by the action.

"You think that there's a connection between what happened tonight and whoever has been sending me those emails, don't you?" she asked.

He swallowed some whiskey and lowered the glass. "I'm going on that assumption until proven otherwise."

She propped an elbow on the counter and rested her chin in her hand.

"You're in this mess because of me."

"Stop," he ordered. "We've already had this conversation. I'm with you because I want to be with you."

"Yes, but—"

"Shut up and drink your whiskey."

She reached for the glass.

He walked around the edge of the counter, sat down beside her and picked up a sandwich. "There is a slight possibility that tonight was all about me. You met my ex this evening."

Grace paused, her whiskey halfway to her mouth. She stared at him, clearly shocked.

"Surely she wouldn't hire two thugs to beat you up."

"Probably not," he agreed. "Diana has led a rather sheltered life. She wouldn't know how to find that kind of muscle on the street."

Grace gave him an odd look. "Who *would* know how to hire the sort of creeps who attacked us tonight?"

"Good question." He took a bite out of his sandwich. "I'm thinking it's probably the same bastard who isn't afraid to handle a dead rat."

"My stalker."

"Yeah." He took another bite and reflected on the evening's events while he munched.

"Mind if I ask a personal question?" Grace said after a moment.

He shrugged. "Go for it."

"You said earlier that the Hastings family company was digging its own grave. Do you really believe that?"

"Hastings is in bad shape and I'm sure the problems are inside."

"Would Edward Hastings be capable of sending a couple of jerks to punish you with a beating?"

"If Ed blames me for his problems, it's quite possible that he'd take drastic measures. But he and I go back a ways. I'm the one who hired him after he had a falling-out with his father and his uncles. Ed wanted to reboot Hastings and take it into the twenty-first century. But the old guard wouldn't let go. So he walked."

"He left Hastings and went to work for you."

"Yeah, for about two years. Then his father had a heart attack and was forced to retire. The uncles realized they couldn't handle Hastings on their own. They asked Ed to come back and take control of the company. He accepted the offer. Hastings started sailing into troubled waters a few months later. My gut tells me that if Ed was convinced that I was behind his troubles, it's a lot more likely that he would walk into my office and take a swing at me, himself."

"He wouldn't hire someone to do that?"

"If he did hire someone to do the job he would have employed higher quality talent. I taught him that if you do use a fixer, you buy the best."

Grace looked at him, eyes widening. "Wow. That's cold."

He shrugged and finished the sandwich. He refused to pretend to be something other than what he was—not with Grace. He'd tried to be someone else once before with Diana. Things had not gone well.

Grace drank some more whiskey with a meditative air and lowered the glass. "Maybe the police will be able to get some useful information out of the guy with the knife."

Julius ran the scenarios in his head the way he did when he was considering an investment, looking for the stuff that was hiding just out of sight in the shadows.

"My guess is that the guy with the knife won't be able to tell the cops much about who hired him," he said. "The deal would have been a cash transaction. No names. No identities. No good descriptions. What with one thing and another, I think we need to try another angle."

"Such as?"

"We need to find a way to draw the stalker out of hiding."

"How do we do that?" Grace asked.

"I'm not sure yet. But one thing is obvious—the bastard has a reason for stalking you. We have to find out what that reason is."

"Well, if it's Nyla, we know she wants the money she thinks I stole from her father's business. I suppose I could offer to talk to her about it but there's not much room for negotiation because I don't have anything to offer."

"What if the stalker's goal isn't the money?"

Grace drank some of her whiskey a little too quickly. She sputtered, coughed and lowered the glass. "What else could it be?"

"You're sure there's no ex in the picture who might have become obsessed with you?"

"Stalkers are by definition delusional and crazy," Grace said. "I suppose it's possible that someone from my past has gone off the rails and decided to fixate on me but I have to tell you, it's highly unlikely."

"I need a list."

She blinked. "Of all the men I've dated in the past?"

He smiled. "That many?"

She grimaced. "I wish."

"Relax, I don't think we need to go back to your high school prom date."

"That's good because I'm pretty sure Andrew isn't my stalker."

"Andrew?"

"My date for the prom. I told you, he spent the evening whining to me because he had wanted to take Jennifer to the prom but she declined. He was deeply depressed about the situation. He asked my advice on how to attract her attention."

"Did you tell him to think positive?"

"Pretty much," Grace said. "First, I told him that Jennifer was all wrong for him. He didn't want to hear that so I reminded him that he had a genius for computers. I told him to invent an addictive online game, get very rich and then go look up Jennifer."

"Did that advice work?"

"Partially. Andrew did invent a successful social media program. He did an IPO that was valued at a few billion dollars and he did get very rich. But he didn't marry Jennifer, which is a good thing because they would have been very unhappy together. He married someone else, instead—another very nice, very smart geek. It was a much better match."

"What happened to Jennifer?"

"She married well and often. She is now on husband number three, I believe, and living in a mansion on Mercer Island. There is, according to Irene, a very big boat parked in the water in front of the house." Grace frowned at the half-empty glass of whiskey. "I'm rambling, aren't I? Way too chatty. I may crash soon."

"That's a good thing," Julius said.

He drank some more of his own whiskey, letting the heat of the liquor relax him.

Grace made a visible effort to concentrate. "About this list you want me to make."

He put down his glass. "I'm not asking for the names of your old boyfriends. What I want is a list of everyone who was closely connected to Sprague Witherspoon—his business and his family."

"You're convinced that whatever is going on in my world is connected to his murder, aren't you?"

"I think it starts there. The vodka bottle thing can no longer be classified as a coincidence."

"No," she said. "Probably not. Okay, I'll make up a list. But I can't do it tonight. I can't seem to focus."

"Think you can sleep?"

She paused in mid-yawn and looked at him with a considering expression.

"What are my options?" she asked.

"Left side of the bed or the right side of the bed."

"Choices, choices."

Julius was watching from the shadows of the big bed as she emerged from the bathroom in a pretty yellow nightgown. She moved, wraithlike, across the room and climbed under the covers on the left side.

He turned out the lights and moved closer to her. She tensed a little when his arm went around her waist. He kissed her shoulder.

"Sleep," he said.

"Okay," she said.

And she did.

Thirty-Two

The old dream rose out of the depths on a dark tide of panic.
    . . . *She tried to control her breathing. She did not want the boy to realize that she was terrified. Her heart was pounding so hard she was afraid he might hear it.*

The boy seemed frozen with horror. She gripped his thin shoulder with one hand. In her other hand she clutched the neck of the vodka bottle. Together she and the boy listened to the monster come down the stairs. Each thud of the boots sent a tremor through both of them.

The narrow beam of the killer's flashlight lanced through the well of night and splashed across the plastic-shrouded body. Then it probed into a far corner of the basement. He was searching for the boy. As soon as he turned around he would see them hiding in the shadows.

"Run," she said to the boy.

She used her grip on his shoulder to haul him out from under the stair-case and propel him toward the stairs. Her stern voice and the physical shove she gave him combined to break through his paralysis.

He charged up the stairs toward the open door.

She followed, taking the steps two at a time. Trager yelled at her. She did not stop.

And then he was on the stairs behind her, moving so fast she knew she could not outrun him. He was so much bigger and stronger.

The boy reached the top of the steps. He paused and looked back.

"Go," she said again. "Don't stop."

The boy disappeared into the gloom that infused the atmosphere beyond the doorway.

Trager caught her jean jacket. She was trapped. She smashed the vodka bottle against the railing, creating a jagged blade. She slashed wildly, felt the resistance when the sharp glass struck skin and bone. Trager screamed. There was blood everywhere.

The crimson rain splashed her clothes, her hands . . .

"Grace. Grace, it's all right. You're safe, I've got you. Just a dream."

It was Julius's voice, pulling her out of the dark fog. She came awake, shivering as she always did after the nightmare. Her eyes snapped open and she gasped for breath. Someone was holding her down—pinning her to the bed.

"No." She struggled, frantic to get free.

Julius released her instantly. She bolted upright, pushed the covers aside and swung her legs over the side of the bed. She tried to go into her breathing routine.

Should have slept in the guest bedroom. Shouldn't have taken the risk. What had she been thinking?

"Sorry," she said. Her voice was tight and thin. "Old dream. Haven't had it in a long time but ever since I found Sprague's body—"

"I understand," Julius said. "Been there."

His voice was calm and steady, as if he was accustomed to being awakened by a woman who was emerging from a nightmare. No, she thought. He was talking about himself.

"You know something about nightmares," she said.

"Oh, yeah."

The breathing exercises weren't working. She lunged to her feet and grabbed the robe that she had left on the wall hook. She looked out the window. It was still dark, still raining, but the cityscape glittered and sparkled in the night.

Breathe.

She turned and watched Julius climb out of bed. He was wearing the T-shirt and briefs he'd put on after the shower. She was suddenly very conscious of the fact that she was enveloped in his robe.

"I know this sounds weird," she said, "but I need to get some air. I need to move. I need to get *outside*."

"Not a problem." He pulled on the jeans he'd left on a nearby chair. "Got meds?"

He sounded so matter-of-fact she knew that he'd meant it when he said that he'd been there.

"Yes," she whispered. "My purse." Desperate to appear normal, she tried to inject some brittle humor into her voice. "I never leave—"

"You never leave home without them. Neither do I. Haven't had to use them in years but I keep them handy."

That reassured her as nothing else could have done in that moment. He really did understand. But the terrible jittery sensation and the tightness in her chest were not improving.

"I'll use them if I need them," she said, "but I think I'll be okay if I can just get through the door—outside."

She rushed into the vast living room. The light coming through the wall of windows was sufficient to guide her to the balcony slider. Julius got there first. He reached out to open the door. His fingers brushed against hers. She jerked back.

"Sorry," she said.

"It's okay."

He unlocked the slider and pulled it aside.

The door at the top of the stairs was open. She had to get through it. There was no other way to escape.

She stepped out onto the balcony. Julius followed her out into the chilled night.

She gripped the railing and went into the breathing exercises.

Julius stood beside her and waited calmly, as if there was nothing unusual about a date who had panic attacks and needed to go outdoors in the middle of the night.

Slowly she got herself under control.

"Sorry," she whispered again. "Among other things, this is really embarrassing."

"No," he said. "It's not. Are the dreams getting worse?"

"Sprague's body. The stalker. The damn vodka bottle. The rat. The trapped feeling. It's been a very heavy couple of weeks. I should have known better than to think I could get away with sleeping in your bed. I never spend the night with . . . with a date."

Gradually her pulse slowed. Her breathing calmed.

When she was sure she was back under control she released her death grip on the railing and straightened.

"Damn," she said softly. "I hate these crappy panic attacks."

"I know how you feel. I told you, I've been there."

"For me it all goes back to that day in the basement at the asylum," she said.

"Reason enough for an anxiety attack."

"Trager tried to stop me." She sucked in a deep breath. "When I ran up the stairs, he grabbed my jacket. I was trapped. I knew that he was going to kill me."

"But you slashed his face with a broken bottle. You escaped."

"Yes. If I hadn't grabbed that bottle—"

"But you did grab the bottle. You saved yourself and the boy."

She took in another deep, square breath and let it out slowly.

"I've been mildly claustrophobic ever since that day. But that's not the worst part. I can handle elevators and airplanes so long as they are in motion. The worst part is the dream. The real bad attacks are always linked to it."

"But you never know when it will strike. That's why you never let a date spend the night."

She nodded, mute.

"Nights were always the worst for me, too." Julius gripped the railing beside her. "It's been better in the past few years. I did my time with the shrinks and with meds. But once in a while it all comes roaring back."

She looked at him. "No decent person could go to war and not be changed."

He leaned on the railing and gazed out over the glowing city. "Things looked different to me afterward."

"Because you were different."

He nodded. "But for a while I made the mistake of trying to pretend that nothing had changed. It was time to move forward with my life and all my big plans. And that's just what I did. Got the job, with Harley. Learned from him. Started my own business. Got rich. Got married."

"You were determined to be normal," she said.

"Absolutely determined."

"You set an objective and you pursued it," she said. "Is that why your marriage fell apart? Because you were focused on trying to get back to normal?"

"No," he said. "My marriage fell apart because I was not the man Diana wanted me to be. Not her fault. I had fooled both of us into thinking I could become that man. Diana is a beautiful woman and she is also a very nice person, at least she is when she isn't attacking my dates in the women's room."

Grace managed a weak laugh. "But otherwise—"

"Otherwise, she's a good person. But I think I was attracted to her mostly because she seemed to fit so perfectly into my fantasy of a new life."

"She completed the normal scenario."

"Right. It took me a while to accept that there is no reset button when it comes to normal. And it soon became clear to Diana that I was never going to fit into her definition of normal, either. The more she tried to transform me into the kind of husband she wanted, the harder I worked to build Arkwright Ventures. I used my business the way an addict uses drugs."

"You pushed each other away," Grace said.

"I knew that I was losing her and that it was my fault. Then I started having the nightmares again. Diana was frightened. I think she also found the situation embarrassing."

"Embarrassing?"

"She'd had to overcome a lot of objections from friends and family to marry me. My money got me through the front door of her world but it didn't give me the social polish, the education and the connections required to really fit in. Diana did her best to smooth the transition. I learned a lot from her. She taught me how to dress and how to pretend to enjoy a cocktail party or a reception. But it soon became clear to both of us that I wasn't going to go through some magical transformation."

Grace smiled. "You probably also made it clear that you weren't going to waste a lot of time trying to be someone else."

Julius's mouth kicked up at one corner. "Busted. You're right. I think the fact that I might be having some post-traumatic stress issues was just one more piece of data confirming that she had made a mistake. She felt she couldn't confide to friends or family. But Edward

Hastings was close enough to the situation to see what was happening. She turned to him. It worked out well for both of them."

"What about you?"

"I had to acknowledge that I was a failure in the long-term-relationship department but the nasty little truth is that another part of me was relieved. I could finally focus on my obsession."

"Right. Your business. It never asked questions. Never tried to change you. Never wondered why you came home late at night. But in the end you found out what every addict learns—there's always a dark side to your drug of choice."

"Yep. The more money I made, the less satisfying it was to make money."

"That's because your life lacked balance."

He smiled. "Is that the problem?"

"I think balance is always the problem. I doubt that anyone ever gets it perfectly right. The trick is to recognize when things are tilting too far in the wrong direction and make course corrections."

"That sounds like one of those dorky Witherspoon Way affirmations."

"I've been told that some people find them annoying," she said.

"Amusing would be more accurate."

Grace took a breath and let it out slowly, with more control this time. The exercises were doing their work.

"You know," she said, "there is a Witherspoon saying that does cover this situation rather nicely."

"Of course there is." Julius looked at her. "What is it?"

"There can be no true definition of normal because life is ever-changing."

"What the hell does that mean?" Julius asked.

"Danged if I know, but I thought it sounded rather pithy when I wrote it."

"Very deep," Julius said.

"Thanks. I used it as a tagline for the recipe for Harmony Vegetable Soup in the cookbook." She paused. "The idea was that no two versions of vegetable soup are ever exactly the same."

"Got it." He did not move. "Feeling better?"

She ran an internal check. All the vital signs were once again green. "Yes." She hesitated. "Thanks."

He nodded once and she knew that he did not need an explanation.

"I made it a rule long ago not to discuss the nightmare or the anxiety episodes with my dates," she said.

"What a coincidence," he said. "I made the same rule."

"Did you?"

"I had the same policy that you have when it comes to spending the night. I shelved the policy for a time for marriage and things did not end well. Lesson learned. I went back to that policy after the divorce."

She smiled. "Cinderella Man. Home by midnight."

"No glass slippers, though. I refuse to wear glass slippers."

"Glass slippers are so last year," she said.

"Good to know." He looked out at the glowing cityscape. "So, to sum up recent developments, we have both broken our own rules."

"Yes," she said. "We have."

She moved her palm along the railing until she was touching the edge of his hand. This time she did not flinch. He was warm and strong and rock-steady. She relaxed a little more.

After a while Julius tightened his fingers gently around hers.

"Okay now?" he asked.

"Yes, I think so."

He led her back inside and back to bed. This time she fell into a dreamless sleep.

Thirty-Three

I've been thinking about your ex-wife and your former vice president," Grace said.

"Don't think about Diana and Edward," Julius said. "I sure as hell don't want to think about either of them."

"But there are issues here that you can't ignore."

"Watch me."

She was doing just that, watching him from her perch on the other side of the kitchen counter. Julius was cracking eggs into a bowl. He did it with an easy, one-handed action. A man who was in the habit of cooking for himself, she thought. A man who was accustomed to living alone.

"I take it you don't believe in getting closure?" she said.

"There is no such thing as closure as far as I'm concerned." Julius tossed the contents of another egg into the bowl. "Things are what they are. You deal with reality and move on."

"Listen up, Mr. Realist, I'm the one who was confronted by your ex in the ladies' room last night. I've got a right to tell you what I think is going on and you should listen to me."

"Why?"

"Because we're sleeping together now, that's why," she shot back. "This is a relationship. In a relationship people are supposed to talk to each other."

Julius groaned. "Okay, talk. But talk fast because we've got other To-Do items on our agenda today."

"I'm aware of that." She folded her arms on the granite and watched him whisk a little cream into the eggs. "Here's my take on Diana. I think she feels guilty."

"About walking out on me? I doubt it. Hell, she had cause. Just ask her."

"I don't think she feels guilty about walking out on you," Grace said patiently. "I'm sure in her mind she did the right thing—she set you both free from a broken relationship that she knew could not be repaired. And what's more, she had the good sense to figure out that things were not going to work before there were any children to consider."

"I'll give you that point." Julius poured the beaten eggs into the frying pan. "So what's she feeling guilty about?"

"She blames herself for being the reason you are trying to destroy her husband's company."

"Except that I'm not trying to destroy Hastings."

"That is precisely what I told her."

"Fine. You did what you could to straighten her out on that score." Julius picked up a spatula and began dragging it slowly through the eggs. "Can we all move on now?"

"I think you should talk to Edward."

"About moving on? Trust me, he's got enough on his plate at the moment trying to save Hastings. He doesn't have time for therapy."

"I was thinking that you could offer to help him salvage the company."

Julius looked at her as if she'd lost her mind. "In case you haven't noticed, I also have a lot going on right now."

"Yes, I know, and I appreciate what you're doing on my behalf but I think your issues with Edward and Diana are important."

"I just told you, I don't have any issues with either of them," Julius said.

"You said you thought the problems were coming from within the Hastings family empire. If that's true, Edward may be too close to the situation. Couldn't you, perhaps, offer to consult for him?"

"He wouldn't want my help, believe me."

"Do you know that for a fact or are you just assuming that he would turn down an offer from you?"

Julius removed the pan from the burner. "I think it's time we brought closure to this conversation and moved on to another topic."

"What topic is that?"

"Your issues with a certain stalker. You're supposed to make up a list of people in Witherspoon's orbit, remember?"

"I did that for the police," she said.

"The cops are looking for the killer." Julius spooned the scrambled eggs onto two plates. "You and I are going after the stalker."

"What if they're one and the same?"

"That will certainly simplify things," Julius said. "I think there's a connection between the murder and the stalking but whether we're looking for one or two people is still an open question."

She did a quick little staccato with her fingertips on the granite counter.

"You're not the first person to come up with that theory," she said. "Kristy suggested that Nyla and Mr. Perfect might have conspired to murder Sprague. Millicent agrees with her."

"It's certainly a viable possibility."

She reached for the tablet of lined yellow paper and the pen he had put on the counter. "Okay, I'll see if I can expand the list."

Her phone rang just as she finished writing *Nyla Witherspoon*. She glanced at the screen and saw her sister's name. She picked up the phone.

"Hi, Alison, what's going on?" she said.

"I don't know," Alison said. "You tell me, little sister."

Alison's voice was too cool and a shade too neutral. She was in lawyer mode. Grace went blank.

"I don't understand," she said. "Is something wrong? Alison, are you okay? Are Ethan and little Harry all right?"

"We're fine. You're the one who showed up on every business and financial blog that covers the Pacific Northwest this morning, to say nothing of social media."

"*What?*"

"You were Julius Arkwright's date for that Seattle business dinner and charity auction last night." Alison's voice started to rise. "There are pictures, Grace. He kissed you right there in front of half of the movers and shakers in the city. There are rumors of a scene with his ex—in the restroom, no less."

"Oh, jeez."

Grace glanced at Julius. He was sitting right next to her. She could tell from the flash of amusement in his eyes that he could hear Alison.

"Just a second, Alison."

Grace jumped off the stool and hurried across the big living room to the window wall. She did not think that Julius could hear the other side of the conversation from that distance.

"Calm down, Alison," she said softly. "I told you that Irene and her husband set me up with a blind date in Cloud Lake. I said the date's name was Julius."

"You never said his name was Julius *Arkwright*," Alison snapped.

"I didn't think it was important. Besides, you didn't ask."

"Good grief, do you have any idea who you're seeing?"

Grace glanced back at Julius, who was now drinking coffee and putting on a good show of pretending to be oblivious.

"Yes, I'm pretty sure I know who I'm dating," she said, speaking in low tones.

"Why are you whispering? Wait. Where, exactly, are you?"

"I'm still in Seattle."

"You gave up your apartment there," Alison said. "Good grief. You're with him, aren't you?"

"Stop talking as if I'm about to single-handedly launch Armageddon."

"Too late," Alison said. "If you're sleeping with Julius Arkwright, the world as you know it is about to be drastically changed. Listen to me, my naive little sister, there are rumors circulating about Arkwright."

"You mean that gossip about him trying to destroy the Hastings family business? Yes, I know. But they aren't true."

"I heard you defended Arkwright to his ex. And I'm inclined to agree with you. Given his reputation, I have a hunch that Hastings would be in much bigger trouble than it is if Arkwright had decided to take down the company."

"Exactly," Grace said.

"But," Alison continued, "that doesn't mean that there isn't a lot of dangerous drama going on between Hastings, Arkwright and the ex-wife. You do not want to get caught in the middle of a three-way war. Do you hear me? That isn't something you can fix with a couple of dumbass affirmations and the application of positive-thinking principles."

"Dumbass affirmations?"

"Pay attention, Grace. This is your life we're talking about."

"Alison, I appreciate your concern, really I do, but I've got things under control. Trust me."

"Said the bunny rabbit just before the wolf ate her."

Grace smiled. "Little Red Riding Hood."

"What?"

"Never mind. I take it that you didn't hear that Julius and I were attacked by a couple of thugs in the garage after the business affair."

"Good grief." Now Alison sounded stunned. "Are you serious?"

"Yes, but don't worry, Julius and I are fine. A little bruised, but okay. Those self-defense exercises finally came in handy. Unfortunately the gorgeous piece of art glass that Julius had to buy at the charity auction was smashed to smithereens. But Julius caught one of the assailants. We're hoping the cops will get some information that will lead to the arrest of the guy who got away."

"I can't believe this. I think I may need to lie down and put a cool cloth on my fevered brow. What in the world are you doing?"

"Don't know for sure, yet, but it turns out that Julius is a pretty good bodyguard."

"He is?" Alison sounded bewildered.

"Marines. Then he worked as a fixer for a man who ran construction sites in various parts of the world. Anyhow, I'm in good hands. But don't tell Mom, okay? Not yet. She'll freak."

"I'm freaking."

"My life will calm down as soon as the cops catch the person who murdered Sprague Witherspoon."

There was a short pause on the other end of the connection.

"Are they making progress?" Alison asked in her lawyerly accent.

Grace decided to go for a positive spin. "They're expecting a big break any day now."

"In other words, no progress."

"Look, I've got to go."

"Promise me that you'll be careful," Alison said.

"Promise. Talk to you later. Love you. Bye."

Grace ended the connection and looked at Julius.

"My sister."

Julius watched her with an unreadable expression.

"Yeah, I got that much," he said. "I take it she doesn't approve of our relationship?"

"She'll be okay," Grace said. "Alison is just somewhat in shock because she got the news through social media instead of from me. Perfectly understandable. And naturally she's concerned about the lack of progress in the murder investigation."

"So am I," Julius said. "But getting back to the subject of our relationship."

She walked across the room and sat down at the counter. "What about it?"

"You're okay with it?"

The present is the only thing that is certain. Live it fully.

She smiled. "I wouldn't be here if I wasn't okay with our relationship."

Julius did not look entirely satisfied with her response but he went back to his coffee. She reached for the yellow pad and the pen.

Another phone rang. Julius's this time. He glanced at the screen and took the call.

"No problem, Eugene. I told you to call me the minute you came up with anything interesting. What have you got?"

Grace put down her pen and waited.

"Thanks," Julius said. "Yes, this is important. Contact Chief Nakamura at the Cloud Lake PD and give him what you've got. He's coordinating things with Seattle. Good work."

Julius ended the connection. "That was Eugene, one of the wizards I asked to follow the money."

"I remember," Grace asked. "What did he find?"

"I told you I asked the wizards to go deeper into the Witherspoon financial records. They found an interesting item marked Medical Expenses."

"What's unusual about that?"

"Every month for the past few months several thousand dollars have been transferred from Witherspoon's private account to an account in New York. The name on the NYC account is William J. Roper. Eugene says he can't find a William J. Roper at the address on the account."

"That doesn't make sense. Why would Sprague have been paying medical expenses in New York? I don't think he had any East Coast connections." Grace stilled. "Wait, is that Nyla's missing inheritance?"

"No, that's definitely gone, probably sitting offshore. This looks more like a slow bleed."

"What's that mean?"

"Blackmail."

Her email alert chimed, startling her. She froze, the way she always did lately when she heard an alert. Julius went still, too.

They both looked at her phone. Grace picked it up, looked at the screen and sighed in relief.

"It's from Millicent," she said. "Not the stalker."

"Millicent gets star billing on our suspect list," Julius said. He looked grim. "What does she want from you?"

Grace pulled up the email and smiled. *"Life is short. Eat more chocolate."*

Julius frowned. "What the hell is that supposed to mean?"

"It was an office joke. Kristy, Millicent and I used to amuse ourselves thinking up funny affirmations. Millicent came up with that particular slogan. She loves chocolate."

Julius glanced at his watch. "It's eight o'clock in the morning. Why is she sending you that email now?"

"I have no idea."

"Does she make a habit of sending you emails like that?"

"No, she doesn't. The line about eating chocolate was just a little joke around the office but Millicent isn't one of those people who emails things like that." Grace glanced at the email and the time. "It is a little weird, isn't it?"

"Call her," Julius said. "Find out why she sent it."

The cool edge on his words sent a chill through Grace.

"I'm sure it's nothing," she said. She eyed the phone. "But I will admit that a funny email at this hour is a little out of character for Millicent. Unless—"

"What?"

Grace made a face. "I'll bet she heard about that little scene last night at the business banquet."

"The scene between you and Diana?"

Grace cleared her throat. "More likely it was that kiss in front of all those people that got her attention. Alison says there were pictures."

Julius did not look amused. He was very intent. "Why would Millicent email you a jokey affirmation because I kissed you at that damn banquet?"

"Got a hunch she'd think it was . . . entertaining. Millicent was always teasing me about my rather boring social life."

"I'm not seeing a connection with chocolate."

"It's a female thing."

"By all accounts, Millicent is very good with money," Julius said. "A lot of it has recently gone missing. In addition, my financial wizards have uncovered something that looks a lot like blackmail. And now this Millicent, who is so good with money, is sending you funny emails at eight o'clock in the morning. Call her. Find out what's going on."

Grace took a breath. "Okay."

She clicked on Millicent's contact info—and got dumped straight into voice mail.

"Try emailing her," Julius said.

Grace looked at him. "You're very serious about getting in touch with her."

"We know she just sent that email. She's on her phone or computer. Go ahead, hit reply."

Grace tapped out *"Everything okay?"*

She drank some coffee while she waited for a response. When none came, she tried leaving another voice mail message. Then she tried a text message.

"This is important. Please call."

There was no response.

"Do you have her address?" Julius asked.

"Yes, of course. She invited Kristy and me over to her apartment occasionally for cocktails and a movie. She lives in the South Lake Union neighborhood."

Julius got to his feet. "Let's go see if she's home."

"Now?"

"Now."

"I'm not so sure this is a smart idea, Julius. As you keep reminding me, it's still early in the morning. Millicent may not be alone. And even if she does answer the door, what, exactly, are we going to talk to her about?"

"Sprague Witherspoon and the missing money," Julius said. "I've got lots of questions."

Thirty-Four

T he apartment building was one of the gleaming towers that had sprung up seemingly overnight in the South Lake Union neighborhood of Seattle. The area between the downtown core and Lake Union—once a sleepy industrial sector—was now a thriving mix of high-rise offices, condos, apartments, trendy restaurants and boutique shops. The sidewalks were filled with upwardly mobile techies and ambitious professionals who liked to live close to where they worked. There were very few suits to be seen. Denim prevailed.

It was only eight-thirty but the coffeehouses and cafés were busy. Julius admired the purposeful way everyone in the vicinity moved. The people around him all looked like they were intent on constructing a grand future. There had been a time when he had possessed a similar sense of drive and purpose, he reflected. But somewhere along the line the thrill had faded. Lately he had been running on autopilot. And then Grace had happened.

Grace had changed everything.

He watched her enter Millicent's number into the apartment building's electronic entry system.

"This is an expensive neighborhood," he said.

"Millicent says she likes living here in South Lake Union because everyone is so busy inventing the future no one has any time to pry into other people's business," Grace explained.

"In other words, she likes her privacy."

"Who doesn't?"

There was no response from the entry system. Julius looked through the glass doors. A man sat behind a high desk doing his best to ignore what was happening on the other side of the front door. He was in his twenties. He might have been working on his computer but Julius thought it was more likely the guy was playing games.

Julius took out his wallet and removed some cash. He folded the bills and slipped them into his pocket.

"Contact that guy at the door station," he said.

Grace raised her brows. "You're going to try bribery?"

"Got a better idea?"

"Now that you mention it, no."

She punched in the door station code on the keypad. The doorman responded to the summons. He got up and crossed the lobby to open the door.

"Can I help you?" he said. He looked as if he hoped the answer was no.

"I'm a friend of Millicent Chartwell in apartment twelve-oh-five," Grace said. "I've been trying to get in touch with her this morning. It's very important. She's not answering her phone but I think she's here. I'm afraid she might be ill."

"We're extremely concerned about her well-being," Julius said.

He palmed the folded bills out of his pocket and shook hands with the doorman. When he retrieved his hand, the cash had vanished.

The doorman appeared significantly more concerned about Millicent's health.

"You think Miss Chartwell might be too sick to come to the phone?" he asked, brow furrowing.

"Yes," Grace said. "Or perhaps she fell in the shower. She doesn't have any family here in town. There's no one I can call to check on her."

The doorman looked hesitant. "Well, we do insist on a signed PTE from every tenant."

"What's a PTE?" Grace asked.

"Permission-to-enter form." The doorman headed toward the elevators. "I'm authorized to go into the units to perform safety checks. I noticed her car in the garage downstairs this morning when I came on duty but she didn't go out for her usual latte."

The elevator doors slid open. The doorman did not say anything when Grace and Julius followed him inside. On the twelfth floor they all got out and went down the hall to twelve-oh-five.

The doorman knocked loudly several times.

"Miss Chartwell?" he called. "Are you home? A friend of yours is here. She's very concerned about you."

"Something's wrong," Grace said. "I know it. Open the door."

"Or we'll contact the police," Julius added. He unclipped his cell phone from his belt.

"Shit, don't call the cops," the doorman said, clearly alarmed. "She'll be really pissed if you do that. So will my boss. Not a good thing to have cops seen in the building. Gives the place a bad rep. Hang on."

He got the door open with a key card and called out loudly again, "Miss Chartwell?"

Still no response. The inside of the apartment seemed unnaturally hushed. The slice of the living room that Julius could see through the partially open doorway looked as if it had been furnished as a model apartment rather than a home. The color scheme was black and white punctuated with touches of red and gray. There was an empty martini glass sitting on the low black coffee table.

It was all very sleek and modern but it was also impersonal, Julius thought, as if Millicent had simply ordered the entire room from a furniture rental catalog. It reminded him of his own condo, although he was pretty sure his stuff had come with a much higher price tag.

Millicent had not put down roots in Seattle, he decided. It looked as if she was prepared to fold up shop and walk out the door on a moment's notice.

"That does it," Grace said. "You two wait out here. I'll go see if she's in there."

She sailed into the apartment before the doorman could argue. Julius stood in the opening and watched her go through the empty living room and past the kitchen. She vanished down a short hall.

A moment later her voice rang out.

"Call nine-one-one. She's still alive."

Thirty-Five

W hen I saw her lying there in bed I thought she was dead," Grace whispered. "She was so still. So pale. Barely breathing. Hardly any pulse."

She stood with Julius and the doorman in the hallway outside Millicent's apartment and watched the medics wedge the gurney into the elevator. Several residents from nearby apartments had gathered to witness the solemn process. Millicent was unconscious. There was an oxygen mask on her face.

"I heard one of the medics talking to someone at Harborview," the doorman said quietly. "Something about the situation looking like a deliberate overdose. Man, I would never have guessed she was the type."

There were several murmurs of agreement from the handful of other residents.

Grace shook her head and folded her arms. "I would never have thought so, either. I can't believe it."

Julius looked at the doorman. "How well did you know Miss Chartwell?"

The doorman shrugged. "She was one of the nicer tenants. Friendly. Tipped well. But we didn't have what you would call a personal relationship."

The muffled wail of the ambulance siren rose and then fell in the street outside the building. The small crowd in the hallway broke up as people drifted back to their own apartments.

"I'd better call my boss," the doorman said. He took out his phone. "Sure hope he doesn't get mad."

"For heaven's sake," Grace said, "you just helped rescue Millicent. If she survives it will be because you performed a safety check or whatever it was you called it."

The doorman perked up a little at that and moved a few feet away to talk on his phone.

The thirty-something woman who had emerged from the apartment next to Millicent's shook her head. "I wonder if she was depressed because of that man she brought home last night."

Grace turned quickly. "What man?"

"I don't know who he was but I'm guessing he was married from the way he acted. They came in around nine or so. He wasn't the first hookup she dragged home from a bar but I could tell by the way she laughed that the guy was different. She seemed really excited, as if he was special."

Julius glanced back into the apartment. "What time did he leave?"

"I don't know. It must have been around ten-thirty because I was getting ready for bed. He didn't stay gone for long, though."

Grace frowned. "What do you mean?"

"I think I heard someone out in the hallway later. The door opened and closed. I assumed it was the same man. But maybe it was one of her previous hookups. Who knows?"

"How long did the second visitor stay?" Julius asked.

"I don't know," the woman said. "I fell asleep."

"Is there anyone on duty at the door station at night?" Julius asked.

"No, just days," the woman said.

"So she had to buzz in the second visitor," Julius said. "She knew who it was."

"Sure," the woman said, a shrug in her voice. "But like I told you, she was always bringing guys home."

Grace went to the doorway of the apartment. From where she stood she could see the empty martini glass on the table. She had to know, she thought. She had to be sure.

"I think I left my cell phone in Millicent's bedroom," she said in a voice pitched loud enough to be overheard by the two or three people who were still hanging around in the corridor. "I'm going to get it. I'll be right back."

Julius gave her a sharp glance. "I'll come with you."

She moved into the apartment and turned to look at him.

"What?" she asked quietly.

"I didn't see any sign of a personal computer," he said. "Never met a numbers person who didn't have one."

"Yes, of course, Millicent had a computer."

"I'm going to take another look around."

He disappeared into the bedroom.

She headed for the small kitchen, dread whispering through her.

She had not imagined it. The liquor bottle stood on the counter. She had caught a glimpse of it earlier when she rushed past on her way to Millicent's bedroom but she had not had time to take a closer look. Now she could see it clearly. She had been right about the label. A cold sensation washed through her.

"Damn," she said softly.

Julius came up behind her.

"No computer," he said.

She felt him go very still when he saw the bottle.

"The same brand of vodka that the stalker left in your refrigerator," he said. His voice was grim.

"The same brand that I found in Sprague's bedroom." She gestured toward the bottle on the counter. "Millicent drinks vodka martinis but that isn't her favorite brand. Whoever is stalking me tried to murder Millicent last night."

Thirty-Six

"Let me get this straight," Devlin said. "You want me to reopen a very old, very closed murder case?"

"We're not talking about reopening it," Julius said. "The Trager murder was solved. What we're looking for is a connection that links that case to the recent Witherspoon murder and Millicent Chartwell's overdose."

"A connection besides the obvious one," Grace added very deliberately, "which would be me."

"Which is you," Devlin agreed. He contemplated her for a moment. "Interesting."

Irene shot him a warning glare.

"Just making an observation," Devlin said.

The four of them were gathered in Grace's kitchen. It had started raining during the drive back to Cloud Lake. The steady drizzle was still coming down.

There were two large pizza boxes on the table and two bottles of beer. There were also two glasses of white wine.

Irene gave Grace an apologetic look. "You were right. I found out that Devlin did ask Julius to get a read on you the other night when you had dinner with us."

Devlin winced. "Now, honey, I tried to explain—"

"Never mind," Grace said. She gave both men a steely smile. "Old history. Water under the bridge. I'm willing to let bygones be bygones. The applicable Witherspoon affirmation, I believe, is *Never let old storms cloud sunny skies.*"

Julius and Devlin exchanged male-to-male looks.

"In other words," Julius said, "she's never going to let me forget that our first date was supposed to be an undercover sting operation."

Devlin picked up his beer and eyed Grace over the top of the bottle. "But you're prepared to let bygones be bygones, right?"

"Absolutely," Grace said. She gave him another overly polished smile. "However, under the circumstances, I'd say you owe me, don't you agree?"

"Hah," Irene said. "Damn right he owes you. And me."

"I agree, I owe you both," Devlin said. He reached down into a small briefcase and took out a laptop. "After I got Julius's call today I pulled up the old file on the Trager murder again. The brand of vodka was not noted on the evidence inventory but there is a photo of the bottle."

Grace caught her breath. "Same brand as the three bottles I've come across lately?"

"I think so," Devlin said. "But it's a little hard to read the label." He hesitated. "Crime scene photos can be . . . disturbing. Are you sure you want to look at these?"

Images of Trager's bloody mask of a face whispered through Grace's mind. She swallowed hard.

"The only photo I want to see is the picture of the vodka bottle," she said. "I need to be sure."

Devlin nodded. "All right. Just the bottle. No need to look at the bodies."

"Thanks," she said.

He tapped a few more keys and then turned the laptop around so that she could see the screen. She thought she was prepared for the image but she was wrong. The sight of the broken vodka bottle splashed with dried bloodstains sent a shock of horror through her. She had killed a man with that terrible weapon.

"Dear heaven," she whispered.

Devlin looked hard at her. "You saved a little kid's life and your own. Never forget that."

"I won't," Grace said. "I can't."

Julius reached under the table and put his hand on her clenched fingers.

Irene watched Grace closely. "Are you okay?"

Grace took a breath and let it out with control. "Yes."

"Well?" Devlin prompted.

"Yes," Grace said. "It's the same brand that I saw in Sprague's bedroom and in Millicent's kitchen. The same brand of vodka that the stalker left in my refrigerator."

"She's right," Julius added. "Same green-and-gold label." He looked at Devlin. "We are not talking coincidence, Dev."

"I agree," Devlin said. "But just so you know, as of this evening the Seattle authorities are still convinced that Millicent Chartwell tried to commit suicide or accidentally overdosed. They have found no evidence of foul play, and Millicent is still unconscious so no one has been able to question her."

"Someone tried to murder her," Grace said. "I know it."

"We need to find something else," Julius said.

"Not much to go on here except the bottle," Devlin said. "Both murders and the possible attempt on Millicent's life were carried out in different ways. Mrs. Trager was beaten to death. Witherspoon was shot. Millicent's situation was made to look like an overdose."

Irene studied Grace. "You said you got an email from Millicent this morning but the authorities think she was unconscious hours before you got to her apartment?"

"Yes," Grace said. "When I talked to the police I pointed out that the email was out of character for her but the consensus is that it was Millicent's way of saying good-bye to me. She didn't have any close family and no serious relationships. But she liked me. At least, I think she did. Damn. How can I even be sure of that? Obviously I didn't know her well at all."

"Speaking of relationships," Julius said, "one of her neighbors said Millicent had a male visitor last night—possibly two male visitors. Or one who left and returned an hour later."

"I told you, Millicent was not averse to the stray bar pickup," Grace said. "She liked adventurous sex but she wasn't stupid about it."

They all looked at her. Neither man said a word. Irene cleared her throat.

"Some people would say that adventurous sex is a working definition of stupid," Irene said. "Maybe Millicent just took the wrong man home. He left, then came back later and murdered her."

"That wouldn't explain the coincidence of the vodka bottle," Julius pointed out. He picked up his beer. "Huh."

They all looked at him.

"What?" Devlin asked.

"The Trager murder was clearly domestic violence," Julius said. "We are assuming that the motive in Witherspoon's death and the attempt on Millicent's life involves money. But there is only one reason why someone would leave the bottles of vodka at the scenes of the crimes."

"To implicate me," Grace said. "Yes, that possibility has not escaped my attention. If the cops ever figure that out—" She broke off and looked at Devlin. "Uh—"

He gave her a humorless smile. "Right. I'm a cop."

"Yes," she said very politely. "I know."

"I am also, believe it or not, your friend," he added.

"Absolutely," Irene said.

Grace gave Devlin a thin smile. "Uh-huh. Right. Thanks."

"Damn, lady, you sure do know how to hold a grudge," Devlin said.

"I never hold grudges," Grace assured him. "They interfere with one's inner balance."

"Good to know," Devlin said. But there was a spark of amusement in his cop eyes.

Julius fixed his attention on Devlin. "Who, besides the Cloud Lake Police, would be likely to have access to the information in the Trager file?"

Devlin shook his head. "No way to tell for sure. It all happened years ago. Before my time here. But anyone who went digging into the records could have found that detail about the bottle. He would have had to look damn hard, though. Like I said, the bottle was entered into evidence but the label was evidently not considered a critical element. At least, no one made a note of it." He gestured toward the image on the screen. "Take a look. You can hardly make it out due to the—"

He stopped. No one finished the sentence out loud. But Grace heard it in her head. *You can hardly make it out due to the bloodstains.*

"As Devlin just told you, he wasn't here at the time," Irene said, interrupting quickly. "It was a huge story locally, of course. Everyone in town knew about the murder and that Grace had used a broken liquor bottle to defend herself. However, I seriously doubt that anyone outside the police would have been aware of the label. I certainly don't remember it and I was paying close attention because my best friend had nearly been murdered."

"So someone went looking for details of the case," Julius said. He leaned back in his chair and straightened his legs under the table. "There seem to be a lot of pieces here."

"The two thugs who tried to mug you in the parking garage at your condo," Devlin said. "What was that about?"

"Could have been a random thing," Irene ventured.

"No," Julius said. "It wasn't random."

"Someone was trying to frighten you off, Julius." Grace turned abruptly in her chair to look at him. "They were trying to scare you away from me. They intended to put you in the hospital—maybe worse. You're too close to me—practically a bodyguard."

They all looked at her.

"She's right," Devlin said. "Someone wants you out of the picture, Julius. It's the only explanation that fits. I know you're keeping company with Grace now but I ordered extra patrols on this street for the next few nights."

"Thanks," Julius said.

Thirty-Seven

She felt Julius leave the bed shortly before dawn. When she turned her head on the pillow she saw him standing at the window looking out over the lake. She pushed the covers aside, got up and went to join him.

"You're planning something," she said. It wasn't a question. Mentally she braced herself for what she knew was coming. "I can tell that you're working on a strategy."

He put an arm around her shoulders and pulled her close against his side.

"I hate to ask this," he said, "but would you be willing to walk me through the crime scene at the Cloud Lake Inn?"

"Somehow I just knew you were going to suggest that we take a look at the place where it all happened."

"Sorry," he said. "But I think it's something I need to do."

"It's okay," she said. "I'm willing to do it but I doubt that there is anything left to find after all this time. I told you, the place has been abandoned for years. Between the kids who have used it for parties and the transients who have camped out there, any evidence that might have been left at the scene will have disappeared by now."

"I just want to see it for myself. I need to figure out what we're missing."

"All right," she said. "The sun will be coming up soon. Let's do it this morning."

Julius turned her in his arms and drew her close.

"I hate to put you through this," he said. "I know it won't be easy for you."

"Going back into that place can't possibly be any worse than wondering why someone is murdering and attempting to murder people I know and leaving those bottles of vodka at the scenes."

"When morning comes, we'll go to the inn."

"Okay." She looked out the window. Dawn was on the way but it would be a while before real daylight appeared. Nevertheless, she knew she would not be able to go back to sleep, not now that she knew what lay ahead. "There's not much point going back to bed. I'll go take a shower and get dressed."

"That's a plan." Julius cupped her face in his hands. "But I've got a better one."

His kiss was all slow-burn seduction and aching need. She wrapped her arms around his neck and gave herself up to the embrace. He picked her up, carried her across the room and put her down on the rumpled bed.

He straightened long enough to strip off his briefs and then he got in beside her. He leaned over her, caging her with his arms. He brushed his mouth across hers.

The sweet, hot tension built deep inside her. She reached up to touch the side of his face with her fingertips. He turned his head and kissed her palm.

"Julius," she said.

She felt his teeth lightly graze her throat and then he began to work his way down her body. He lingered over her. By the time his mouth reached her breasts, she was twisting beneath his weight. When he reached her belly she sank her nails into his shoulders.

"Julius."

She almost screamed when his tongue touched the inside of her thighs. She did scream when he found her tight, full core. Her release flashed and sparked through her.

Before it was over he shifted. He rolled onto his back and pulled her down on top of him.

And soon it was his low, rumbling growl of satisfaction that echoed in the bedroom.

Thirty-Eight

"This place was a magnet for teenagers back in the day," Grace said. "But not so much anymore. The local kids have found other places to party."

They were standing on the path in front of the old asylum. Julius had a small box of tools in one hand. Grace was surprised at her own inner calm. She felt remarkably steady and absolutely determined. There was still the possibility that the sense of claustrophobia and an accompanying anxiety attack would strike when they entered the boarded-up building. But for now Julius's belief that returning to the scene would provide some answers had a strengthening effect on her resolve.

It would do no good for him to go inside on his own, she told herself. He needed her to give him the visuals. She could do this.

It had stopped raining but the trees still dripped and the surface of the lake mirrored the steel-gray sky. There was another storm on the way.

"I can see why a series of owners tried to turn the asylum into an inn." Julius studied the front of the decaying structure. "Good bones, as they say. Classic Victorian architecture."

"It dates from an era when people believed that the hospital buildings designed for patients with mental health issues should be part of the cure," Grace explained. "The theory was that tall windows, high ceilings and tranquil landscaping would lift the spirits and soothe the nerves."

"Not a bad theory, as theories go. Probably should have built the hospital someplace where there's more sunlight, though."

"Yes," she said. "It is very dark at this end of the lake because of the woods and the hillside." She looked at him. "How do you want to do this?"

Julius considered briefly. "What made you go inside that day?"

"Sheer teenage curiosity. I was on my way to visit Irene that afternoon. I took the lake path, as usual. When I got to this place I stopped to take a look around inside."

"Was that usual, too?"

"I didn't always stop," she assured him. "But there were rumors that some of the A-list kids had held a party in the asylum that week. Sex and drugs were assumed to have been involved. The question of which A-list girl was sleeping with which A-list boy was always a hot topic. I decided to take a look to see if any clues had been left behind. When I saw that the plywood on one of the side doors had been removed, I knew I was onto something. So, I went inside."

"Which door?"

"That one." She pointed toward the sheet of plywood that covered the door. "It's boarded up now."

"Let's go."

Julius led the way alongside the building. When he reached the boarded-up door he stopped and set down the toolbox. She watched him open the box and remove a crowbar.

It didn't take long to pry off the sheet of plywood. Julius set it aside. Grace moved to stand beside him. Together they looked into the deep gloom of what had once been a large kitchen. The door sagged on rusty hinges. All of the old appliances had long since disappeared. The walls were battered and worn.

Julius took two flashlights out of the toolbox. He handed one to Grace.

"Ready?" he asked.

He looked concerned and serious, she realized. But she could see that he did not expect her to lose her nerve. The knowledge that he had faith in her fortitude strengthened her resolve.

"Yes," she said.

She switched on her flashlight and moved into the kitchen.

"All right, you entered here to see if you could find any remnants of the party," Julius said. "Tell me what happened next."

"I walked through the kitchen and into the hall. I remember my footsteps echoed."

She retraced the path she had taken that day. The chill of dark memory and old nightmares raised goose bumps but she kept going. Julius followed close behind.

The basement door was shut. She stopped in front of it.

"I heard thumping sounds," she said.

"Go on," Julius said.

"Something about the thumping sounded urgent—frantic. I opened the door."

"It wasn't locked?"

"No, I suppose there was no way for Trager to lock it, that day. But I don't think he was worried that anyone would go into the basement. He knew the boy couldn't escape because he was bound hand and foot with duct tape. Mark's mouth was taped shut, too. I couldn't believe it when I saw the poor kid at the bottom of the stairs. I thought some bully had left him there."

"How did he get your attention?"

"He heard me come into the house. He couldn't scream for help but he used his feet to kick a wooden box that was on the floor. He kept kicking the box until I opened the door."

"Smart kid."

"Yes. He told me later that he made the noise because he could tell my footsteps were different from Trager's."

"Did you know Mark?"

"No. His family lived on the other side of town, next door to the Tragers, as it turned out."

"Let's go down and take a look," Julius said.

I can do this, Grace thought.

She switched on her flashlight and started down the stairs. When she reached the bottom she stopped and looked around.

"I didn't see the body at first. I got Mark out of the tape and he started crying. He clung to me and wouldn't let go. At that point I was still thinking that it was the work of a local bully. But Mark kept saying *Mrs. Trager is hurt. Mrs. Trager is hurt.* I saw what I thought was a sleeping bag. It turned out to be Mrs. Trager's body wrapped in plastic."

"Did Mark understand that Trager had murdered Mrs. Trager?"

"Not exactly. He told me that Mr. Trager had hurt Mrs. Trager and that now she was asleep and wouldn't wake up. I didn't know much about domestic abuse in those days. I'd heard the term but I didn't fully understand. It wasn't something I'd ever had to contend with, thank heavens."

"Where was the body?" Julius asked.

The calm, deliberate way he spoke helped her focus.

"Over there." She walked slowly across the space and stopped again, remembering. "When I got close I could see Mrs. Trager's face through the layers of plastic wrap. Her eyes were open. I will never forget what she looked like. It finally dawned on me that I had stumbled into a murder scene. I started to tell Mark that we had to get out of the house and get help. That's when we heard it."

Julius aimed his flashlight into the shadows. "What did you hear?"

"A truck engine in the yard out front. I told Mark that was a good sign. It meant there was an adult who could help us. But Mark was suddenly paralyzed with fear. He recognized the sound of the truck, you see."

"What happened?"

"He said it was Mr. Trager coming back and that he was going to hurt both of us just like he hurt Mrs. Trager. The kid was so calm about it. I think he was beyond crying at that point. After all, there was a monster coming for him. What could you do when facing a monster?"

"Where was the vodka bottle?" Julius asked.

"Next to the body. I grabbed it because there was nothing else around to use as a weapon."

"Where did you and the boy hide?"

"Over there, under the stairs."

Grace made herself cross the damp concrete floor to the dark shadows alongside the stairs. "I told Mark that we would get away but that for now he must not make a sound. I told him that when I said *run*, he was to head straight up the stairs and get out of the house as fast as he could and keep going until he found an adult."

"He did what you told him?"

"Yes. He was so scared I think he would have obeyed any adult in that moment. It took Trager a few seconds to realize that Mark wasn't where he had left him. Trager evidently assumed the kid was huddling in some corner of the basement and started to search the place with his flashlight. I hauled Mark out of the shadows and told him to go. He dashed up the stairs. I tried to follow him but Trager caught hold of my jacket. I smashed the bottle against the railing and slashed at Trager's face with the broken glass."

"Good girl," Julius said quietly.

"There was suddenly blood everywhere. It was raining blood."

Julius said nothing but he came to stand beside her. He put one arm around her shoulders.

Breathe.

She steadied herself. "Trager screamed when I cut him. He let go of my jacket and toppled backward. I kept going up the stairs. When I reached the top Mark was already outside, running along the lakeside path. I caught up with him. The nearest lakefront houses were empty. They were summer homes in those days and this all happened in winter. My mom and sister weren't at home that day but Mrs. Gilroy was."

"She's the one who called the police?"

"Yes. She locked all the doors to keep us safe from Mr. Trager in case he chased after us. Then she got her big pruning shears out of the closet. I will never forget the sight of her holding those shears, ready to defend us against Trager. But he didn't come after us. Because he was dead at the bottom of the basement stairs."

"You did the world a favor, Grace. But there is always a price to be paid for that kind of thing."

"Yes."

Julius removed his arm and walked slowly around the basement. The beam of his flashlight swept back and forth in a search pattern.

"There isn't any logic to what has been going on when we look at things in terms of the present," he said. "We need to view them from the past."

"How do we do that?"

Julius was silent for a long moment. "You said that Mrs. Trager was watching the boy for her neighbor that day."

"That's right. The poor kid just happened to be in the wrong place at the wrong time. As Devlin said, the police believe that Trager intended to drown Mark and hope the authorities would think the death was just another lake accident."

"What about the family?" Julius said.

"The Ramshaws? I don't know much about them. They moved to California soon after the Trager murder. Mom said they felt they needed to get Mark away from the town where he had been kidnapped. I'm sure he's had a few nightmares over the years, as well."

"Not the Ramshaw family," Julius said. "Trager's family. Did he and his wife have any children?"

"No," Grace said. Then she stopped for a beat, remembering some of the things she had overheard in the past. "But Trager had been married before. I remember my mother talking to Billings, the chief of police at the time. I overheard him saying something about Trager having a history of domestic violence and that his first wife had divorced him. Why?"

"I'm not sure. Just looking for connections."

Grace managed a shaky smile. "Is this how you go about analyzing investments?"

"Pretty much. The trick is to look for the stuff that is hiding in the shadows."

"You know, there's a Witherspoon affirmation that sums up your approach to problem solving."

"What's that?" Julius asked.

"Look deep. The important things are always just beneath the surface."

"I think I'll stick to my rules."

"Trust no one and *Everyone has a hidden agenda."*

"When it comes to words to live by, I believe in simplicity," Julius said.

"Whatever."

"Don't tell me that's a Witherspoon affirmation."

"Sometimes it's the only appropriate response to a situation," Grace said.

Thirty-Nine

R alph Trager had two children by a previous marriage, a boy and a girl," Grace said. She studied the information she had pulled up on her computer. "The names were Randal and Crystal. The first wife never remarried but she moved in with a series of boyfriends for a while."

"I'll bet that didn't go well," Julius said.

"It looks like she had really bad taste when it came to men. A couple of the boyfriends sold drugs for a living and one was arrested for abusing the daughter." Grace sat back in her chair. "How many times have we heard that sad story?"

Julius picked up the coffeepot and carried it across the kitchen to the table. "What happened to the first wife and kids?"

"Let's see." Grace leaned forward and scrolled through more data. "Looks like the former Mrs. Trager and the daughter, Crystal, died in a car crash. Randal, the son, went into foster care, moved through a series of homes and then just sort of disappeared for a couple of years."

"Probably decided life was better on the streets. Anything else?"

Grace scrolled through some more data. "Randal held a series of part-time contract jobs, most of them involving computers and programming. Looks like he had an aptitude for that sort of thing."

Julius looked out over the lake. "Go on."

Grace went back to her screen. "He came to a bad end. He was arrested on fraud charges and got six months and probation. He died in a boating accident soon after he was released."

"So it looks like everyone in Trager's family is dead."

"Yes." Grace picked up her mug. "What a tragic scenario."

Julius leaned back in his chair and swallowed some coffee. "It's also a very convenient scenario."

Grace looked at him over the top of the mug. "Are we back to *trust no one*?"

"We are," Julius said. "In light of this new evidence, we need to reevaluate our findings on all of the characters in our little drama."

"What's to reevaluate? We've already checked out everyone involved."

"But now we'll do it from another perspective," Julius said. "We've got a situation that involves fraud, and at least one character in our story did time for fraud."

"Yes, several years ago, but Randal Trager was killed after he got out of jail."

"Maybe."

"Devlin's right, you really do think like a cop. Maybe you missed your calling."

"I don't like guns," Julius said.

"Okay, that might have been a problem for you if you had pursued a career in law enforcement."

A phone rang. Julius this time. He glanced at the screen and took the call.

"What have you got for me, Eugene?" he said.

He listened attentively for a few minutes.

"That would explain a few things," he said. "Including his career path. Thanks, Eugene. You've done some really fine work on this. Yes, I will let you know how it all comes out. No, you cannot quit to go work for the FBI. It doesn't pay nearly as well as Arkwright Ventures does."

Julius hung up and looked at Grace.

"Well?" she prompted.

"It appears that Sprague Witherspoon may have had a secret past, one he tried to bury a long time ago. It may explain the blackmail."

Grace's heart sank. "Oh, no. Please don't tell me Sprague was a criminal."

"He did time under another name for fraud."

"Damn." Grace closed her eyes. "I really, really admired him, you know."

"I know," Julius said gently.

She opened her eyes. "I'll bet that after he got out of prison he reinvented himself for good and committed himself to helping other people make new lives for themselves. When you think about it, that's a very inspiring story."

"That's definitely one way of interpreting the facts," Julius said.

She beetled her brows. "It's my interpretation of the facts until proven otherwise."

"There is the little issue of his possible gambling addiction and the embezzlement thing."

She glared.

He moved one hand in a dismissive gesture. "Fine. Innocent until proven guilty. Whatever."

The rumble of a vehicle pulling into the drive stopped Grace before she could start asking questions. She got to her feet and went out into the living room. The familiar logo of an overnight package delivery company was emblazoned on the side of the large van parked in front of the house. She watched the uniformed driver climb out. He came up the front steps, a box in one hand.

She opened the door.

"Grace Elland?" he said.

"That would be me."

"Got a package for you."

"Thanks," Grace said. She glanced at the return address and recognized the name of the Seattle chocolatier. "Candy. This is a surprise."

"Sign here, please."

She scrawled her name and took the package. The deliveryman got back into the truck and rumbled down the drive toward the road.

Grace carried the box of chocolates back into the kitchen and set it down on the table. She tore off the outer wrapping.

"Truffles," she said. "My favorite. Someone knows me well."

Julius eyed the box with narrowed eyes. "Boyfriend?"

"I told you, I don't have one at the moment." She picked up the envelope that had been taped to the top of the box. "Well, except for you, that is."

"Good to know that I count as a boyfriend."

She ignored the sarcasm and ripped open the envelope. For a moment she could only stare at the signature.

"Oh, shit," she said.

"Not what most people say when they open a box of truffles," Julius said. "Don't keep me in suspense. Who sent the candy?"

"Millicent."

Forty

This is too creepy," Grace said.

She sat at the kitchen table and stared at the rows of elegant chocolates. It might as well have been snakes or scorpions in the box, she thought. All right, maybe not quite that bad. Nevertheless, she was very sure she would not be eating the truffles.

"According to the label, the box was sent yesterday directly from the store," Julius said. He looked down at the chocolates from the opposite side of the table.

"Overnight delivery," Grace said. "But Millicent was unconscious all day yesterday and last night. As far as we know she still isn't awake She couldn't have sent this box of candy."

"You got an email from her yesterday morning and all indications are that she was unconscious at the time it was sent," Julius said. "If Millicent is the sender, she could have scheduled the email and the chocolates before she was drugged. Probably thought she could cancel both if everything went according to plan."

"But something went wrong, so the email and the chocolates got sent automatically. But why me?"

"Looks like you were her backup plan," Julius said. "Better take a close look at that candy."

"Not the candy." Grace held up the small white card. "It's all right here in the note."

She read it aloud.

Grace, if you're reading this, it's probably because I'm dead. I don't think that there are any good affirmations for this situation. It sucks. Consider this my will. I'm leaving my retirement savings to you even though I know you'll probably hand it over to that ungrateful bitch, Nyla. I can't bring myself to do it, that's for sure. I hope you will at least keep a commission for yourself, but you probably won't do that either. It must be hard always trying to do the right thing. But I will say it was rather entertaining watching you do it. It was fun knowing you for the past year and a half, so at least do me a favor and enjoy the chocolates.

The note was followed by the name of a bank Grace had never heard of and a long string of numbers.

"Offshore account?" Grace asked.

"I think, under the circumstances, we can assume that's the case." Julius sat down at the table and opened his laptop. "Easy enough to find out."

A short time later he had the answer.

"It's an offshore account, all right. And all you need to access it is that number she wrote on the card. There's a sizable sum involved here. A few million."

"So she was embezzling from Sprague." Grace propped her elbows on the table and cupped her chin in both hands. "She seemed—seems—like such a nice person. Always so cheerful. Lots of positive energy."

"I have a hunch that knowing she was raking in a tidy little fortune and setting it aside for her retirement was the reason she was always so cheerful and positive."

"Well, this does answer one question," Grace said. "We now know where the money went. And we know that Sprague wasn't embezzling the funds."

"We know something else, too," Julius said. "Miss Cheerful probably didn't try to kill herself. She was looking forward to an early retirement and the pleasure of spending the cash that she had stashed in that island bank. I wonder how she planned to bring the money back to the States without arousing the interest of the authorities."

"In a suitcase?" Grace suggested.

"Carrying a few million bucks through customs is a high-risk game." Julius shook his head. "This kind of money needs to be scrubbed clean."

"I suppose the next step is to call Devlin," Grace said without much enthusiasm. "And then I'll have to chat with the Seattle cops. Again."

"Dev comes first." Julius took out his phone. "Someone is going to get the credit for what amounts to a very big break in the case. Might as well be him."

"I suppose so," Grace said.

Julius smiled briefly. "Trust me, Dev is on our side."

"I'll take your word for it. But I'm going to call Nyla and tell her that I think we found her inheritance."

"That note and the account number are evidence," Julius pointed out in a neutral tone. "We are going to give both to Dev."

"Fine, whatever," Grace said. She took out her phone. "But Nyla has a right to know that we found her money."

Julius checked his watch. "I've got a meeting in Seattle this afternoon. No sense dragging you along. Can I trust you to stay with Irene at her shop?"

Grace glared. "I'm not a kid. I don't need a babysitter."

"You're a woman with a stalker—a stalker who may be escalating. You need a babysitter."

"Right. Yes, of course, I'll stay at Irene's shop. When will you get back?"

"I should be home by dinner. Just make sure you are with Irene and Dev until I return."

Forty-One

I t was all falling apart. The biggest score of his life was crashing and burning around him. If he didn't get out fast he would get crushed in the rubble.

Burke tossed the hand-tailored, neatly laundered and folded shirts into the suitcase and went back to the closet to zip the designer jackets into a carrying bag. He had spent a fortune on the clothes he knew he needed for the job. He was not going to leave them behind.

He had put the plan together with the precision of a military commander preparing for battle. Every detail, from a résumé so solid it could have withstood a high-level government background check—not that the government was that good at background checks—to the dates on his driver's license, had been engineered to perfection.

The timing had been perfect at every step of the way until that first mistake. He had told himself that leaving the vodka bottle at the scene of Witherspoon's death was a harmless whim. It was an error but a survivable one.

Finding out that Nyla's inheritance had vanished had come as a stunning shock, however. He'd almost cut his losses the day he realized that someone else had gotten to the money first. He'd torn the Witherspoon offices apart and then hacked the three computers in a desperate effort to find the key to the cash. He knew the thief had to be a member of the staff. It was the only answer that made sense.

Then Millicent had made him an offer that seemed too good to be true. For a while it looked like it would be possible to salvage the situation.

Now Millicent was in a drug-induced coma and might wake up and start talking at any minute. Another mistake. She should have died. He'd searched her apartment and gone through her computer but he had found no clue to the missing money. Without the account info, there was no way to get at it. It might as well be buried at sea.

The old rage rose out of nowhere, washing through him in a red tide. He had planned so damned carefully.

He dropped the suit carrier on the bed and slammed a fist against the wall of the bedroom. It hurt like hell and it dredged up old memories from his childhood—stuff that he hated remembering—but he felt better almost immediately. His heart rate slowed and his breathing went back to normal. Sometimes a man just had to let off a little steam.

The apartment security intercom buzzed, startling him. He debated whether or not to answer it and then decided to pick up.

"This is Grayson at the door station. Miss Witherspoon is here to see you, sir."

Shit. The last thing he needed was a visit from Nyla. But he survived by adhering to certain rules. The first rule of a well-run con was to stay in the role until you were out of town. With one person dead and another in the hospital, it was very, very important to stick to the rules.

"Please send her up, Grayson," he said. "Thanks."

He ended the call and looked around the bedroom. He had to make certain that Nyla didn't realize he was planning to fly out of Seattle that afternoon.

He left the bedroom, closing the door on the scene of the open suitcases.

The doorbell chimed. He took a breath and focused on channeling Burke Marrick, scion of a wealthy Southern California family that had made its money in real estate.

When he opened the door he saw Nyla's face and knew at once that everything had changed. She was in tears but they were tears of joy.

She threw herself into his arms.

"I just got a call from Grace," Nyla said. "I can hardly believe it, but she says they found my money. That bitch Millicent Chartwell was the embezzler. I should have known. She handled all of Dad's money. She hid millions in some damn island bank and more money is going in every day, thanks to the website and blog revenue."

Forty-Two

It was four-thirty by the time Julius walked out of the office. An early winter twilight, made even darker by a heavy cloud cover, had settled on the city.

He paused just inside the parking garage and did a quick visual scan. There were a handful of other people heading toward their cars. Office workers, he concluded. Nothing looked or felt wrong.

One little mugging and you start acting like you're back in a war zone every time you walk through a garage. Get a grip, man.

He took a last look around before he opened the driver's-side door of the SUV. Again, nothing appeared out of place. He got behind the wheel, took out his phone and called home.

Home. Where had that thought come from? He wasn't calling home, he was calling Grace. But somehow it was all one and the same.

She answered on the first ring.

"How did the meeting go?" she asked.

"The meeting went fine," Julius said. "The deal will net a sizable chunk of change within five years. My staff is celebrating at the closest bar."

"But you're bored."

"It was a very dull meeting. I'm on my way back to Cloud Lake now. Should be there in a little over an hour, depending on traffic. I'll stop by my place and change clothes. Then I'll walk to your house. You're still with Irene?"

"Yes, indeed, as promised. We're at her shop. Devlin is going to join us as soon as he leaves his office. We'll pick up some takeout and then go to my place."

"Sounds like a plan. See you soon."

"Drive safe," Grace said. There was a slight catch in her voice, as if she had been about to say something else but she stopped herself. "Good-bye."

"See you soon."

He ended the connection and paused for a moment, wondering what it was that Grace had almost said. *I miss you*, perhaps. Or, maybe, *I'm looking forward to seeing you again*. That was probably it. The chances that she had been about to say *I love you* were slim to none. It was way too soon. And Grace's track record indicated that she was very cautious when it came to relationships. Still, a man could dream.

He hadn't been doing much in the way of dreaming until Grace arrived on the scene. Grace changed everything.

He fired up the SUV and reversed out of the parking space. He was in a strange mood, one he could not quite define. Whatever it was, it was not connected to closing the Banner deal. The only thing involved there had been money.

By the time he drove out of the garage and into the river of downtown traffic he was pretty sure that the little rush of energy he felt was anticipation. Soon he would be back in Cloud Lake, where Grace was waiting. For now she was safe with friends.

It was full-dark by the time the exit sign for Cloud Lake came up in the headlights. Another little rush hit him when he pulled off the freeway. Not much longer.

Coming home.

Fifteen minutes later he cruised slowly through the neat little town and turned off onto Lake Circle Road. He checked the Elland house when he drove past and was satisfied when he caught a glimpse of the windows glowing warmly through the trees. Dev's police vehicle was parked in the drive. Grace was where she was supposed to be. She was safe.

With any luck Devlin would come through with a solid connection between the crimes and Burke Marrick. There had to be one. No con artist was perfect. Theoretically, now that Marrick had the money in sight again he would stop trying to murder people who stood in his way. Theoretically.

Julius turned into his own driveway, parked and got out. He grabbed his laptop and started toward the front steps.

The door of the neighboring house banged open. Harley appeared. The porch light shone on his bald head.

"Thought I heard you," Harley called a little too loudly. "How'd the Banner deal go?"

"It went the way deals always go. Banner is happy. My investors are happy. My staff is happy."

Harley snorted. "So why aren't you happy?"

"I'm thrilled, can't you tell?"

"You know what your problem is?"

"Grace tells me I'm bored. What's your opinion?"

"You're not building anything. You're just making money. After a while, that's not enough. When I was in business, we built things all over the whole damn world, remember? Water treatment plants. Hospitals. Hotels. Apartments. And it's all still standing. People got clean water and jobs and places to live because we put in the infrastructure you need for those things to happen."

"I'm in a bit of a hurry here, Harley. Your point?"

"I'm thinking maybe Grace is right. All you do these days is make money for yourself and your investors. You're bored."

Julius went up the steps and unlocked his front door. "Now, see, there's where you're wrong. I'm not bored, not any longer."

Harley laughed. "That's because you're heading out to spend the night with Grace."

"I don't want her to be alone until the cops pick up the psycho who's been stalking her."

"Right. You're just a regular Boy Scout doing a good deed." Harley chuckled. "Face it, you're in deep there. The scary part is that she understands you better than you do yourself. That kind of woman can be dangerous."

Julius paused in the doorway and looked at Harley. "Got any advice?"

"Sure. Same advice I always gave you when I sent you out to salvage a job that was in trouble. Don't screw up."

Harley went back inside his house. His front door slammed shut.

Julius went through his own door and switched on some lights. He stood quietly for a moment, listening to the silence. The place felt empty, just like his condo in the city. But that no longer mattered. He would be with Grace soon.

Nevertheless, the yawning emptiness seemed almost eerie this evening. He walked across the front room, his footfalls echoing on the wooden floor.

There had to be a connection to Burke Marrick. What the hell was taking the Seattle police so long to find it?

His imagination was spinning into overdrive. He needed to change clothes and go find Grace and his friends.

He hauled the duffel bag into the bedroom and dropped it on the bed. He was in the process of unzipping it when he heard the faint, muffled *whoosh* of an explosion.

Instinct and old habits took over. Without thinking, he flattened himself against the nearest wall, automatically seeking cover. He crouched and pulled the pistol out of the ankle holster before he even had a chance to consider the possibilities. His pulse kicked up and the battlefield focus infused his senses.

You're probably overreacting. Just someone fooling around with fireworks out on the lake. You're not going to be any good to Grace if you don't stay in control.

Outside the window the night was suddenly lit up with flames. He eased the curtain aside and saw that Harley's boathouse was on fire.

Harley burst out of his kitchen door and charged across the porch. He grabbed the garden hose and dragged it toward the dock.

"Arkwright, get out here and give me a hand. We got a fire."

Julius thought about the fuel, the flares and all the other combustible items that were stored in the boathouse and on board the cruiser.

He shoved the pistol back into the holster and headed for the kitchen door. When he was outside on the back porch he took out his phone to call 911.

"Harley, get away from that damn boathouse," he shouted. "The whole thing could explode at any minute."

Harley continued to haul the hose toward the dock. "It's my boat inside that boathouse, damn it."

"You've got insurance. Besides, we both know you can afford to buy two or three more."

Julius punched in the emergency number.

"Nine-one-one. What is the nature of your emergency?"

"Fire," Julius said. "Twenty-eleven Lake Circle Road. Harley Montoya's place. The boathouse."

"I've got vehicles on the way."

Julius ended the call and started down the steps. "Forget it, Harley. There's nothing you can do. Stay clear. Fire department's on the way."

"You gonna give me a hand or just stand there and tell me the fire department's coming?" Harley shouted.

"Stay away from the boathouse, you stubborn—"

Julius caught the flicker of movement out of the corner of his eye just as he reached the bottom step. A neighbor coming to help, he thought. But the nearest house was some distance away. No one could have run that fast.

The porch light glinted darkly on a metal object in the newcomer's hand.

. . . And Julius was thrown back into a war zone.

He dropped to the ground just as the gun roared. He felt cold talons slash open his right side. The pain, he knew, would come later. At that moment he was riding a wave of adrenaline.

Another shot slammed into the porch boards just above his head. He was flat on his belly on the far side of the steps. It occurred to him that he had made a fine target standing there in the light while he called 911. *Idiot.*

He pulled the gun back out of his ankle holster and watched the dark figure advance cautiously across the yard. When the gunman reached the edge of the porch light he paused, searching for his target in the shadows.

"What the hell are you doing, Julius?" Harley shouted. He started across the gravel lane that separated the two houses. "Are you shooting a damn gun? I've got a problem over here, in case you didn't notice . . . Shit."

"Harley," Julius shouted. "Get down."

Harley finally saw the gunman.

"Son of a bitch," he bellowed. "You set that fire, didn't you?"

The shooter was already swinging around toward Harley, who was clearly silhouetted against the flames.

Julius took a breath, let it out partway and squeezed the trigger.

The force of the shot took the gunman down. He collapsed into the ring of porch light.

Julius got to his knees, his weapon in one hand. He clamped his other hand against his side.

"The gun," he said.

"I've got it." Harley scooped up the weapon the gunman had dropped and hurried toward Julius. "Shit, son, where'd that SOB hit you?"

Julius considered the question closely. It was getting hard to focus, but there was warm liquid spilling over his hand now, he was pretty sure of that.

"Right side. I think. Kind of damp there."

Sirens wailed in the distance.

"Damn, you're bleedin', all right." Harley ripped off his flannel shirt and bunched it into a tight bandage. He pressed it firmly against Julius's side. "The fire trucks will be here in a minute. They'll have some medical supplies."

"Okay." Julius did not take his eyes off the fallen man. "Keep an eye on that bastard."

"Don't worry, I will. You know him? He's not from around here, that's for sure."

"Burke Marrick," Julius said. "Grace . . . Tell her . . ."

"Shut up and concentrate on stayin' right here with me. You can tell Grace whatever it is you want to tell her, yourself. Got a hunch she'll be along right quick."

Forty-Three

He drifted in and out of a medication haze, vaguely aware that Grace was somewhere nearby. He tried to focus because he had things to say to her but he kept slipping back into a murky dream world. Machines hummed and beeped endlessly in the shadows. Figures appeared and disappeared, startling him because they moved so quietly. He finally realized what was happening and glared at the nurse who was getting ready to inject another dose of the drug into the IV line.

"No more," he ordered. The words were thick and ragged.

The nurse, a tall, heavyset man with red hair, studied him closely. "You sure?"

"I'm sure."

Grace materialized at the side of the bed. "Don't be an idiot, Julius. Take the pain meds."

"No more," Julius said. "Not now. Need to think."

"Your call," the nurse said. "Let me know if you change your mind."

He left the room. Grace leaned over the railing and touched Julius's hand very gingerly, as if she was afraid he might break. He gripped her fingers and held on tight.

"Marrick?" he croaked.

"He survived but last time I checked he wasn't awake. Devlin has an officer stationed outside his door. His surgery was a lot more extensive than yours. The doctor said that in your case no vital organs were hit. They just had to stitch you up."

"Feels like they did it with red-hot needles."

"You heard the nurse," Grace said. "You can have more pain medication if you want it."

"No, thanks. The meds don't make the pain go away, they just take you to a different place. But everyone around you thinks you're no longer in pain so they feel better."

She smiled. "That's very philosophical."

He pushed himself up against the pillows and groaned when the pain punished him.

"Julius?" Grace looked worried.

He took a cautious breath. "I'm okay."

He surveyed the room and saw a large leather chair. There was a hospital blanket draped over the back. The window glowed with watery morning light.

"Hell, it's tomorrow, isn't it?" he said.

Grace smiled. "It's today. You were shot last night."

"You spent the night here?"

"Of course I did. You scared the daylights out of me. When Devlin got that call saying that two males had been shot at the scene of a fire at Harley's house and that you were one of them—" She broke off and took a breath. "Yes, indeed, I spent the night."

"You didn't have to do that," he said, but he knew it sounded weak. He was thrilled that she had stayed with him. "But thanks."

"You told me you don't like guns," she said.

"I don't. Never said I didn't own one. Used to carry it when I worked for Harley. Dug it out after we got mugged in the garage."

"That turned out to be very farsighted of you." She gave him a misty smile. "How are you feeling?"

"Best not to ask. Does Devlin have any more information?"

"Yes. He'll fill you in on the details but I can give you the short version. Devlin ran Burke's prints and got a hit. They belong to a man named Randal Trager."

"Trager's son by his first wife."

"Right. Randal's prints were in the system because he did time several years ago, remember? I pulled up the details when we researched Trager's family."

"I remember. That fits."

"It gets better. The Seattle police searched Millicent's apartment and found Burke's prints in Millicent's bedroom. He must have been the man she took home that night. Randal, or Burke or whatever his name is, was nailed for his crimes only once long ago but the cops think that he's probably been a successful, mid-level con artist all of his life. Nyla Witherspoon's inheritance would have been a big score for him."

"But only if she got her hands on her money."

"Devlin has been in contact with the Seattle police. It won't be long before Nyla discovers that Mr. Perfect is a scam artist." Grace shook her head. "It's just so sad."

"Now you're feeling sorry for Nyla Witherspoon? Hell, woman. That's right up there with feeling sorry for that dead rat that was in your refrigerator." Julius stopped. "Which reminds me—"

"The mugging, yes, I know. Devlin says the Seattle police picked up the other man who attacked us. Evidently they are violent career criminals with the usual rap sheet. Their main business is drugs but they are available for hire as enforcers. They told the cops that a man paid them to quote, send you a message, unquote."

Julius mulled that over. "Did they run the prints on the vodka bottle we saw in Millicent's apartment?"

"Yes. No prints on the bottle but, as I told you, they did find Burke's prints in her bedroom."

"He wiped the bottle clean of his own prints but forgot about the prints in the bedroom?"

"That's how it looks," Grace said. "The cops think Marrick was very sure that everyone would attribute Millicent's death to an accidental overdose."

"But if they did consider the possibility of murder, the vodka bottle would point toward you," Julius said.

"That's the theory. Millicent is awake, by the way, but she's still disoriented. She told the police that she doesn't remember anything about what happened the night she supposedly took an overdose. Everyone tells me that is not unusual in such situations. But she swears that she never tried to kill herself and that she doesn't do heavy drugs. Beyond that, she's not talking."

"Smart woman. She doesn't want to incriminate herself."

"The cops traced the email about eating chocolate and the online order for the candy delivery. As you guessed, Millicent had scheduled both to go out if, and only if, she did not personally cancel the arrangements every morning before eight o'clock."

"The email and the candy order went out right on time the day we found her in a drug coma."

"Yes," Grace said.

For some reason the thought amused him. "Wonder if she remembers that she sent that email and those chocolates to you and that by now you have the number of that offshore account."

"I don't know. According to Devlin, she's got partial amnesia."

"Or doing a very good job of acting the role of a patient who has lost her memory."

Grace winced. "Just goes to show, you never really know someone. I liked Millicent."

"Don't feel bad. In her own way, she must have liked you, too. That's why she left all the money to you."

"Well, there is that, I suppose," Grace said. She seemed to brighten a little at the thought. "But I wonder why Millicent got involved with Burke. I always had the impression that she was sure he was a con man."

"That's probably exactly why she did get involved with him," Julius said. He tried to connect dots through the remaining drug fog. "She knew who and what she was dealing with—or thought she did. Looks like they were partners in the scam. They murdered Witherspoon and tried to make you look guilty."

"The vodka bottle at the scene?"

"They knew the cops would be looking for someone close to Witherspoon. If their own alibis didn't hold up they wanted to point the finger at you. Burke Marrick knew the brand of vodka that was in the basement that day because he researched his father's death."

"When I think of how many times I went out for after-work drinks with Millicent—"

Julius ignored that, following the bright red line that connected the dots. "Things must have gone wrong between Millicent and Burke. Maybe he thought she was going to betray him and keep all the money for herself. Whatever the case, he tried to kill her and failed. He took her computer, assuming that he could find the offshore account. But he didn't."

"Millicent was very, very big on encryption," Grace said. "She was obsessive about it. Marrick may be good but I'll bet you Millicent was better when it came to hiding stuff online."

"Marrick must have been ready to pull the plug on the whole operation. But suddenly Nyla informs him that she has recovered her inheritance and he realizes he's got a second chance."

"But he knew you wouldn't quit turning over rocks," Grace said. "He was afraid that sooner or later you would ask one question too many and expose him for the fake that he was."

Devlin appeared in the doorway. "We'll get more answers out of Marrick when he wakes up. How are you doing, Mr. Venture Capitalist with a gun?"

"Let's just say I'm not focusing on a lot of positive thoughts at the moment," Julius said. "But I do have some negative things I'd like to go over with you."

Grace smiled. "You two spend some quality time together. I'm going home to take a shower and get something to eat. I haven't had any sleep and the hospital cafeteria food is downright hazardous to the health. Wall-to-wall fried things."

"Okay," Julius said. He knew he sounded grudging about it. He couldn't help it. He didn't want her to leave. He still had things to say to her. Not that he could say them in front of Devlin.

She leaned over the bed and kissed him on the forehead. She stepped away before he could figure out how to hang on to her.

"Are you coming back?" he asked before he could stop himself. He was immediately stricken with guilt. The woman had spent the night keeping watch at his bedside. She deserved a shower and a nap, at the very least. It wasn't like he had a right to have her dance attendance on him. It wasn't like he had any rights at all where she was concerned. Still, he did not want her to leave.

Grace paused in the doorway. "Don't worry, I'm going to make up a batch of the Witherspoon Way Harmony Vegetable Soup for your lunch."

"Yikes," he said. But something inside him relaxed. "Will there be an affirmation included?"

"Absolutely. I'll bring you some fresh clothes, too. They're saying you can probably go home later today."

"Home sounds good," he said.

Grace vanished out into the hall.

Devlin waited until she was gone. Then he smiled a beatific smile.

"I knew the two of you were perfect for each other," he said. "Am I born for matchmaking or what?"

"Bullshit." Julius levered himself up a little higher on the stack of pillows. He sucked in a deep breath and waited for the pain to retreat. "You suspected that she might have killed her boss."

"I never actually believed that," Devlin said. "I just wanted to be sure. Now, do you want to hear the details of my big case or not?"

"I want the details," Julius said. "All of them."

Forty-Four

After an hour of tossing and turning, Grace gave up trying to nap. The sleepless night in Julius's hospital room had left her feeling wired. She never had been able to sleep during the day, anyway.

She took a shower instead. It did wonders.

She breakfasted on a high protein meal of scrambled eggs and whole-grain toast and then she set about the task of making up a batch of Harmony Vegetable Soup.

She was slicing the carrots when she heard a car in the driveway.

She put down the knife, grabbed a paper towel to dry her hands and went into the front room. She pulled the curtain aside and watched Nyla get out from behind the wheel of a gray sedan.

She stifled a groan. The last thing she wanted was an extended conversation with Nyla but the woman had been traumatized twice in recent days. The loss of her father followed by the discovery that her fiancé was probably the killer would have been too much for anyone.

If Nyla wanted to talk, it would be unkind to refuse to listen, Grace thought.

She opened the door and stepped out onto the porch.

"Nyla, I'm so sorry," she said.

Nyla came up the steps, her sharp face tight and bleak. She clutched the strap of her purse as though it were a lifeline.

"I'm the one who needs to apologize," she said. "That's why I'm here. I accused you of murder and embezzlement. I'm sorry, Grace. I can't really explain why I was so sure you were the one who killed Dad and stole the money. I think it must have had something to do with the fact that you were the person who had done so much to make the Witherspoon Way successful. Dad was always singing your praises. I guess I was just flat-out jealous. But that's no excuse."

"It's okay, I understand. Please come in. I just made a pot of coffee. Would you like some?"

Nyla blinked, evidently surprised by the offer. Some of the tension went out of her face, exposing the attractive, elfin features that had been concealed all along. Regret and a deep weariness were also revealed.

"Coffee would be very nice," she said. "Thanks."

Agnes's front door banged open.

"Hello," Agnes sang out. She waved her pruning shears. "How are things over there?"

"Just fine," Grace said. "This is Nyla Witherspoon, Sprague's daughter. You remember she visited the other day."

"Yes, of course," Agnes said. She beamed at Nyla. "Your father was a good man, dear. He was all about positive energy. The world needs more of that commodity, doesn't it?"

Nyla flushed. "Yes, it does."

She went up the steps and moved cautiously into the living room. Once there she stopped, clearly uncertain what to do next.

"This way." Grace shut the door and led the way into the kitchen. She gestured toward a chair. "Have a seat."

She had long ago concluded that something about kitchens made it easier for people to relax.

Nyla sank slowly, tentatively, into the nearest chair. "Is Julius Arkwright going to be okay?"

"Julius will be fine. Thanks for asking." Grace set a mug of coffee in front of Nyla. "I just came from the hospital. The doctors expect him to make a full recovery."

There was a short pause. "What about Burke? I was told his condition was listed as serious."

"All I know is that he is out of surgery. I got the impression that he's expected to survive."

Nyla shook her head. "I couldn't believe it when I got the call from the police this morning. Or, maybe I should say I didn't want to believe it. But somewhere deep down inside I knew that Burke was just too good to be true. The perfect man. Dad was right about him all along."

"If it makes you feel any better, I was just as shocked to find out that Millicent Chartwell was embezzling from your father, even though in hindsight, she was the most logical suspect. Frankly, after it was discovered that the money was missing, I thought Millicent was just too obvious. I mean, really, the company bookkeeper skimming off the profits? How ordinary is that?"

"That's probably why she almost got away with it."

"I think you're right," Grace said. She glanced at the colorful heap of vegetables on the kitchen counter. "I was about to make some soup. Do you mind if I continue?"

"No, of course not." Nyla cradled the mug in both hands and looked out the window at the lake. "I suppose my father must have discovered what was going on and confronted her or maybe Burke."

Grace picked up the knife and began slicing the red peppers. "Probably."

"I wonder which one actually killed him?"

"No one knows for sure, not yet. But given the fact that Burke used a gun to try to kill Julius last night, he's probably the one who murdered your father."

"The police implied that Burke was sleeping with Millicent." Nyla's jaw clenched. "How could I have been so blind?"

"A successful sociopath has to be brilliant when it comes to deceiving others," Grace said gently. She pushed the peppers aside, rinsed her hands and snagged a paper towel off the roll. "The ability to charm you and look you right in the eye while they lie to you and break your heart is their natural camouflage."

"Are you and Kristy going to be okay?" Nyla asked. "I mean, will you be able to find new jobs?"

"We'll both be fine." Grace tossed the carrots and peppers into the simmering broth. "Kristy will probably take a position with Rayner Seminars. Larson Rayner could use her expertise. She's very good with scheduling and she's got excellent relationships with the clients. I expect she could move most of them to Rayner Seminars."

"I don't know how many times Kristy said that Sprague was like a father to her." Nyla sighed. "I can't begin to tell you how much I hated hearing that. Sometimes I got the impression she said it because she knew it upset me."

Grace went to work on the kale, stripping the leaves from the tough stems. "I think she was trying to convince you that she had your father's best interests at heart. She didn't realize how her words would be interpreted."

"It wasn't just the way she talked about Dad. I thought she might be trying to get her hooks into Burke."

Grace paused in mid-rip and considered that comment. Then she shook her head. "That does surprise me. I never saw anything going on between the two of them. She was as suspicious of Burke as Millicent and I were."

"But then, you didn't know that Millicent and Burke were partners in the scam, did you?"

"No," Grace admitted. "What made you think that Kristy was after Burke?"

"I was so worried about losing him. Like I said, deep down, I knew that he was too damned perfect. So I hired a private investigator to watch him for a while. I was told that Burke met another woman on at least one occasion quite recently at a coffee shop on Queen Anne. The PI took a photo of the two."

"Who was the woman?"

"There's no way to be certain. In the shot she's wearing dark glasses and a tracksuit with the hood pulled up over her head. But the investigator followed her back to the apartment complex where Kristy lives. I was sure it was her."

Grace picked up the knife and began chopping the kale. "Well, Kristy did mention running into Burke at a coffee shop on one occasion. It didn't seem to be any big deal. It was after that meeting that she said she thought there was something a little off about him. She said she got the impression he was trying to pump her for information on your father's business affairs."

"That was probably exactly what happened, but at the time I was convinced that she and Burke were sneaking around behind my back. I confronted him about it. He gave me the story about the accidental meeting at the coffee shop, too. At the time, I believed him."

"Kristy was inclined to be chatty. Burke may have hoped to take advantage of that fact."

"Yes, I suppose so."

Grace tossed the kale into the broth and turned to look at Nyla. "I need to ask you again if you're the one who sent me those weird affirmation emails from your father's account. And this time I'd like the truth."

"I never sent you any emails from Dad's account, I swear it. I don't even know the password." Nyla frowned over the rim of the coffee mug. "Why would I do such a thing?"

"I have no idea, but someone sent me emails with Witherspoon affirmations for several nights in a row after your father was murdered. I think they were intended to rattle me."

Nyla's brows scrunched together. "It must have been Burke who sent the emails."

Burke sent the emails for the same reason he left the vodka bottles at the scenes of the crimes, Grace thought. He was after the money but he could not resist stalking her. He would have known about the forty-eight-hour deadline that Nyla had set down. He had wanted to exact some revenge for his father's death at her hands.

"Yes," she said. "That makes sense."

Nyla put down her mug. "I should let you get on with your day. You probably want to return to the hospital to see Arkwright. I just wanted to thank you for letting me know about the money."

"It's yours," Grace said. "Your father wanted you to have it."

"It's strange."

"What is?"

"I thought that if I got my inheritance from Dad, I would feel better. Now all I can think about is that he's gone and there's no way to make up for the disaster of our relationship. I blamed him for my mother's suicide, you see. But it wasn't his fault. It wasn't anyone's fault. I wish I had understood that sooner."

It dawned on Grace that Nyla still did not know about her father's other life as a con man. The truth would probably come out at some point but there was no need to be the one to tell her.

"I can think of a couple of affirmations that might give you some comfort," Grace said.

Nyla turned wary. "What are they?"

"Well, the first one is *You can't go back to change things but you can move forward on a different path.* Your father loved you and regretted the way things were between the two of you. Leaving you that money was his attempt to make amends. The best way to honor his memory is to accept your inheritance and try not to repeat the mistakes of the past as you move into the future."

Nyla's expression was ruefully amused. "That's a very Witherspoon Way thing to say. What's the other affirmation that applies?"

Grace smiled. *"Don't look a gift horse in the mouth."*

Forty-Five

================

G race added the rest of the vegetables to the pot and left the soup to simmer gently. She sat down at the kitchen table and opened her laptop. One by one she went through the stalker's emails. They must have been sent by Burke. But he had been after the money and he was evidently a professional con man. The taunting emails didn't seem like something a pro would risk sending.

But in this case, the pro had also wanted revenge. He had left a vodka bottle at the scenes of the crimes to point the police toward her. Sure, he had wanted the money but he also wanted vengeance.

One thing was true of Burke Marrick—he was a professional liar. That meant everything he had told Nyla was false.

Julius's words echoed soundlessly in the kitchen.

Rule Number One: *Trust no one.*

Rule Number Two: *Everyone has a hidden agenda.*

Grace gave up and closed down the laptop. There was no point wasting time on the emails. That was a side issue. The important thing was that Burke and Millicent were both under guard in the hospital.

The soup was starting to smell very good. The ginger, soy and kombu-based broth spiced the atmosphere of the kitchen. Grace got to her feet and went back to the stove. Picking up the big wooden spoon, she stirred gently.

Kristy had told Nyla that Sprague was like a father to her.

But Kristy had the picture of the perfect family on her office desk. She did not need another father figure in her life. Her father was perfect. Just ask her.

And Burke had appeared to be the perfect fiancé. Just ask Nyla. Except that he was a con man and probably a killer.

Just ask Julius and Devlin.

Burke had invented one life story, why not two? He wasn't the kind of guy to do favors—except, perhaps, for someone who was in a position to do *him* a favor. Or someone in the family. Hey, even sociopaths had families, right?

Trust no one.

This was not good, Grace thought. She was starting to think like Julius—the same Julius who was currently in the hospital recovering from a gunshot wound because she had involved him in her positive-thinking world.

Kristy and Burke had met at least once for coffee. But Burke hadn't needed a second source in the Witherspoon offices, not if he had been working with Millicent from the start. Why risk trying to get info from Kristy? He must have known that Nyla would be upset if she found out—which was apparently what had happened.

But Burke hadn't appeared on the scene until about three months ago. Millicent had started skimming Witherspoon money long before that. Burke had, in fact, arrived shortly after Kristy had been installed as the receptionist.

Sprague was like a father to me.

That was a lie. Sprague had been a good employer but he had not tried to be a father figure to any of his employees. He had enough trouble with his real daughter.

Grace took the spoon out of the pot and set it in the small dish on the counter. She went to the table and picked up her phone, intending to call Julius. The sound of heavy footsteps on the back porch stopped her.

. . . And she was sixteen years old again, nearly frozen with panic, listening to the echoing thud-thud-thud of the killer's boots. Trager was returning to the scene of the crime. He had come back to kill the witness.

Breathe.

She looked at the kitchen door, double-checking to make certain it was still locked. The bolt was in place.

This was ridiculous. It was not yet night. *Don't even think of looking under the beds. Don't go there. You don't want to make the compulsion any worse by firing up a daytime ritual.*

Trager was dead. She had killed him. His son, who may have wanted revenge, was in the hospital. There was no way either of them could be on the back porch today.

That left Kristy but it was not Kristy's footsteps she heard on the back porch.

More solid footfalls shattered the stillness.

She put her back to the wall next to the window and peered out through the crack in the curtain.

Agnes, dressed in her gardening clogs, sunhat, jeans and a loose-fitting flannel shirt, raised her gloved hand to knock.

The wave of relief was so overwhelming Grace started to shiver. She wasn't in the middle of a scene from a horror movie, after all. She lowered the phone and opened the door.

"Agnes," she said. "Are you okay? Is something wrong?"

"I'm so sorry, dear," Agnes said. There was a mix of anger, fear and guilt in her eyes.

"What on earth?" Grace said.

More footsteps sounded—light and quick this time.

Kristy appeared from the far side of the porch where she had been concealed behind the old refrigerator. She had a bottle of vodka in one hand. There was a gun in her other hand.

"Drop the phone," Kristy said. "Do it now or I kill the old lady first and you next."

Grace dropped the phone.

Forty-Six

I t's all coming together," Devlin said. "The Seattle investigators are convinced that Marrick was working the scam with Millicent Chartwell. The partnership went bad."

"No, it's not that simple." Julius paced the small hospital room. The medication and the painkillers had finally worn off. The pain was back but he could think clearly again. "We're overlooking something."

"We'll fill in the missing blanks when Marrick wakes up and starts answering questions."

Julius stopped at the window and looked out at the view of the street. "Marrick is a professional. He should have cut his losses and run a few days ago."

"Everyone has a weak point," Devlin said. "Seems clear that in Marrick's case, it was the need for revenge."

"No," Julius said. "The timing is off. Millicent was embezzling from the Witherspoon accounts over a year before Burke Marrick showed up."

"Two cons passing in the night, recognize each other and hook up for a score," Devlin said.

"No, this was about revenge from the start," Julius said. "And it only started a few months ago." He went to the nightstand and picked up the phone. "I want Grace where I can see her."

He keyed in her code.

And got tossed into voice mail.

"She's not answering," he said.

"Maybe she's in the shower or taking a nap. She spent the night here at your bedside. She needs some rest."

"I don't like it." Julius opened the tiny closet and discovered that it was empty. "Where the hell are my clothes?"

Devlin raised his brows. "Locked up in evidence bags. Grace is bringing you some clean clothes when she returns with the soup, remember?"

"Screw the clothes. Where's my gun?"

"That's in evidence, too."

Julius swung around. Pain lanced through his side. He ignored it and looked down at Devlin's ankle. "You've got a spare. You always carry an extra."

"Your point?"

"Let's go." Julius headed toward the door, the tails of the hospital gown flapping in the breeze.

Devlin followed. "Do you think it's possible you're overreacting?"

"No," Julius said. "Call Harley. He's closer to the Elland place."

Forty-Seven

*A*ct as if you are in control, especially when you know it's not true. *Your mind will clear and you will be able to see opportunities that are veiled by chaos.*

"Agnes needs to sit down," Grace said. "Can't you see that she's about to collapse? She has serious health issues, don't you, Agnes?"

She focused on Agnes's eyes, willing her to play along.

Agnes gasped and clutched at her chest. She started to pant.

"My heart," she wheezed. "It's beating so fast. I think I'm going to faint."

Rage flashed across Kristy's face. For an instant she appeared confused. She had not made allowances for small adjustments in her plan—always assuming there was a plan.

Using Agnes as a hostage had been an impulsive decision on Kristy's part, Grace decided, one that had probably been made at the last minute when it became clear that the grand scheme to exact revenge had fallen apart.

Because that was what this was all about, Grace thought. The vodka bottle that Kristy had set on the kitchen table made it clear. This was about vengeance.

"Sit down." Kristy jerked the nose of the gun toward one of the chairs and glared at Agnes as if she was nothing more than a nuisance now that she had served her purpose.

"Move, you stupid old woman," Kristy hissed when Agnes did not move fast enough.

Agnes staggered rather dramatically toward the nearest chair. Grace remained where she was in front of the stove. She watched the gun in Kristy's hand. It was trembling ever so slightly. That was not a good sign.

Kristy was in the grip of an obsession. There was nothing else that could have caused a smart woman to risk two more murders when there was nothing to be gained except revenge. Burke was in the hospital and under guard. He would start talking soon. Millicent was recovering and in time would provide answers to the questions the police were asking. It was all over.

Kristy should have been on the run and hiding under a new identity. Instead, here she was, confronting her target. Vengeance was a harsh taskmaster.

"I'll give you credit for your skill at hiding in plain sight," Grace said. "You and Burke must have spent a long time working on your business plan, so to speak. It went perfectly, at least for a while."

"Burke and I didn't learn the truth about our real father's death until a year ago," Kristy said. Her eyes burned with the fever of her rage. "Mom left Dad while we were still babies. We had no memory of him. She changed our names and our life histories because she was terrified of Dad. Told us he died in a car crash. She never gave us the truth."

"She was probably trying to protect you," Grace said gently.

Kristy giggled. "Sure. She didn't want us to know about the bad genes on that side of the family."

"If your mother was so frightened of Trager, she must have kept an eye on him from afar," Grace said. "She would have been aware of his death."

"Wrong." Kristy smirked. "She never knew what happened to him because she was killed in a car accident, herself, shortly before you murdered Dad. Talk about karma, huh? Witherspoon would have loved that. Mom lies to us about Dad's death and then she dies in the exact same way he supposedly died. But his death wasn't an accident, was it? You murdered him."

The gun in Kristy's hand trembled more violently. Grace held her breath. Agnes sat very, very still.

Kristy used both hands to tighten her hold on the gun. She appeared to regain a measure of her control.

"Mother died with her secrets," she said. "Burke and I went into foster care."

"Was it bad?" Grace asked, trying to make the conversation sound normal—reasonable.

Kristy grinned. "Let's just say it was very educational. One of our foster parents taught Burke how to sell drugs, and I learned how to make money in . . . other ways."

"Someone pimped you out?"

"Not for long." Kristy shrugged. "Burke and I gave it a few months and then decided we could manage much better on our own. Burke has a real gift for the tech stuff, and I was the perfect saleswoman. We did pretty well, considering we were a couple of amateurs at the time."

"And then Burke got busted for running a pyramid scheme."

Kristy raised her brows. "You know about that, do you?"

"The cops know everything now."

"Doesn't matter," Kristy said. "This will all be over soon and I will disappear. Yes, Burke did time. He learned a lot inside. First thing we did when he got out was make up some new identities. We've had several over the years. Burke and I die and get reborn on a regular basis. Talk about positive thinking."

"Burke buried your past by changing the records to make it appear that you died as a little girl in the car accident that took your mother's life. He faked his own death after he got out of prison."

"I'm impressed," Kristy said. "You really have done your research."

"What made you come looking for me?" Grace asked.

"Burke discovered the truth when he was preparing the set of identities that we're using now. He got the bright idea of researching Mom's family tree. There's so much ancestry information available online. Amazing, really. Anyhow, that's when he figured out that she had lied to us about our past. Once he started peeling back the layers, it didn't take him long to find the connection to Cloud Lake and our real father."

"How long did it take him to find me?"

"Are you joking?" Kristy smiled. The fever in her eyes rose a couple of degrees. "The girl wonder of Cloud Lake. The young heroine who saved a little boy from a vicious killer. The brave, resourceful teen who killed a man with a liquor bottle. Oh, yeah, your name popped up right away—once we started looking in the right place."

"You started making plans," Grace said. "Nice work landing the receptionist's job at the Witherspoon Way."

"The fact that Sprague needed a new receptionist at the time was just good luck," Kristy said. "But even without that opening, I would have found a way to get close to you, Grace."

"How?"

"Simple. Burke and I would have rented space in the same office tower and set up shop as a pair of investors. It's easy. One way or another I would have become your friend. I wanted to get to know the woman who murdered my father, you see. I wanted time to decide just how I would make you pay for what you did to my family. I wanted to destroy you slowly but surely."

"You intended to start murdering the people around me and leave a bottle of vodka at the scenes?"

"I knew it would take a while for the police to get the significance of the vodka. But that was fine by me. I was sure you would understand immediately that this was all about the past. I wanted to see you suffer and fall apart. I wanted to destroy you."

"Burke was on board with the revenge plan, then?"

Kristy grimaced. "Burke is all about the money. He didn't get excited until he realized how much revenue Sprague Witherspoon was pulling in with his motivational seminar business. That's when he sat up and paid attention."

"He set out to marry Nyla."

Kristy's smile was thin and cold. "I was patient. I gave him the time he required to set up his con, but when I told him I was ready to start putting my plan into action, he got upset. He wanted to ride the Witherspoon Way gravy train for another year or so. He figured the income would double or even triple in that time frame, thanks to you."

"So he didn't want you to take any action that would jeopardize my position at the Witherspoon Way, at least not until he thought that he had maxed out the profits."

"We quarreled."

"Right. That day when you met him at a coffee shop on Queen Anne."

"Shit, you really do know too much." Kristy frowned. "Burke didn't want to meet me but I insisted. I had already waited long enough. I had given him his shot at Nyla. He stood to make a few million. He was getting greedy. He knew that Sprague had to die before Nyla could get the inheritance. It was just a matter of when. He finally agreed."

"Are you the one who murdered Sprague?"

"Yes." Kristy smiled, pleased. "I knew the code to override the household alarm system because I was the one who volunteered to look after Sprague's plants while he was out of town, remember? Sprague also authorized me to buy stuff for him using his credit card."

"That was how you made it look as if he had purchased the vodka that you left in his bedroom."

"Exactly." Kristy beamed. "I let myself into his mansion shortly after midnight and shot him while he slept. He never even woke up."

"The next morning when we all started to wonder why Sprague hadn't come in to the office, you were the one who suggested that someone should check on him," Grace said. "I was the logical one to do that because I lived closest to the office. My car was in my apartment garage, only a few blocks away."

"It was so easy," Kristy said, almost crooning. "Things went exactly as I had planned. Burke was pissed because he figured he'd lost a few million but he was still going to do okay out of the con and he knew it."

"Until he found out that Nyla's inheritance was missing."

Kristy snorted. "I told him, easy come, easy go. He didn't like it but there wasn't much he could do about it. But he called me right after he left her apartment. Told me the con was back up and running. He said Millicent needed someone to launder her money. She told Burke they could run the same embezzlement scheme at Rayner Seminars."

"So you tried to murder her, too."

"She was next on my list, anyway," Kristy said.

"What went wrong?"

"The bastards I bought the drugs from cheated me." The gun shivered again in Kristy's hands. She took a moment to regain control. "I was in a hurry. I knew I had to move fast. I got to Millicent's about an hour after Burke left. I was in tears. I told her I needed to talk to someone because I had stumbled across some information about Larson Rayner that indicated he was a con. I said we had to talk about it before we agreed to work for him."

"You lied."

"Of course. It's one of my many talents. But Millicent wanted the information she thought I possessed. We had a couple of drinks together. I put the drug in her glass. When she started to pass out, I dragged her into the bedroom and injected her with more of the junk. She should have been dead by morning."

A faint burning odor wafted through the kitchen. The soup was starting to scorch.

"You're the one who sent the late-night emails," Grace said.

Kristy smiled. "Thought those would make you nervous. You knew someone was watching from the shadows but you had no idea where to look. I loved that part."

"Which one of you sent those thugs after Julius?"

Kristy stopped smiling. "That was Burke's idea. We knew Arkwright was getting too close to you. Burke thought a good beating would scare him away. After all, Arkwright was just a businessman. He should have been a soft target."

"A bit of a misjudgment on Burke's part, I'd say. And he certainly didn't hire high-end talent to deliver the message."

Kristy grimaced. "Same bastards who sold me the drugs that were supposed to take care of Millicent. Burke and I were from out of town. We didn't know how to find reliable help here in Seattle. Burke asked around shortly after we arrived. Someone recommended that pair of idiots."

"Were they the ones who put the dead rat and the vodka bottle in my refrigerator?" Grace asked.

"No." Kristy beamed. "That was me. Pretty cool, huh? I had a lot of fun with that bit. Wish I could have seen your face when you opened the refrigerator that day."

"Things really went off the rails after you failed to kill Millicent," Grace said. "Burke must have been shocked when he realized Millicent had sent me the key to the money and that I had given it to Nyla."

"He said there was still a chance to save the con because Nyla still trusted him. But he had to get rid of Arkwright once and for all because Arkwright was too close to the truth."

"But Burke screwed up last night and now everything is falling apart, isn't it?"

The smell of scorched broth was getting stronger.

"Do you mind if I take the pot off the fire?" Grace asked. "The soup is burning. It might set off the fire alarm."

Kristy hesitated but she obviously wasn't quite ready to pull the trigger. She wanted more time to explain exactly why she had gone to so much trouble.

"Move the damn pot," she said. She gestured with the gun.

Grace turned toward the stove and carefully gripped the heat-proof handle. She lifted the heavy pot off the gas burner and shifted it to the other side of the stove. She did not turn off the burner that she had been using to heat the soup.

Casually she reached for a paper towel to wipe her hands. She pulled the leading edge toward the stove and left it lying on the counter. Then she placed one hand on the counter as if she needed support.

She turned halfway around to look at Kristy.

"You came here today to finish what you started, didn't you?"

"Yes," Kristy said. Hot tears burned in her eyes. "This was about punishing you for what you did to me and my brother."

"What I did to you?"

"If you hadn't murdered my father—my real father—everything would have been different for Burke and me."

"You think your biological father would have taken you in? Cared for you? The guy beat his second wife to death and would have murdered a little boy, just to cover up the crime. Try a reality check, Kristy. What kind of father do you think he would have been to you if he had lived?"

"We would have been a family."

"The perfect family," Grace said softly.

"Yes, damn you."

Grace moved her hand slightly on the counter, guiding the trailing edge of the paper towel into the fire of the gas burner.

The towel burst into flames that raced across the counter, consuming paper towels with stunning speed. The thick roll caught fire. Smoke billowed.

The smoke detector screamed.

Kristy stared at the smoke and the fierce flames. "What did you do? Stop it. *Stop it.*"

Agnes climbed to her feet. She had the heavy pepper mill in one hand.

"Hang on, I'll take care of everything," Grace said.

She looked at Agnes as she spoke. Agnes got the message and hung back.

Grace turned toward the counter as if she were going to try to tamp down the blaze. But she seized the handle of the pot instead, swung back around and hurled the scorching soup straight at Kristy.

Distracted by the smoke and fire, Kristy didn't see the hot soup coming her way until it was too late. Her scream of rage and panic was louder than the shrill squeal of the fire alarm. She fell back, swiping madly at the soup that had splashed across her face and chest.

The gun roared. The shot went wild. Grace sent the heavy pot sailing across the room. It struck Kristy on the shoulder, spinning her sideways.

She was frantic now. In her desperation to get the soup off her skin, she dropped the gun.

Agnes moved quickly and seized the weapon. She aimed it at Kristy with the steady calm of a woman who is accustomed to handling dangerous implements.

"You'd better do something about that fire, dear," Agnes said to Grace. She pitched her voice above the screech of the fire alarm. "Or you'll lose the house. That would be a shame."

"I'm on it," Grace said.

She rushed to the counter, grabbed the long-handled soup spoon and used it to push the blazing roll of paper towels into the sink. She heard the SUV engine in the drive just as she turned on the faucet.

Footsteps thudded on the back porch. She glanced out the window, heart pounding, and saw Harley Montoya. He had a gun in his hand. He kicked open the door before she could get to it and stormed into the kitchen.

Simultaneously, Julius and Devlin arrived through the front door with the ferocity of an invading army. It had clearly been a move the three men had coordinated.

Julius, Devlin and Harley slammed to a halt and took in the situation. They lowered their weapons.

The last of the flames died in the sink. The draft created by the open doors took care of the smoke. The screech of the fire alarm stopped abruptly.

Devlin moved to take charge of the gun Agnes was holding on the sobbing Kristy.

"Thanks, Agnes," Devlin said. "I'll take it from here."

"She's all yours," Agnes said.

She sat down abruptly on the nearest chair. Harley went to stand behind her. His fingers closed around her shoulder. She reached up and touched his big hand.

Julius looked at Grace. His eyes burned. The right side of his hospital gown was wet with fresh blood.

"You might be interested to know that I did a hell of a lot of positive thinking on the ride from the hospital to this house," he said.

She walked straight into his arms. He caught her close with his free arm.

"I told you, it works," she mumbled into the hospital gown.

"Are you okay?" he asked. His voice was raw.

"Yes," she said. "Yes, I think so. I'll probably have an anxiety attack when this is all over but I'll postpone that for a while."

"Grace."

That was all he said. But it was the only thing that needed saying.

Forty-Eight

"**T**rust no one," Grace said. *"Everyone has a hidden agenda."* She shook her head. "I hate to admit it but in this particular case, your affirmations are the ones that seem to fit best."

"You were the target of a carefully planned and executed strategy," Julius said. "It almost worked but it failed because you managed to outmaneuver your opponents."

"Because I had your help."

"Well, it was three against one, if you count Millicent," Julius said. "Seems only fair that in the end you had reinforcements. Even if they did show up late."

They were on the sofa in the living room of her house. Julius was back in jeans and a worn denim shirt that fit loosely around his freshly bandaged side. His sock-clad ankles were stacked on the coffee table.

Grace had her legs curled under her. Earlier Julius had built a fire in the big stone fireplace. Dinner had consisted of takeout and a bottle of wine. It should have been a very cozy, very romantic setting, she thought. There was even an affirmation that suited the scene:

Recognize the good moments and cherish them. But night had descended on Cloud Lake and in spite of the wine, she was still wired. She did not think that she would sleep. She did not want to sleep.

That afternoon she had worried about Agnes spending the night alone after the disturbing events. But Agnes had declined the offer of the spare bedroom, saying somewhat vaguely that she had a friend who was coming over to stay with her. Grace had understood when she saw Harley's old truck pull up in front of Agnes's house. For the first time in the recorded history of Cloud Lake, Harley had arrived at the Gilroy house with what appeared to be an overnight bag.

"I know Millicent was conspiring with Burke but it was all about the money as far as she was concerned," Grace said. "She had nothing to do with Sprague's murder. I'm sure she had no idea that Kristy is Burke's sister, let alone that Kristy was plotting revenge against me."

"That's certainly Millicent's story," Julius said.

"You don't believe her?"

Julius's smile took a grim twist. "The woman is an embezzler, Grace. Are you sure you want to think of your relationship with her as a friendship?"

"Okay, maybe friendship isn't the right word. But she left all of her ill-gotten gains to me, if you will recall." Grace looked into the fire. "She did that because she literally has no one else in the world. That is just so sad."

"Something tells me she'll make all sort of friends in prison, assuming she actually ends up doing time."

"You are so cynical." Grace thought for a minute. "Maybe Millicent will become one of those white-collar criminals who gets recruited by the FBI to detect other embezzlers."

"I wouldn't be surprised if she manages to talk her way into a job like that."

"I still can't quite believe that this was all about revenge," Grace said.

"And money," Julius said. "Two of the most compelling forces in the world."

"No." Grace pulled away from the protective embrace of his arm. She knelt on the cushions and caught Julius's face between her palms. "I refuse to believe that revenge and money are the strongest forces in the world."

He watched her with the controlled hunger that always shadowed his eyes.

"Are you going to tell me that positive thinking is the strongest force in the world?" he asked. "Because if you are, I need another drink first."

She smiled. "What I'm going to tell you is that love is the strongest force on the planet and maybe in the entire universe."

"Is that one of your affirmations?"

"Nope. It's just the truth, at least for me. I love you, Julius Arkwright."

He went very still. For a moment he looked at her as if she had spoken in some language that he might have known long ago but had forgotten.

Then he moved. He took his feet off the table and set his glass down with great precision.

"Grace."

He said her name as if he could not quite believe that she existed. As if it could work magic.

She put her own glass on the table and leaned into him—careful not to touch his freshly bandaged side. She brushed her mouth against his.

"I know you've got trust issues and I know that you don't go for the feel-good, positive-thinking stuff," she said. "I get all that because I've got some issues of my own. None of our issues are as important as the fact that I love you."

JAYNE ANN KRENTZ

"Grace."

He kissed her with a desperate passion. It was the kiss of a man who had been thirsting for love for so long he did not know how to ask for it politely. Instead, he seized it with both hands.

"I've been looking for you all of my life," he said simply. "I love you."

The truth was there in the stark wonder that infused his words. The night would be a long one but she would not be alone. Neither would Julius.

"We will hold on to this," she said.

"Yes," he said. "We're both fighters. We know how to hang on to what is important."

She awoke from a ragged dreamscape that involved darkness, a flight of stairs and an empty doorway.

She sat up, suddenly wide awake but not in the shaky, breathless way that indicated an impending panic attack.

"Julius?" she whispered.

"Over here," he said.

She looked toward the window and saw him. In the glow of the night-light she could tell that he was wearing his T-shirt and jeans.

"Bad dream?" he asked.

"Started out that way." She sat up on the edge of the bed and automatically went into the breathing exercises. "What about you?"

"I couldn't sleep," he said. "Every time I closed my eyes I thought about that damned vodka bottle sitting on your kitchen table."

"Yeah, the vodka thing was creepy. Kristy is creepy. But when I think about what a dreadful childhood she had—"

"Don't," Julius said. It was a command. "Don't go there. I am not going to listen to you make excuses for a psychopath."

She thought about that. "You're right. Sometimes there are no excuses."

"Zero in this case. How's the breathing going?"

She did an internal check. "Okay, I think."

"Need your meds?"

"No. No, I'm fine, really."

"Was your dream the old one that you told me about?"

"At first. I was back in the basement of the asylum, trying to get to the top of the stairs. Trager grabbed my jacket but I broke free. This time I made it through the doorway. I found what I was searching for on the other side."

Julius came toward the bed and took her into his arms. "So, your dream is changing. That's a good thing, right?"

"Yes, I'm sure it is."

Her nerves were still on edge but the sensation—like the dream—was different this time. A great rush of expectation sparkled through her.

"What did you find on the other side of the door?" Julius asked.

She smiled. "You."

"Good," he said. He sounded pleased.

"And my new career path," she added.

"I'm your new career?" He sounded more than pleased now. He sounded exultant. "I can definitely live with that."

"No, no. Sorry for the confusion. You aren't my new career. Well, not exactly. More like my first employee. I'm going to offer you a job."

Julius considered that for a couple of beats.

"You want me to work for you?" he said finally.

"Not full-time, of course. I can't afford you full-time."

"Honey, you can't afford one hour of my time, at least not in your current financial situation. However, I am willing to negotiate."

"That's good because I'm going to need a first-rate consultant."

"I see." He kissed her forehead and then the tip of her nose. When he got to her mouth he put his hands around her waist. "Why don't you come back to bed and tell me all about this new career of yours?"

"Sure," she said. She wriggled out of his arms and headed for the hallway. "But first I'd better make a few notes. You know what they say, inspiration often strikes in the middle of the night. If you don't write it down, you'll forget it by morning."

"I've never heard that. But as it happens, I'm feeling inspired, myself, at the moment. Inspired to go back to bed."

"Wait," she yelped.

He started to scoop her up in his arms. He stopped suddenly, his eyes tightening in a spasm of pain.

"Shit," he said. He took a deep, careful breath. Gingerly he touched his right side. "Okay, let's talk about your new career path."

She told him all about her vision of her glorious new future.

His reaction was swift and certain.

"That'll never work," he said. "Forget it. Find another career path."

"No," she said. "This is what I was born to do. You've got two options, Julius Arkwright. Either you agree to consult for me, or I'll find someone else who will."

His mouth curved faintly. "Is that a threat?"

"Definitely."

He appeared to give that some thought.

"Well?" she said after a moment.

"You do realize that you'll be the first client I've ever had who got away with blackmailing me."

"Really? Others have tried?"

"Sure. Not often but, yes, occasionally one has tried to put me in a corner. And failed."

"Don't think of it as blackmail," she said earnestly. "Think of me as a protégée."

"No, I'm pretty sure this is blackmail. What I'm thinking is that I'm going to let you get away with it."

"Excellent decision," she said.

He kissed her. Then he raised his head and smiled his lion smile.

"Now, let's discuss my fees," he said.

Forty-Nine

Irene poured more coffee into Grace's cup. "You're back on the high-octane stuff today. Are you sure you're okay?"

"Yes, I'm fine, really," Grace said. "Didn't sleep a lot last night but that was only to be expected under the circumstances. I was more concerned with Agnes, to tell you the truth."

They were in Irene's office. On the other side of the window business in Cloud Lake Kitchenware was brisk. The sun had come out and so had the locals and tourists. Customers browsed the elegantly displayed pots and pans and the gleaming kitchen knives with the same pleasure that was usually reserved for art galleries and jewelry stores.

"Agnes is a tough lady," Irene said. "Which reminds me—word around town this morning is that she did not spend the night alone, either."

Grace smiled. "I can report that for the first time ever, Harley Montoya did not leave before dawn. In fact, he stayed for breakfast. I saw them in the kitchen together."

"About time. Maybe they'll finally get married."

"Don't be so sure of that. I think last night was a special-circumstances thing. Agnes always says that she and Harley like things just the way they are. Gardening club rivals by day, lovers by night. After all these years, I'd say it works for them."

"Each to her own, I suppose." Irene sipped her coffee. "What about you and Julius?"

"Julius needs a home and a career," Grace said. "I plan to help him make that happen."

"He's got both."

"They aren't working for him. I'm going to fix the problem."

"Why would you do that?" Irene asked. "I thought you had decided to get out of the fixing business."

"Turns out, I need some of the same things fixed in my life that Julius needs fixed."

Irene laughed. "I've been aware of that for a long time. Why do you think I went to the trouble of arranging that blind date?"

"You're a good friend. I take back everything I said about blind dates always being a bad idea."

"Next question. Why Julius?"

"Discovering that someone wants to kill you has a way of focusing the mind," Grace said. "It has become clear to me that I love Julius."

"I see." Irene leaned back in her chair. "And Julius?"

"He loves me, too."

Irene looked pleased. "I knew it. It's in his eyes every time he looks at you. Heck, it was there that first night. Devlin tells me that it's usually like that for men. Hard and fast. So tell me about this new career path of yours and the job you've lined up for Julius."

Grace told her.

Irene laughed. "I can't see Julius going for it, not in a million years."

"It's a done deal. I applied Arkwright's second rule—*Everyone has a hidden agenda*. I found out what Julius really wants and I intend to give it to him."

Fifty

The office of the president and CEO of Hastings, Inc., was located in the southwest corner of the forty-seventh floor of a gleaming office tower. The rain had stopped but it would return soon. The rain always came back in Seattle. But for now the clouds were scattering. Sunlight sparkled on the snow-capped peak of Mount Rainier and flashed on the waters of Elliott Bay.

The wraparound view made for an iconic postcard, Julius thought. This was Seattle at its most spectacular. Sure, Mount Rainier—an active volcano considered one of the world's most dangerous—was only sixty miles away. And the waters of the Puget Sound were cold enough to kill you within half an hour if you fell off one of the picturesque ferries. It was also true that the region was laced with major seismic fault lines. The experts were always warning that it was just a matter of time before the next Big One struck. So what? That just made life all the more interesting.

"What are you doing here?" Edward asked.

"Consulting," Julius said.

"No one asked you to consult for Hastings."

"That is not entirely accurate," Julius said. "Someone did ask me to do just that. My client."

Edward sat forward and clasped his hands on top of his desk. "I hope that your client is paying you because I sure as hell don't intend to. Can't afford you."

"Don't worry about it," Julius said. "My fee will be covered. Now, do you want my advice or not?"

Edward thought that over for a moment and then he sat back in his chair.

"All right, I'll bite," he said. "What's the free advice you're offering?"

"I told you, it's not free."

Edward snorted softly. "There's always a price. I learned that much from you."

"You should have learned something else from me. *Trust no one.*"

Edward's eyes narrowed. "Including you?"

"Your choice, of course. I know there's a theory going around that I somehow sabotaged Hastings in the past eighteen months. But do you really believe I'm the one behind your problems?"

Edward looked at him for a long time.

"No," he said eventually. "I don't. I never did believe it."

"Why not?"

Edward's mouth twisted in a grim smile. "For the same reason your new companion gave Diana—you'd have done a better job of it. I'd be standing in the smoking ruins of the company by now. Instead I'm being slowly bled to death. That's not your style. You can be cold-blooded but you aren't into long-term pain and suffering."

"What security steps have you taken?"

"The usual. I brought in an outside forensic accountant who conducted a full-scale audit. I also had a security firm run new background checks on all employees. Nothing. The clients are just quietly fading away. Contracts aren't being renewed. New ones aren't being signed. I'm in a death spiral. I need financing and I can't get it because of the rumors. Some of my best people are looking for jobs with other firms. You want the truth? I'm starting to think a merger is my only option."

"You're in no position to negotiate one that will be favorable to you and your employees," Julius said.

"Don't you think I know that? But the alternative is to let the company go under, and that would be worse for everyone, including my employees and the family."

"You said you brought in a security firm to investigate your employees."

Edward steepled his fingertips. "They came up with nothing."

"What about your board of directors? Did you have everyone on it investigated?"

Edward did not move. "Are you serious? You know damn well that every member of the board is a member of the family. Each and every one has a strong, vested interest in the success of the company."

"You know what they say about family feuds. And I can tell you from recent experience that people rarely think logically in situations that present them with an opportunity to punish someone they think deserves punishment."

Edward tapped his fingers together and looked thoughtful.

"Damn," he said very softly.

"People tell you that they operate on logic and reason but that's not how it works," Julius said. "I thought you learned that from me as well. The truth is, most folks make their decisions based on their emotions. After the decision is made, they can always find reasons to justify the action."

"*Everyone has a hidden agenda.* Arkwright's Rule Number Two." Edward got to his feet. He walked to the window and looked out at the city. "It's true, not everyone on my board likes the idea that I'm in charge now. But it's one thing to be resentful or angry. It's something else altogether to attempt to destroy the whole damn company."

"When it comes to revenge, some people will go to any lengths." Julius gripped the arms of his chair and pushed himself to his feet. "Speaking as your outside consultant, my observations these past few months indicate that the source of your problems is very close to home."

There was a long silence before Edward exhaled slowly.

"Richard," he said.

"Your half brother? I agree. That's where I'd start looking if I were in your shoes."

Edward nodded, more resigned than dismayed. "He has always resented me. Things got worse when the family put me in charge of the company after Dad died. There have been times when I wondered if he was somehow involved in the problems at Hastings but I kept telling myself that he wouldn't do anything that was against his own best financial interests."

"He's probably telling himself that if he can convince the rest of the family that you aren't up to the job of managing Hastings, the others will push you out and put him in charge."

"That's the kind of short-term thinking that can ruin a closely held business like Hastings."

"Yes, it is." Julius crossed the room and joined Edward at the window. "What are you going to do?"

"Have a talk with Richard." Edward rubbed the back of his neck. "I'll make it clear that if he doesn't agree to give up his seat on the board and leave quietly, I'll take the issue to the rest of the family. He'll step down. He won't want the other members of the family to find out that he was trying to sabotage their main source of income— not to mention their social status."

"I think you're right. Richard will leave. But you'd better watch your back from now on."

"A cheerful thought." Edward grimaced. "I can handle Richard. But it would be good to know that I had someone I could trust on the outside to help me keep an eye on him, someone who always seems to know what's going on in the shark pool."

"Me?"

"You."

"I'll do what I can to watch your back," Julius said.

"Thanks." Edward's expression tightened. "About Diana—"

"Diana and I were mismatched from the start. My fault. I convinced both of us that I could become the kind of man she wanted me to be. That was never going to be true. The two of you belong together."

"I just want you to know that, in spite of what you suspect or the rumors that went around at the time, we were never together—not physically—until after Diana left you and after I handed in my resignation."

"Don't you think I know that?" Julius smiled. "You were the knight in shining armor—for both of us. You saved Diana and me from a marriage that was doomed from the start."

Edward eyed him warily. "That's a very generous way of looking at things."

"I'm in a different place these days. I've had plenty of time to think about the past and put things into perspective." Julius paused a beat and then grinned. "What's the matter? Afraid I'm playing you?"

"No," Edward said. "I think you're telling me the truth. You're trying to close a few doors on the past so that you can move forward into the future, aren't you? That's why you came here today."

"You have to excuse me. I've been hanging out with a positive-thinking expert lately. I'm learning to look for the silver lining. Going with the glass-half-full approach, blah, blah, blah."

Edward raised his brows. "Blah, blah, blah?"

"Don't worry, I haven't completely lost my mind. Just moving in a different direction." Julius started to turn away. He stopped. "One more thing. You're going to need some financing to pull out of the dive."

Edward looked at him. "Are you offering to help arrange a cash infusion?"

"Are you asking?"

Edward thought about it and then nodded. "There's no one else I'd rather deal with at the moment. No one else I can trust. The situation is . . . fragile."

"I know."

"I've got the whole damn family and more than a thousand employees depending on me, Julius."

"You can turn this around."

"With a little help from a friend," Edward said. He smiled. "Thanks."

"Forget it."

"No, I won't forget it. If you ever need anything from me, just ask."

"Thanks. I appreciate that."

They stood there in silence for a time, watching the ferries glide across Elliott Bay.

"That was a good after-dinner talk you gave the other night," Edward said eventually. "Definitely your personal best. I don't think a single person in the audience dozed off."

"I had some coaching."

Edward's mouth twitched at the corners. "Grace Elland?"

"Yes."

"According to the media, the two of you have been living dangerously lately."

"The good news is that the excitement is over," Julius said.

"It wasn't just the after-dinner talk that was different," Edward said. "You seem different."

"Grace changed everything."

Edward smiled. "Diana said she thought that might be the case."

"Did she?"

"You sound surprised." Edward laughed. "Sometimes others see things more clearly from the outside. Your advice to me today would be a prime example."

"You didn't see the truth about the problem on your board because you were unwilling to look in the right places."

"Isn't that always the case?"

"Yes." Julius winced. "Sounds like one of those damn Witherspoon affirmations, doesn't it?"

Edward chuckled. "Yes, it does."

Julius glanced at his watch. "I'd better get going. If I hang around here any longer people will start to think that I'm going for a hostile takeover of Hastings."

"You don't want to swallow my company?"

"No." Julius moved toward the door. "I've got another project in mind."

"Yeah?" Edward watched him. "What is it?"

"Grace is going to establish a foundation. I'm her consultant."

"You? In the do-good business?"

Julius shrugged. "Something a little different for me."

"No offense, but working for a charitable foundation doesn't sound like a good fit for you, Julius. You can't help making money. It's your gift."

"That's what Grace says. She's going to take advantage of my talent to finance her foundation."

"Sounds like she spent too much time working for that positive-thinking guru, Witherspoon."

"You want to know a little secret?" Julius asked. "Grace was the brains of that outfit."

"Yeah?" Edward looked intrigued. "How's that?"

"She wrote the cookbook and the blog. Came up with the affirmations. Figured out the target audiences. Directed the online marketing. She took Witherspoon from a mid-level player straight to the big leagues."

"Grace is that good when it comes to business?"

"She's a natural when it comes to marketing. Unfortunately, she's only interested in a business model that has a feel-good mission."

"Thus your newfound interest in charity work," Edward said. "Got it. What will you be doing, aside from backing her up with funding?"

"Her instincts are great when it comes to marketing, but where people are concerned, she has a bad habit of focusing on the positive. Way too trusting. Tends to see the best in people."

Edward nodded in somber understanding. "That kind of naiveté leads to trouble every damn time."

"Which is why I'll handle the personnel end of things at the foundation. In addition to the hiring, I'll also vet the funding applicants. Grace needs someone to filter out the con artists and the daydreamers."

"What's the goal of Grace's foundation?" Edward asked.

"Lots of people think they want to open their own business."

"Sure, it's one of the big American dreams. Statistically speaking, most entrepreneurs lose their shirts."

"Usually because they don't have someone to teach them the ropes," Julius said. "That's what Grace's foundation is all about. She sees it as a sort of start-up university for people who otherwise wouldn't be able to get a foot in the door because they lack the connections and the financing and the knowledge of how to navigate the system."

Edward laughed. "You mean you actually intend to follow through on that advice you gave in your after-dinner talk? You plan to offer your services as a mentor?"

"Grace says my title will be consultant. I'm clinging to that."

"You, Julius Arkwright, will offer free consulting advice," Edward said neutrally.

"I'm not saying I'd be averse to making a little money on the side." Julius smiled. "A certain percentage of those proposals that the foundation funds will prove profitable, I'm sure."

"Now that sounds more like the Julius Arkwright I know."

"Wait until I tell Grace," Julius said.

"Tell her what?"

"She says no one ever remembers the details of an after-dinner speech. She claims that all the audience recalls are the emotions they felt during the talk."

"Depends on the speech," Edward said. "By the way, you never told me the name of your client, the one who hired you to consult here at Hastings today."

"Grace."

Edward got a knowing look in his eyes. "I had a feeling that might be the case. Should I ask about your fee?"

Julius opened the door and looked back over his shoulder. "She's buying me lunch today."

Edward laughed. Julius saw heads turn in the outer office. The expression on the receptionist's face and on the faces of the three people waiting to speak with Edward were priceless.

Automatically, he ran the scenario in his head. The news that Arkwright and Hastings were back on good terms would be all over Seattle by the end of the day. Carefully plotted strategies designed to take advantage of the Hastings business situation would collapse. Mergers-and-acquisitions experts would look elsewhere for targets. Headhunters would think twice about trying to lure away some of

Hastings's best executives. Employees who had stayed awake at night worrying about their jobs would relax.

Julius crossed the hushed reception room, smiling a little. Grace was right about one thing, the future could be changed. And she was just the woman who could do it.

Fifty-One

She waited for Julius downstairs in the coffee shop. The grande-sized cup of organic, free-trade decaf coffee she had ordered was still nearly full because after ordering it she had concluded that her tightly strung nerves could not handle even decaf.

Like most of the other customers around her, she had her laptop open. She was supposed to be working on the mission statement for the new foundation but she had discovered that she was not yet ready to concentrate on target audiences and marketing strategies. The meeting between Julius and Edward seemed to be taking forever. A good sign, she told herself. Or maybe not a good sign.

She refused to go negative.

The moment she saw Julius walk into the coffee shop, she knew she could stop fretting. His face was as unreadable as ever, but when he got closer, she saw his eyes and knew she could relax.

"I'm hungry," he said. "I'm ready to collect my first paycheck. Where are we going for lunch?"

"I know a nice little place that caters to vegetarians on First Ave. near the Market," she said.

"Oh, joy."

"But first tell me how the meeting went. I want a report."

Julius shrugged. "I doubt if we'll be having Thanksgiving with the Hastings family this year but Ed and I reached an understanding. He knows I'm not after his business and he knows what he has to do to save his family's company. By the time you and I finish lunch, the rumors that Ed and I are doing business together again will have filtered through half of Seattle. The other half will get the gossip before they sit down to dinner this evening."

"Excellent." She smiled, satisfied. "The rumors alone will change the business dynamic of the situation for the Hastings empire."

"Yes, they will, but here's the thing—I don't want to talk about business anymore today," Julius said. "I want to talk about us."

She paused in the act of closing her laptop. A frisson of hope mingled with uncertainty making her go very still. No negative thinking, she told herself. But her future was on the line and she knew it.

"Okay," she said. "Do you want to have this conversation over lunch?"

"No. I want to have it here. Now."

"What, exactly, do you want to discuss?" She felt as if she was walking over quicksand. One false step . . .

He reached across the little table and took her hand in his. "I love you, Grace Elland. I don't think I ever understood what love was until I met you. It changes everything."

It wasn't the first time he had told her he loved her, but she knew she could never hear the words often enough. Her emotions were so dazzled that she feared she might burst into tears, right there in front of the baristas and everyone else. The atmosphere in the busy coffeehouse was suddenly crystalline; pure and perfect.

"Meeting you changed things for me, too," she said, lowering her voice because of the people at the nearby tables. "I love you, Julius."

"I know this is all new for both of us and that we should give ourselves some time. But I don't want to waste any more time." He tightened his grip on her hand. "Will you marry me? Make a home with me? Make a family with me?"

"Yes," she said. "Yes. And yes."

Julius got up and pulled her to her feet. He looked at the baristas and the customers.

"She just said yes," he announced.

Applause broke out.

Grace flushed. She knew she was turning scarlet but she was also aware that she had never been happier in her life.

Julius kissed her, right there in front of the talented baristas and all the people who were drinking coffee and working on computers and phones.

The applause got louder.

Julius released her long enough to pick up her laptop. She grabbed her jacket and bag. The cheers followed them outside into the glittering, rain-polished afternoon. The sidewalks were crowded, as they always were in Seattle when the sun came out to play. Sunglasses were everywhere, appearing as if by magic.

"Got an affirmation for this moment?" Julius asked.

"The one you came up with works for me," Grace said. "Love changes everything."

"That's not an affirmation," Julius said. "That's a promise."

GARDEN OF LIES
Excerpt

S imon Roxby regarded Ursula through the lenses of his wire-rimmed spectacles. "What the devil do you mean you won't be available for the next few weeks, Mrs. Kern? We have an arrangement."

"My apologies, sir, but a pressing matter has come up," Ursula said. "I must devote my full attention to it."

A disturbing hush fell on the library. Ursula mentally fortified herself. She had been acquainted with Simon for less than a fortnight and had worked with him on only two occasions, but she felt she had an intuitive understanding of the man. He was proving to be a difficult client.

He had very nearly perfected the art of not signaling his mood or his thoughts, but she was increasingly alert to a few subtle cues. The deep silence and the unblinking gaze with which he was watching her did not bode well. She sat very straight in her chair, doing her best not to let him know that his unwavering regard was sending small chills down her spine.

Evidently concluding that she was not responding as he had anticipated to his stern disapproval, he escalated the level of tension by rising slowly from his chair and flattening his powerful hands on the polished surface of his mahogany desk.

There was a deceptively graceful quality about the way he moved that gave him a fascinating aura of quiet, self-contained power. The dark, unemotional manner characterized everything about him, from his calm, nearly uninflected speech to his unreadable green-and-gold eyes.

His choice of attire reinforced the impression of shadows and ice. In the short time she had known him she had never seen him in anything other than head-to-toe black—black linen shirt and black tie, black satin waistcoat, black trousers and a black coat. Even the frames of his spectacles were made of some matte-black metal—not gold- or silver-plated wire.

He was not wearing the severely tailored coat at the moment. It was hanging on a hook near the door. After greeting her a short time ago, Simon had removed it in preparation for work on the artifacts.

She knew she had no right to critique the man on the basis of his wardrobe. She, too, was dressed in her customary black. In the past two years she had come to think of her mourning attire—from her widow's veil and stylish black gown to her black stacked-heel, ankle-high button boots—as both uniform and camouflage.

It flashed across her mind that she and Simon made

quite a somber pair. Anyone who happened to walk into the library would think they were both sunk deep into unrelenting grief. The truth of the matter was that she was in hiding. Not for the first time, she wondered what Simon's motives were for going about in black. His father had died two months ago. It was the event that had brought Simon home to London after several years of living abroad. He was now in command of the Roxby family fortune. But she was quite certain that the black clothes were indicative of a long-standing sartorial habit—not a sign of mourning.

If even half of what the press had printed regarding Simon Roxby was true, she reflected, perhaps he had his reasons for wearing black. It was, after all, the color of mystery, and Simon was nothing if not a great mystery to Society.

She watched him with a deep wariness that was spiked with curiosity and what she knew was a reckless sense of fascination. She had anticipated that giving notice, especially in such a summary fashion, would not be met with patience and understanding. Clients frequently proved difficult to manage, but she had never encountered one quite like Simon. The very concept of managing Simon Roxby staggered the mind. It had been clear to her at the start of their association that he was a force of nature and a law unto himself. That was, of course, what made him so interesting, she thought.

"I have just explained that something unforeseen has arisen," she said. She was careful to keep her voice crisp and professional, aware that Simon would pounce on anything that hinted at uncertainty or weakness. "I regret the necessity of terminating our business relationship. However—"

"Then why are you terminating our arrangement?"

"The matter is of a personal nature," she said.

He frowned. "Are you ill?"

"No, of course not. I enjoy excellent health. I was about to say that I hope it will be possible for me to return at a later date to finish the cataloging work."

"Do you, indeed? And what makes you think I won't replace you? There are other secretaries in London."

"That is your choice, of course. I must remind you that I did warn you at the outset that I have other commitments in regard to my business which might from time to time interfere with our working arrangement. You agreed to those terms."

"I was assured that, in addition to a great many other excellent qualities, you were quite dependable, Mrs. Kern. You can't just walk in here and quit on the spot like this."

Ursula twitched the skirts of her black gown so that they draped in neat, elegant folds around her ankles while she considered her options. The atmosphere in the library was rapidly becoming tense, as if some invisible electricity generator was charging the air. It was always like this when she found herself in close proximity to Simon. But today the disturbing, rather exciting energy had a distinctly dangerous edge.

In the short time she had known him she had never seen him lose his temper. He had never gone to the other extreme, either. She had yet to see him laugh. True, he had dredged up the occasional, very brief smile, and there had been a certain warmth in his usually cold eyes from time to time. But she got the feeling that he was more surprised than she was when he allowed such emotions to surface.

"I do apologize, Mr. Roxby," she said, not for the first time. "I assure you I have no choice. Time is of the essence."

"I feel I deserve more of an explanation. What is this pressing matter that requires you to break our contract?"

"It regards one of my employees."

"You feel obligated to look into the personal problems of your employees?"

"Well, yes, in a nutshell, that is more or less the situation."

Simon came out from behind the desk, lounged against the front of it and folded his arms.

His sharply etched features had an ascetic, unforgiving quality. On occasion it was easy to envision him as an avenging angel. At other times she thought he made a very good Lucifer.

"The least you can do is explain yourself, Mrs. Kern," he said. "You owe me that much, I think."

She did not owe him anything, she thought. She had taken pains to make her terms of employment clear right from the start. As the proprietor of the Kern Secretarial Agency, she rarely took assignments herself these days. Her business was growing rapidly. The result was that for the past few months she had been busy in the office, training new secretaries and interviewing potential clients. She had accepted the position with Simon as a favor to his mother, Lilly Lafontaine, a celebrated actress who had retired to write melodramas.

She had not expected to find the mysterious Mr. Roxby so riveting.

"Very well, sir," she said, "the short version is that I have decided to take another client."

Simon went very still.

"I see," he said. "You are not happy in your work here with me?"

There was a grim note in his voice. She realized with a start that he was taking her departure personally. Even more shocking, she got the impression that he was not particularly surprised that she was leaving his employ; rather, he seemed stoically resigned, as if it foretold some inevitable doom.

"On the contrary, sir," she said quickly, "I find your cataloging project quite interesting."

"Am I not paying you enough?" Something that might have been relief flickered in his eyes. "If so, I am open to renegotiating your fee."

"I assure you, it is not a matter of money."

"If you are not unhappy in your work and if the pay is satisfactory, why are you leaving me for another client?" he asked.

This time he sounded genuinely perplexed.

She caught her breath and suddenly felt oddly flushed. It was almost as if he were playing the part of a jilted lover, she thought. But, of course, that was not at all the case. Theirs was a client-employer relationship.

This is why you rarely accept male clients, she reminded herself. There was a certain danger involved. But finding herself attracted to one of her customers was not the sort of risk she had envisioned when she established the policy. Her chief concern had been the knowledge that men sometimes posed a risk to the sterling reputations of her secretaries. In the case of Simon Roxby she had made an exception and now she would pay a price.

GARDEN OF LIES

All in all, it was probably best that the association was ended before she lost her head and, possibly, her heart.

"As to my reasons for leaving—" she began.

"Who is this new client?" Simon said, cutting her off.

"Very well, sir, I will explain the circumstances that require me to terminate my employment with you, but you may have a few quibbles."

"Try me."

She tensed at the whisper of command in his tone.

"I really do not want to get into an extended argument, sir—especially in light of the fact that I hope to return to this position in the near future."

"You have already made it clear that you expect me to wait upon your convenience."

She waved one black-gloved hand to indicate the jumble of antiquities that cluttered the library. "These artifacts have been sitting here for years. Surely they can wait a bit longer to be cataloged."

"How much longer?" he asked a little too evenly.

She cleared her throat. "Well, as to that, I'm afraid I cannot be specific, at least not yet. Perhaps in a few days I will have some notion of how long my other assignment will last."

"I have no intention of arguing with you, Mrs. Kern, but I would like to know the identity of the client you feel is more important than me—" He broke off, looking uncharacteristically irritated. "I meant to say, what sort of secretarial work do you feel is more critical than cataloging my artifacts? Is your new client a banker? The owner of a large business, perhaps? A lawyer or a lady in Polite Society who finds herself in need of your services?"

"Two days ago I was summoned to the house of a woman named Anne Clifton. Anne worked for me for two years. She became more than an employee. I considered her a friend. We had some things in common."

"I notice you are speaking in the past tense."

"Anne was found dead in her study. I sent for the police, but the detective who was kind enough to visit the scene declared that in his opinion Anne's death was from natural causes. He thinks her heart failed or that she suffered a stroke."

Simon did not move. He watched her as though she had just announced that she could fly. Clearly her response was not the answer he had expected, but he recovered with remarkable speed.

"I'm sorry to hear of Miss Clifton's death," he said. He paused, eyes narrowing faintly. "What made you summon the police?"

"I believe Anne may have been murdered."

Simon looked at her, saying nothing for a time. Eventually he removed his spectacles and began to polish them with a pristine white handkerchief.

"Huh," he said.

Ursula debated another moment. The truth of the matter was that she wanted very much to discuss her plan with someone who would not only understand but possibly provide some useful advice—someone who could keep a confidence. Her intuition told her that Simon Roxby was good at keeping secrets. Furthermore, in the past few days it had become blazingly clear that he possessed an extremely logical mind. Some would say he took that particular trait to the extreme.

"What I am about to tell you must be held in strictest confidence, do you understand?" she said.

His dark brows came together in a forbidding line. She knew she had offended him.

"Rest assured I am quite capable of keeping my mouth shut, Mrs. Kern."

Each word was coated in a thin layer of ice.

She adjusted her gloves and then clasped her hands firmly together in her lap. She took an additional moment to collect her thoughts. She had not told anyone else, not even her assistant, Matty, what she intended to do.

"I have reason to suspect that Anne Clifton was murdered," she said. "I intend to take her place in the household of her client to see if I can find some clues that will point to the killer."

Turn the page to hear more about the world of Jayne Ann Krentz, Jayne Castle and Amanda Quick!

RIVER ROAD

Jayne Ann Krentz

It's been thirteen years since Lucy Sheridan was in Summer River.
The last time she visited her aunt Sara there, as a teenager, she'd
been sent home suddenly after being dragged out of a wild party,
by the guy she had a crush on, just to make it more embarrassing.
Obviously Mason Fletcher – only a few years older but somehow a
lot more of a grown-up – was the overprotective type who thought
he had to come to her rescue.

Now, returning after her aunt's fatal car accident, Lucy is learning
there was more to the story than she realized at the time. Mason
had saved her from a very nasty crime that night – and soon
afterward, Tristan – the cold-blooded rich kid who'd targeted her –
disappeared mysteriously, his body never found.

A lot has changed in thirteen years. Lucy now works for a private
investigation firm as a forensic genealogist, while Mason has quit
the police force to run a successful security firm with his brother –
though he still knows his way around a wrench when he fills in at
his uncle's local hardware store. Even Summer River has changed,
from a sleepy farm town into a trendy upscale spot in California's
wine country. But Mason is still a protector at heart, a serious (and
seriously attractive) man. And when he and Lucy make a shocking
discovery inside Sara's house, and some of Tristan's old friends
start acting suspicious, Mason's quietly fierce instincts kick into
gear. He saved Lucy once, and he'll save her again. But this time,
she insists on playing a role in her own rescue . . .

THE HOT ZONE

Jayne Castle

The world of Harmony has its wonders, one of them being Rainshadow Island. Just beneath its surface, a maze of catacombs hides a dangerous secret . . .

Halloween – with its tricks and treats – is a dust bunny's dream come true. Just ask Lyle, Sedona Snow's faithful sidekick. But for Sedona, it's a nightmare. Though her new job managing a small hotel and tavern on Rainshadow is helping her move on from her tragic past, a bizarre disaster down in the catacombs has brought a pack of rowdy ghost hunters to her inn.

And now, Sedona's ex has arrived on the island, claiming he wants to get back together, just as a newcomer appears to have a strong interest in her. Cyrus Jones is the new Guild boss in town. He has his own agenda when it comes to Sedona, but even the best-laid plans are no match for the passion that springs up on Rainshadow . . .

OTHERWISE ENGAGED

Amanda Quick

One does not expect to be kidnapped on a London street in broad daylight. Yet Amity Doncaster barely escapes with her life after meeting a man in a black silk mask who whispers the most vile taunts and threats into her ear. Her quick thinking, and her secret weapon, save her – for now.

But the monster known in the press as the Bridegroom has left a trail of female victims in his wake, and will soon be on his feet again. He is unwholesomely obsessed by Amity's scandalous connection to Benedict Stanbridge – and Benedict refuses to let this resourceful, daring woman suffer for her romantic link to him – as tenuous as it may be.

For a man and woman so skilled at disappearing, so at home in the exotic reaches of the globe, escape is always an option. But each intends to end the Bridegroom's reign of terror in the heart of the city they love, which means they must also face feelings neither of them can run away from . . .